Achilles Daunt

In the Land of the Moose, the Bear, and the Beaver

Adventures in the Forests of the Athabasca

Achilles Daunt

In the Land of the Moose, the Bear, and the Beaver
Adventures in the Forests of the Athabasca

ISBN/EAN: 9783337177188

Printed in Europe, USA, Canada, Australia, Japan

Cover: Foto ©Andreas Hilbeck / pixelio.de

More available books at **www.hansebooks.com**

STALKED BY INDIANS.

Page 226.

IN THE

LAND OF THE MOOSE, THE BEAR, AND THE BEAVER.

Adventures in the Forests of the Athabasca.

By

ACHILLES DAUNT,

Author of "*Frank Redcliffe*," "*The Three Trappers*,"
&c. &c.

WITH ILLUSTRATIONS.

London:
T. NELSON AND SONS, PATERNOSTER ROW.
EDINBURGH; AND NEW YORK.

1890

Contents.

CHAPTER V.

CHAPTER VI.

CHAPTER VII.

CHAPTER VIII.

CHAPTER IX.

CHAPTER X.

CHAPTER XI.

CHAPTER XII.

CHAPTER XIII.

CHAPTER XIV.

CHAPTER XV.

CHAPTER XVI.

CHAPTER XVII.

CHAPTER XVIII.

CHAPTER XIX.

CHAPTER XX.

CHAPTER XXI.

IN THE LAND OF THE MOOSE, THE BEAR, AND THE BEAVER.

CHAPTER I.

THE vast territory of North-Western Canada, comprising an area almost equal to that of Europe, offers an attractive field to the explorer or hunter. Here may be found the deer, the moose, the elk or wapiti (*Cervus Canadensis*), the fierce grizzly bear, and the cougar, or "painter" as he is styled by the backwoodsman. Fur-bearing animals, persecuted for many generations by the hardy employés of the Hudson Bay Company, exist still in considerable numbers in the tangled forests; but the buffalo, once the staple of subsistence of many tribes, no longer thunders across the plains in countless thousands. Only in scattered bands do these shaggy monarchs of the wild still survive. Continual slaughter by the half-breed hunters, and the ceaseless war waged against them by the Indians, who live almost solely on their flesh, have at last told upon their numbers.

Before the Pacific Railway was made, the buffalo herds ranged from the Great Slave Lake in the north to the fertile prairies of Texas in the south. But now the myriad droves which formerly blackened the plains no longer exist, and the few survivors of the southern herds find temporary security in the wild territories of New Mexico, Arizona, and Panhandle Texas, while those in the north are driven deeper and deeper into the wilderness each successive year.

In the extensive forests of the Athabasca, there is an animal of the same species — the wood bison— larger and fiercer than his brethren of the plains; but he too is scarce. It is possible that this animal was originally identical with the common buffalo, but that, forced by circumstances to the shelter of the forests, he, as has occurred in the case of other animals, became somewhat modified in habit and appearance, in order to conform to the requirements of his new habitat.

In the immense regions lying north-west of Manitoba many other valuable animals are to be found. These we shall describe in the course of this narrative of adventure.

The geography of these wild regions is little known to the general reader. Chartographers, and the few persons who have travelled there, are almost the only individuals acquainted with the physical aspect of the country. For upwards of two centuries the Hudson Bay Company have been virtual rulers of the land; and in the prosecution of the fur-trade they have established their posts in the wildest and most inaccessible districts. Their *voyageurs* and *coureurs des bois* are famous in every country for hardihood and skill in the prosecution of their calling. Fierce conflicts between them and the savage Redskins have frequently taken place, as thrilling as those which render attractive the pages of Fenimore Cooper.

Not alone with the nomads of the plains have these fierce hunters joined issue in deadly conflict. Another company—the North-West Fur Company—many years ago pushed its trade into regions over which the Hudson Bay Company assumed authority in virtue of their charter; and more than one pitched battle was fought between the rival employés.

It is estimated that the population of the Hudson Bay Company's territories is about one hundred and fifty thousand—of which number probably one-tenth is resident at the Red River Settlement. The population of that district, however, is now increasing with such marvellous rapidity that it is difficult to state its exact amount. The remainder consists of the various scanty tribes of Indians and the employés of the Fur Company. Thus almost the whole of the country north-west of Red River is a wilderness. Boundless prairies stretch for hundreds of miles between the white settlements at Winnipeg and the Rocky Mountains, broken here and there by isolated hills—such as the Touchwood, Two Peaks, and Eagle Hill.

Forests of immense extent clothe some districts, while others are pleasantly diversified by an admixture of wood and prairie, which gives a park-like aspect to the scenery. Such is the case in the country comprised between both arms of the Saskatchewan. From the junction of these streams, stretching northward for several hundred miles, to Lake Athabasca, is perhaps the largest forest-covered section in the Territory. This is the great preserve of the Hudson Bay Company, for within the gloomy recesses of these woods fur-bearing animals are plentiful, while the pelts are of the first quality.

In the west, the Rocky Mountains rear their snow-clad peaks among the clouds, while their lower slopes are clad with dense forests, which extend along the chain for many hundreds of miles.

Among these grim mountains numerous rivers take their rise; of which some find their way eastwards across the prairies, after cutting a passage through tremendous cañons, the summits of which frown three thousand and four thousand feet above the foaming torrent below. Such are the Peace, the Athabasca, and Saskatchewan. Others find their way westward to the warm waters of the Pacific through alternate plains and mountains—the former often fertile and adorned with groves, while the latter are usually heavily timbered.

Again, other rivers, having their sources within British territory, flow northwards, and debouch in the Arctic Ocean, after traversing hundreds of miles of desert solitudes. Of these, the chief are the Youkon, the Turnagain or Liard's River, and the Mackenzie. The last flows out of the north-west corner of the Great Slave Lake, and carries with it almost to its debouchure a milder climate than prevails in the regions contiguous to its course. Thus along its banks timber of larger growth is found than is elsewhere yielded by the sterile and frost-bound soil; for here the ground is ever frozen, the summer heats not penetrating more than a few feet beneath the surface. The winter cold often reaches 40° and even 50° below zero, while the heat in summer, on the other hand, rises to 100° in the shade!

At the junction of the Liard with the Mackenzie, in latitude 61° north, is situated Fort Simpson, a post of the Hudson Bay Company; and in spring, when the ice breaks up in the rivers, a scene at once grand and terrible is witnessed by the inhabitants. Among the Rocky Mountains to the south the Liard has its source; and swollen by the melting of the snows on the hills, it rushes impetuously northwards, pouring its foaming flood into the still ice-bound Mackenzie. For a short time the ice resists the action of the waters, but soon gives way with a crash like thunder. Roaring and tumbling

in the turbid stream, it rolls madly along, piling vast
blocks along the banks, and tearing from their founda-
tions huge boulders, and uprooting trees, which are
splintered like matchwood by its resistless force. Bar-
riers of ice-blocks sometimes bridge the stream across,
and check the movement of the ice-floe. But the
confined waters surge wave on wave, rising to the
height of forty feet, and with their accumulated pressure again force a passage with a thunderous roar
which can be heard for miles.

The destruction occasioned by these floods can easily
be imagined. Forests are levelled with the ground ; and
even the trading-posts of the Fur Company, although
placed for safety on the higher grounds, do not always
escape. Fort Good Hope, situated about one hundred
and twenty miles south of Fort Simpson, was swept
away some years since by a flood, and the inhabitants
had only just time to leap into a boat which, provi-
dentially, happened to be at hand.

On the north-east of the Territory, on the western
shores of Hudson Bay, lies a country extending over
several thousand square miles, called " The Barren
Grounds." The rock formation is primitive, and the
soil sterile. It is a country of rugged eminences and
numerous valleys, each of which has its stream and
lake. Vegetation is scanty and poor: a few brakes
of willows, with an occasional clump of dwarf pines
in the valleys, and several species of lichen on the
stony hills, constitute almost the only vegetation.

A country so poor is naturally destitute of animal life, and, as a consequence, in these desolate regions but few species are to be found. The reindeer and that quaint-looking animal the musk-ox are the principal quadrupeds, and form the staple of subsistence to the few wretched tribes which dwell on the outskirts of this dreary land. Wolves are also found; and along the coasts of Hudson Bay walruses, seals, narwhals, and polar bears furnish food for the wandering Eskimos.

From the shores of the Great Bear Lake, and reaching to the Coppermine River, lie the hunting-grounds of the Dog-rib Indians. Here reindeer abound, and their flesh and skins afford food and clothing to the natives. These Indians are a well-formed and athletic tribe, and are the terror of their more peaceful and less powerful neighbours.

The various tribes inhabiting the country along the banks of the Mackenzie and the regions reaching inland from that river, are all members of the Chippewan family, and are called Slaves, Dog-ribs, Rabbit-skins, and Gens des Montagnes. Along Peel River is found a tribe which speaks a language different from the Chippewayan; but these are migrants, and are believed to have come from within the Territory of Alaska. They are called Loucheux or Squint-eyes.

Although the different tribes constituting the great Chippewayan group inhabit districts widely distant from each other, and have done so for many generations, it is remarkable that their various dialects are intelligible to all. In their manners and usages there is also a very close resemblance. Their treatment of their women offers a strong contrast to the custom of all other tribes on the American continent. Instead of making them the drudges of the village, hewers of wood and drawers of water, the men take all the manual labour on themselves. They hew the poles for the lodge; they draw them from the forest, and erect them. They clear the snow from the encampment; they even bring home the produce of the chase. It is singular that this family should stand in such marked contrast with not only the surrounding tribes, but with all others in America, whether north or south. Everywhere else savage man debases woman, and makes her his slave. These Indians are a mild, inoffensive race, lovers of peace, and good hunters.

Prior to the settlement of whites amongst them, they, in common with the Eskimos, had no ideas of religion. "Ya-ga-ta-that-hee-hee," or "the man that lies along the sky," is their mode of reference to the Deity. Religion, however, is not their strong point; and they, like all savages, are the dupes of their medicine-men or magicians, to whom they pay great respect.

Notwithstanding their kind treatment of their women, polygamy is not uncommon among the Slaves and Rabbit-skins. Want of forethought in the summer, when game is plentiful, exposes them in the winter to the severest distress. Instances of cannibalism have often occurred, too horrible to be credited, if not supported by good authority. We have heard of a husband, travelling towards a post of the Hudson Bay Company in search of relief, packing up his wife as provision for the journey. This supply becoming exhausted, the monster next sacrificed one of his children. This, too, being consumed before he reached the fort, the cannibal was found by an officer of the Company roasting the remains of his last child at the fire! A little forethought during the season of plenty would prevent this terrible distress: but everywhere savage man seems incapable of foresight; he lives only for the present, and allows the future to take care of itself.

It is singular that among these aborigines of the North-West Territory the tradition of the Deluge should exist—although they preserve no legend of their migration from other lands to their present home. Thus, if questioned as to whence they originally came, their usual reply is: "For hundreds of moons *since the lands were covered with water* our fathers have hunted here; and the white man it was who first told us that other countries existed." The Algonquins in Canada preserve a similar tradition; and among the savages of the Orinoco, in South America, Humboldt found the story of the Deluge. Surely this is strong confirmation of the truth of the sacred narrative. The rocks and mountains, too, bear their testimony in its favour. And yet people who accept without question other historical narratives are sometimes but too ready to be led astray by any trifling difficulty in reconciling the sacred text with scientific discoveries.

A line drawn from the south-east corner of the Great Bear Lake to the sixtieth degree of north latitude on the shore of Hudson Bay, will form the north-eastern and eastern boundaries of the woods. Towards Hudson Bay and the northern coasts from this line lie the Barren Grounds. The principal river of this section is the Great Fish River; also called the River Back, after a gentleman of that name who explored its course about the year 1834. But during this story we shall not be concerned with these barren wildernesses. Let us, therefore, turn to more attractive regions.

The Mackenie River district is by far the richest in furs of any in the Territory; and this is more especially the case with regard to the beaver. But although large game is still abundant, in former times it was much more so. Moose and cariboo, or the woodland reindeer, existed in extraordinary numbers; but the slaughter necessary to supply the employés of many forts as well as the Indians has somewhat thinned their ranks. Great numbers of these animals, however, still exist, and afford sport and food to the wandering hunter.

With this rough outline of the country and its productions, let me introduce to my boy-reader some old friends.

CHAPTER II.

IT is usual to commence a story of this nature by diffusing a roseate hue over the landscape, and by representing the hero or heroes as enjoying their situation to their hearts' content.

I regret that I am unable to deviate so far from facts as to imitate this seductive example. On the contrary, when the incidents occurred from which I draw this veracious tale, the rain poured in torrents, plashing against the rocks, and seething in the furrowed surface of the Clearwater River. Murky clouds concealed the sky behind their dripping folds, and threw an inhospitable gloom over a scene which, even under such unfavourable circumstances, was eminently picturesque.

This effect is heightened by the sudden manner in which the prospect bursts upon the view. A steep hill ends the portage La Loche; and this surmounted, the eye falls first upon a beautiful hill of emerald greenness which rises abruptly from the banks of the Clearwater River. An extensive range of hills, of which this is the most remarkable, runs parallel with the stream, their sides clothed with forests, and often traversed by deep ravines opening back from the water. The sinuous course pursued by the river frequently conceals it behind wooded promontories; and, as often, its rapid waters issuing from their shelter are visible at intervals as it flows down the valley.

From among the trees which grow on one of the most heavily-wooded of these promontories a dense smoke is issuing, and hangs in thick clouds above the summits of the trees. Evidently it is an encampment. We will approach and see who they are who journey in this vast wilderness.

As we near the spot, an immense fire, formed of the entire trunks of decayed trees, shines ruddily among the thick foliage of the spruces, and combats for supremacy with the thickening twilight. By its light we see a hut—a mere temporary shelter, composed of the dense branches of the pines. In the doorway, which fronts the fire, and is of ample size to accommodate them, we behold three figures. They are busily engaged in superintending the cooking of their evening meal; and for this purpose they have raked large and clear embers from the main fire nearer to their hut, and upon these sputter sundry parts of a deer, the remainder of which hangs from a branch near by.

These travellers are evidently hunters, as may be

inferred from their accoutrements. They are of different ages, too. The eldest—a dark-visaged, spare man, of sinewy aspect—seems, as far as can be judged from a few grizzled locks which straggle from beneath his greasy coon-skin cap, to be about sixty years of age. His eyes are small, black, and restless. They wander everywhere, above and around, not vacantly, but with a quick keenness, which is, doubtless, born of the necessity of keeping a sharp outlook. His equipments are apparently much the worse of wear; his bullet-pouch and straps reflect the firelight from their greasy surface; while the individual himself seems as if he had not washed for many a day.

His companions are much younger than this veteran; but between these also there is an evident disparity of age. The elder, naturally of dark complexion, is apparently swarthed to a still deeper hue by long exposure to the elements. His equipments are of a more modern appearance than those of his older comrade; but they too seem to have seen much service.

The youngest of the party is not much more than a lad; but while years have not had time to impart a manly air, the nature of his calling has impressed him with a boldness of glance and action which go far to make amends for his youthfulness.

Within the hut, muzzles downwards, hang three rifles. Of these, two are Winchester repeaters, while the third is an old-fashioned rifle of the Kentucky pattern. The travellers apparently reached their present encampment by water, for a cedar-wood canoe rests bottom up upon the shingly beach within a few yards of the fire. Under the shelter of the hut are stowed the articles of the freight.

The party seem in high good humour notwithstanding the downpour of rain which hisses in the embers. They are amused, apparently, by some anecdote which their grizzled companion is narrating in the intervals between his attacks on a venison rib which he holds across his mouth in both hands, gnawing it from right to left, and left to right. We will draw a little nearer, and share in the amusement of the two youths :—

" Wal, boyees, that wa'n't a sarcumstance to what happened last time I wur at the fort. Some mountainy men wur thur, a tradin' thur plunder, an' you bet they wur on fur a big drink ! They wur squenchin' thur thirst this-a-way one day, an' talkin' o' what they cud do wi' thur rifles, when a dispute riz between two o' 'em, which wur the best shot. " ' 'Tis easy to settle that,' sez Gadwell Green. ' Hyur's my old shootin' stick, and thur's yourn. We'll rig up a mark fast enuff, I'll allow, an' the boys'll jedge atween us.' T'other fellur agreed at oncest, an' looked round fur his rifle, which he had leaned agin the wall. I wur thur at the time, an' seed one o' the lads put down somethin' as wa'n't powder in the rifle afore handin' it to the owner, who didn't see what wur goin' on. A nail wur druv in a tree sixty yards away, an' the thing wur to hit that on the head;—whoever did that fust wur the best shot.

"Wal, to make my story short, Green an' t'other chap—I forgets his name—loads thur rifles an' takes thur stand, an' tosses fur fust shot. The toss fell to Green, an' arter a kearful aim he fired an' jest a'most touched the nail. The boys cheered the shot, an' that made t'other'n savage as a meat-axe. 'Shet yer mouths, ye blatherin' pack,' sez he, 'an' wait till *I* shoots to cackle!' Wal, he aims away, an' pulls; but thur wur no report, I guess. 'Blank this 'ar gun,' sez he, 'but I wur dead on that nail, an' 'ud 'a made a hit sure as pison! Hyur goes agin!' No shot kem this time eyther. Boyees, the talk that fellur went on with 'ud rise yer ha'r! He pranced round cussin' awful, an' drivin' home his ramrod to put down the charge. He wur jest a-goin' to put on another cap, when one o' the boys he sez, 'What'n thunder ails yer rifle, old coon? Why, blank ef she ain't got the tapeworm!' You bet we all rolled about in fits o' larfin. Sure enuff thur wur a long whitey thread a-pokin' out o' the nipple o' the fellur's rifle, which wur *cheese!* O' coorse the gun cudn't go wi' that behint the powder.

"The way that fellur got on wur a sight to see, I reckon! But it wur nigh havin' a bad endin', as he wanted Green to fight; but the boys wouldn't let that go on, an' arter a while they got him to think the hull thing a joke. Ye-es, that wur a funny sight, I guess, an' tickles this coon as often as I thinks o' it."

The language and appearance of the old hunter and his companions seem familiar;—beyond a doubt we have met them before. It is Pierre and his companions Gaultier and old Jake, with whom we travelled on the Saskatchewan. From their remarks it is evident that now they are upon a similar expedition through the wild countries of the North-West. We propose to accompany them, and to chronicle their various adventures, for the instruction and amusement of our young readers.

The party finished their supper, and made arrangements for spending the night beneath the shelter of their hut. Bear-skins and blankets were unrolled and spread over piles of white cedar boughs, which furnish a couch at once fragrant and elastic. Enormous logs were heaped on the fire, which sent volumes of sparks up through the pall-like foliage overhead, and the flaring light gleamed on the rushing river, and glistened on the wet tree trunks.

The storm, however, soon thickened; fierce gusts tore down the gorge, sometimes drowning the rush of the river, and bending the trees like reeds; while branches torn from the parent trunks were whirled about, and strewed the ground round the camp. Rain in sheets hissed through the woods, and notwithstanding the care with which the hunters made their hut, it found its way through, and trickled faster and faster on their faces, making this refuge untenable.

The hoarse thunder of the Clearwater plunging madly

through the darkness, the groaning of the trees as they swayed to and fro beneath the force of the tempest, the rending of branches and the crash of falling trunks, filled the air, and, together with the soaking rain, prevented the party from sleeping. Indeed, they preferred to sit cowering over the fire, which, despite pine-knots in plenty, they could scarcely manage to keep a-light.

The hilarity which they had displayed earlier in the evening now gave place to silent gloom, occasionally broken by a dissatisfied growl from old Jake. A few yards from the camp, on the windward side, stood a clump of large pines, two of which were dead, and stretched abroad their white and scathed branches. The old hunter glanced uneasily at these once or twice, when suddenly a gust fiercer than usual howled down the valley, and, with a report like a field-piece, the larger of the two trees snapped across, and fell with a crash almost across the fire.

"I knowed it," said Jake; "that blamed tree wur a wheezin' an' a coughin' at us all night. I guess we'd better shift the canoe out o' whur it is. That old stack o' faggots wur nigh on doin' fur it!"

Accordingly the lads rose, and with old Jake's assistance carefully lifted the canoe and put it in a place of safety. None too soon had this precaution been taken, as they now perceived that, swollen with the rain, the river had risen to within a few inches of the spot on which the boat had lain.

Towards morning the gale moderated and the rain

ceased; but, drenched and shivering, none of the hunters were able to obtain any sleep. They therefore spent the remainder of the night at the fire, which burned badly, and almost choked them with dense smoke. At length the dawn streaked the eastern sky, from which the clouds in ragged masses trailed slowly away. The warm sun soon dispelled the chilly feeling which early morning always occasions, and our hunters shortly began to feel brighter under the influence of his genial rays. Birds twittered and fluttered through the thick foliage of the spruces; ducks quacked upon the river, and the passing flights soared higher with a rush as they perceived the party at the camp. Everything seemed to rejoice at the departure of the gloomy, uncomfortable night, and at the advent of cloudless skies and warm sunshine.

Old Jake busied himself in building a fire, which he easily effected with sheets of birch-bark and pitch-pine knots, which existed in plenty in the neighbourhood, and which are full of bitumen, and highly inflammable. Gaultier filled the camp kettle and hung it over the blaze; Pierre cut the venison for their meal from the carcass of the deer; and as soon as breakfast was ready, the three hunters seated themselves round the fire, which drew the steam in clouds from their wet garments. This, however, little incommoded them, as they were well inured to the *désagréments* of a trapper's life. Old Jake, indeed, seemed in unusually good spirits.

" It diz this coon's gizzard good," he said, " to get

back to the woods agin. I wur a wearyin' down thur at the settlement to get out o' the crowds. I never yet seed any use in a crowd—a lot o' fellurs 'ithout a notion o' a trail or a rifle, an' tearin' round like all creation arter cows and pigs from one end o' the week to the other. Wagh! it a'most pisons me to think sich fellurs ur goin' on wi' thur doin's whur I rec'lects shootin' buffler some years agone!"

"I suppose buffalo were plentiful in those days?" said Pierre.

"Ye may say that," replied the old trapper; "I've seed the time that I cud shoot a thousand o' the critters in a week. The half-breeds from Red River used to take a skirr out arter 'em, an' as often as not 'ud go back wi' five thousand karkidges. Ye-es; them wur the times when a man cud 'arn his livelihood easy. But now, what atween Injuns, half-breeds, an' buffler-skinners, I guess the game's druv off the peraras."

Here the old hunter heaved a deep sigh, no doubt at the disappearance of his favourite game from its former haunts, and the advent of colonists whom he looked on as enemies of the most malignant type. The meal proceeded in silence, broken only by the rush of the river, the occasional note of a bird, or the hollow tapping of the wood-pecker, who was busily engaged in extracting his breakfast from the decayed trunks of the trees. All having at length satiated their appetites, they lolled a little round the fire before breaking up camp.

"Boyees," said Jake, "did I ever tell yer about the fust gun I ever got my claws on?"

"No, Jake," answered Gaultier; "do tell us about it."

"Wal, it wur a funny thing too," continued the old hunter. "Ye see I wur fond o' shootin' since I broke the shell; and when I wur about seven year old, I determined to get a gun somehow. Now, I seed jest what I wanted over the chimbly at Uncle Silas's, whur I wur sent to stay fur my health, bein' a bit back'ard for my age. Wal, the thing wur twice as long a'most as myself, but I guess that wur no diffeeculty; so one fine mornin', bright an' airly, I skips out o' bed, an' wi' the help o' a table an' cha'r, I gets my claws upon the gun, a-leavin' the bag behint wi' a stick in it to keep it stiff. I reckon I didn't greatly admire it now I had a holt of it; but it wur a gun, an' that wur everything. I stole out to the wood-shed to look it over, an' to ile the lock, which o' coorse wur a flint. I soon diskivered, hows'ever, that the hammer wouldn't work—anyhow, I guess I cudn't make it—an' I wur a-gwine to put the old blunderbox back agin, when who shed look in but Pete Sniggers, as bright an imp as arey a one round them diggin's. Pete, who wur a kupple o' years older'n me, no sooner sees the old gun than he says, 'Jake, you've sloped wi' that thar gun, and I'm jest a-gwine to tell old Silas about it—*I* am—ef we don't run it on shares. Say.'

"'Wal, Pete,' says I, 'I don't say agin that. I've

got the gun; an' do you get the fodder, an' I'm in wi'
yer.'

"'That's fair an' squar' enough,' says Pete. 'I knows
whur I kin make a raise o' powder. But let's hev a
squint at the gun.' Pete turned it this away an' that
away, an' pulled an' tugged, but 'twur no go; the
blamed thing wouldn't cock for us. He then said he'd
take it along wi' him an' get it fixed by an Irish carpenter as lived clost to his own house. Wal, in a
kupple o' days I walked over an' asked ef Pete Sniggers hadn't left my old gun fur repairs. 'Yerra,
Johnny,' says Paddy, 'I'm afeerd ye'll be mad at me;
but Biddy b'iled the kittle fur tay wid it—bad manners to her that didn't know better! But it can't be
helped. Anyhow, sure you had no bisness to have a
gun; you're too young, child, and 'ud only shoot yer-
self; so you ought to be thankful instead o' sorry.' I
wur mortal vexed, you bet, an' most of all when I
thort o' what Uncle Silas 'ud say when he found the
old musket gone. But, as Paddy had said, it cudn't be
helped; an' so I went home sad enuff.

"Three days arter this, one mornin' at breakfast,
Uncle Silas says to me, 'Lucky fur you, Johnny,' says
he, 'that you're not like that sneakin' cuss, Pete Sniggers. He stole a gun somewheres, an' it busted an'
blowed the hull arm clean off him!' Wal, I a'most fell
under the table. I felt green, white, an' red by turns;
an' only Uncle Silas wur a-pokin' down in his plate, he
must have smelt out I knowed somethin' about it. Arter

breakfast I skims over to Paddy the carpenter, an'
hearin' a rumpus a-goin' on, I jest stopped at the door.
Biddy wur givin' Paddy a bit o' her mind. 'Ye're a
blaguard, that's what ye are,' I heerd her a-yellin', 'to
sell a gun that wasn't yours, and thin to say I burned
it under the kittle. It's only a mane blaguard 'ud do
the like. Why didn't ye tell the little nagur the ould
gun wasn't safe? You'd sell yer ould sowl for a dollar
any day, let alone somebody else's, ye low, mane man.'

"I guess I didn't go in. I heerd enuff, an' seed how
the trail lay. I wur well quit o' the gun, though, that's
a fact. I reckon Pete didn't come loafin' round our
wood-shed agin lookin' fur guns. No; that he didn't."
Here the old hunter laughed heartily at this reminis-
cence of his juvenile days.

CHAPTER III.

OUR hunters now prepared to continue their journey.
The canoe was carried to the river and launched;
Gaultier stepped in, and held on by a branch, while
Pierre and Jake busied themselves in placing on board
the different articles of their outfit. This accomplished,
these also took their places; and Gaultier releasing his
hold on the branch, the light boat, obedient to the dip
of the paddles, shot out into the stream.

The freshet of the previous night had not yet run
itself out, and the river still rushed swiftly down the
glen, bounding in long, smooth undulations where the
water was deep over hidden rocks, and boiling in foam-
crested surges round boulders which projected here and
there above the surface. The navigation was therefore
difficult, and in not a few spots even dangerous. A
slight graze against the jagged edges of some of the
boulders which strewed the bed of the stream would

have torn a hole in the frail side of the canoe, and sent its occupants to the bottom. Neither of the youths, therefore, breathed freely until this portion of the river was left behind, and until they again found themselves floating on quiet water, which reflected the dark shadows of the pines along the banks.

It was yet early morning, and the sun poured a flood of light upon the forest, which here consisted principally of coniferous trees. A resinous perfume was wafted on the air, extracted from the pines by the warmth of the sun. Ducks sprang with a quack and a rush off each successive reach of the river, as the boat and its occupants became visible.

Several large birds were observed from time to time over the summits of the trees, but swooped again out of sight before the boys could obtain a shot. These were bald-headed eagles, no doubt in pursuit of the wild-fowl which abounded on the river. Ospreys circled high in air, eying the water below. Occasionally one would close its wings and shoot downwards with the velocity of an arrow, burying itself amid a cloud of spray in the river, from which it reappeared almost invariably carrying a fish in its talons. Many of these birds were at work along the river; and that they kill an immense number of fish the party had evidence, as they rarely seemed to make a swoop in vain. Many of them seemed to be fishing to supply their young, as the boys observed several nests in the top branches of pine trees which stood close by the banks of the

OSPREY FISHING.

river. To these the fish were conveyed by the parent-
birds, who, by their hoarse cackling and croaking, attracted the attention of their young ones, and incited
them to eat. Some of the birds had ceased to fish,
and, balanced on the bare tops of dead pines, they
seemed to view the labours of their associates with
subdued interest—bending their necks to observe the
result of a swoop, or occasionally glancing upwards as
they heard the rushing sound made by a bird in its
descent. They did not pay much attention to the boat,
as ospreys are rarely molested by man, and hence
have not that dread of him which characterizes other
species.

Since leaving the camp, the voyageurs had seen no
game, with the exception of the ducks and a few swans,
which tantalized them by taking to wing before the
canoe got near enough for a shot. Pierre, indeed, had
cut some feathers from a trumpeter, a large bird of
this species, at the distance of nearly four hundred
yards; but there his success ended.

Since entering the Clearwater they had had no sport,
with the solitary exception of a deer which old Jake
had secured. They therefore kept a very sharp look-
out both in advance and on either side the river as
they sailed along. The day was beautifully fine, and
the warm sunshine lighted up the woods, falling upon
mossy banks and on thickets of young birches within
the shelter of the forest, and enhancing their emerald
greenness.

Overhead was a sky of the deepest blue, in which floated a few light clouds, that hardly dimmed the sun whenever they interposed between him and the earth. It was one of those days in the first half of summer when all nature seems buoyant, and filled with gladness at the departure of dark and sterile winter. The air was deliciously warm ; and whenever a light breeze blew from the forest, the hunters perceived the aromatic fragrance of the pines whose shadows darkened the water near the banks, and the serrated outlines of whose summits were relieved against the sky.

The boat had now approached a bend in the stream formed by a projecting tongue of land, which was clothed to the point with a thick growth of firs. Pierre, who had often journeyed by this route, cautioned the party to have their rifles ready, as he considered it very probable that several deer would be seen feeding along the banks of the next reach, which were bare of trees.

" I guess this coon knows a likelier trick than that," cried old Jake. " Jest let us land this side o' yonder p'int, an' still-hunt the critturs from the cover of the timber."

As this plan met the approval of Pierre and Gaultier, the three hunters accordingly landed ; and having secured the canoe, they looked to their rifles, and in Indian file entered the forest. The distance across the promontory was not more than one hundred yards, and the trappers soon reached a position from which they could obtain a good view down the lower reach of the river. Here a spectacle met their eyes which caused all three to start.

Two persons sat by the verge of the stream, on which floated a light birch canoe. One was a lady evidently young, while her companion, a man of gentlemanly appearance, seemed considerably her senior. The latter was busied over a fire, at which he appeared to be cooking; while the lady, engaged with her pencil, was sketching the pretty view down the river.

"Wal! this is a caution, now it is!" exclaimed old Jake. "Who'd a thort to see a buck an' a doe like that in this hyur location? But, thunder, fellurs! do ee see what ur a-gwine on behint—at the edge o' the timber?"

The boys, startled by the vehemence of the old hunter's manner, looked in the direction indicated. At first they were unable to perceive anything; but shortly they observed two Indians crouching from bush to bush, trailing their rifles, and evidently stalking the travellers, who were engrossed by their respective occupations, and wholly unsuspicious of danger. That the intentions of the two savages were hostile was apparent from their attempting secrecy in their approach; and that they would effect their murderous purpose was also evident, unless frustrated by the intervention of the trappers. The edge of the timber was about one hundred yards from the river; but several bushes and young pines grew here and there in the intervening space, and afforded good cover for the lurking savages, who, when they had got directly behind their unsuspecting victims, availed of these and crept swiftly from one to the other.

They soon reached a position scarcely sixty yards from the fire; and here they bent forward with rifles cocked and ready, glaring upon their intended victims like tigers couched to spring.

They were now about ninety yards from where the three trappers stood concealed, and from this position a clear view was obtainable of both the travellers and the prowling savages.

" Now, young fellur's the time to show yer shootin'," cried Jake to Pierre.   " I guess old Plumcentre ur a pantin' to be let go at one of them red skunks.   Do ee take the fellur as is kneelin', an' I'll take t'other'n. Now !"

At the word, the two rifles cracked together.   Never did a just Nemesis overtake criminals more opportunely.   The savage at whom old Jake had fired leaped from the ground with a cry, and plunged heavily forward, falling dead upon the body of his companion, who was shot through the brain.

The astonishment and consternation of the two travellers can hardly be described, when, at the reports of the rifles, they started from their positions and first saw the bodies of the Indians lying on the grass, and then beheld the trappers advancing to them from the cover of the woods.   At first they seemed to apprehend a fate for themselves similar to that which had overtaken the Indians; and, filled with this idea, they ran towards the canoe, into which the gentleman handed his companion, and was preparing to follow himself when Pierre called out,—

"Don't fear, sir! we are friends."

"Ay," said old Jake, "we're the raal articles, I guess. 'A friend in need,' they say, 'is a friend indeed;' and I reckon that's just what we ur."

The gentleman, however, seemed only half assured, and looked uneasily towards the hunters, who were not now many yards from the boat.

"Don't be skeert, old hoss," said Jake; "though ye mout 'a been, a leetle agone, if you'd knowed who wur behint yer. But I guess ye're safe enuff now."

Pierre now explained what had occurred; and when the gentleman had recovered from his surprise, he accompanied Jake and Gaultier to the spot where the bodies of the savages lay.

No sooner did the stranger see these than he exclaimed,—

"Ah! I know these fellows, and I see now what prompted them to attack us. You must know," he continued, "that I am a chief trader in the Hudson Bay Company's service, and these two Indians applied to me some time since for a further advance of goods of one sort or another, while at the same time they refused to pay for what they had already got, notwithstanding that they had had a good hunt and had plenty of furs. Seeing that they could not obtain their object, they became very insolent, and finally left the fort threatening vengeance. They learned at the fort, I suppose, that I was returning from one of the posts with my daughter, and they waylaid us as you saw."

Meanwhile Pierre was doing the amiable with the young lady, who thanked him with much warmth for the great service he had rendered both her father and herself. Pierre bashfully assured her that neither he nor his companions were entitled to any gratitude, as their intervention was solely the result of accident.

Jake now approached and received the thanks of Miss Frazer (for that was her name), with the manner of one unused to speak to the other sex. His awkwardness afforded much amusement to the two youths, who, however, did not allow Jake to perceive their merriment.

" Wal, ma'am," said the old trapper, " 'tain't much of a sarvice to brag of, I guess. Them two skunks meant mischief, sure ; but thur wa'n't much difficulty in introjoocin' Plumcentre hyur" (tapping his rifle) " to the varmints. Ef it had been a couple o' grizzlies now, thur mout 'a been something to talk about. Old Eph'm's onkimmon tough—*that* he ur! and it'd been pretty considerable o' a skrimmage afore *they* went under—that's a fact."

As it was now near mid-day, the trappers resolved to halt ; and Gaultier was despatched for the canoe, with which he soon returned. The whole party then dined together, Pierre helping Miss Frazer to the daintiest morsels with great gallantry. Mr. Frazer, on learning that the trappers intended to pass Fort Pierre, which was his post, cordially invited them to stay there on a visit as long as they wished.

He was much astonished and pleased to find that one of his new acquaintances was the hero of the adventure which bestowed the name of the fort as a *sobriquet* on its bearer. Pierre modestly refused to give the particulars of the *fracas*. But old Jake had no such scruples, and gave an account of the affair which even Pierre failed to recognize, so filled was it with the exaggerations and strange conceits peculiar to the old hunter.

Miss Frazer listened with eager interest, and at the conclusion fixed her eyes on the young trapper, who blushed crimson under the ordeal. It was evident, even at that early stage of the acquaintance, that Pierre was "a gone coon."

Chatting thus pleasantly together, the dinner hour passed speedily. To persons living in civilized communities it may seem strange that a young lady could so soon forget the terrible event that had so recently occurred, and take her dinner with apparent *sang-froid* within view of the corpses of her would-be murderers. But life in the wilderness soon strengthens the nerves, and the most sensitive become callous to impressions which seem a part of our nature. Perhaps it is as well that it should be so. It by no means follows that persons who can behold terrible scenes unmoved are destitute of the better feelings of humanity. These are merely subdued, and are only permitted to regain the ascendency when it is proper they should do so.

After the travellers had finished their repast, Mr. Frazer and his daughter re-embarked in their canoe, and led the way down the river, the voyageurs sometimes floating alongside, and at other times following close behind.

It was not a little remarkable that Pierre, who was ordinarily rather reserved, now manifested great interest in Miss Frazer's conversation. Old Jake once or twice muttered something which discomposed the young hunter considerably, and at which Gaultier laughed heartily. As often as these sallies were repeated, Pierre glanced uneasily towards Miss Frazer, to ascertain whether the old hunter's jokes had been overheard; and guessing by the unmoved expression of the young lady's face that she was unaware of the cause of the mirth, he usually suffered the canoe to fall behind that of the strangers, when he rated Gaultier soundly for the impropriety of his conduct. He was well aware of the utter uselessness of remonstrating with old Jake. Indeed, to have done so would most probably have led to an *exposé* of the matter, of which Pierre was by no means desirous.

This by-play seemed to give Jake exquisite delight; and to Pierre's great chagrin his allusions to " gone coons," " gizzards," and " squaws " became more pointed and frequent. To put an end to this annoyance, Pierre, who steered, directed the canoe to the nearest bank, and taking up his rifle he stepped ashore and plunged into the woods.

For some time the young hunter walked swiftly forward, very much incensed against his companions, and taking note neither of the declining sun nor of the direction in which he was going.

Descending a thickly wooded glen, he presently found himself in a natural basin some hundred yards across, quite free of timber, and covered with a thick growth of rich succulent grass. Through the serried summits of the pines on the western bank of this depression the golden beams of the setting sun found their way, and fell on a mossy knoll beneath the branches of a maple. Here Pierre threw himself on the ground, and mused on the vexations to which he had been subjected.

With his reflections I do not propose to trouble my readers, nor am I anxious to fix the proportions in which the sweet and the bitter were mingled. After lying nearly motionless for more than an hour, Pierre at length rose and looked around. The sun had set and twilight had fallen. The edges of the woods looked dim and dark, and here and there a gray trunk stood out, relieved against the mysterious shade of the forest behind.

A sudden snapping of twigs caught the hunter's ear, and quietly cocking his rifle he glanced in the direction of the sound. At first nothing was visible; but soon

Pierre made out the figure of a tall animal standing between two trees which grew very close together at one end of the open space. After a careful inspection, he perceived that it was a bear seated on its haunches, and apparently engaged in taking a reconnaissance of the intruder on its domains. For some moments the animal continued this inspection, and then, suddenly dropping on all fours, advanced towards Pierre, uttering harsh snarling growls. The young hunter now for the first time perceived that two smaller animals followed close to the old one. It was evidently a female bear and her cubs. The presence of the latter explained the boldness of the parent. Usually the black bear avoids man, and will only attack when obliged to do so in self-defence. To this rule there are, of course, exceptions, as temper varies in bears as well as in human beings. In the rutting season, and when accompanied by its young, the bear becomes very aggressive, and at these seasons is a dangerous antagonist, if it can get to close quarters with the hunter.

On the present occasion Pierre was well aware that he would have either to fight or to run ; and as he felt it beneath his manhood to retreat, he braced his nerves for the encounter.

The twilight had thickened considerably, and a dusky gloom, which seemed to advance from the surrounding forest, rendered objects indistinct at a few yards' distance. Pierre, however, advanced towards his assailant, whose attention was somewhat divided between her rising anger against the hunter and her maternal solicitude for the safety of her progeny. She would rush forward a few steps, showing her teeth and growling ferociously; and then, turning to her cubs, she would apparently endeavour to induce them to retreat to the shelter of the woods, accompanying them a little way herself. She would then suddenly turn round, and bound forward towards Pierre, uttering savage snarls. The dim light, combined with the quick movements of the beast and her dark colour, which rendered her extremely indistinct, prevented Pierre from taking a certain aim.

He therefore advanced quickly with his rifle at his shoulder, with the intention of firing at close quarters, and ending the contest with one shot. The bear, nothing daunted by the boldness of the hunter, rushed to meet him. Pierre took a hasty aim and pulled the trigger. No report followed. Before he could throw down the lever of his rifle the savage beast was on him. With a blow of its paw it sent the rifle flying from the hunter's grasp, and immediately closed with him, hardly giving him time to draw his knife!

Embraced in a deadly hug, with the shining teeth of the monster at his face, Pierre gave himself up for lost. He did not, however, lose his presence of mind, but fought madly on, plunging his knife into the side of his antagonist, and trying to keep his feet. Suddenly he stumbled over a root, and in a moment lay on his back with the bear above, its eyes glaring into his, and its fetid breath pouring hot on his face. A sensation of weakness overpowered the hunter, objects swam before his eyes, and he fainted.

How long he lay in this state he never ascertained. When he regained consciousness he found himself where he had fallen. At a little distance he could perceive the bear, apparently dead, while round its carcass snuffed and gambolled the two young ones.

On endeavouring to rise, he was glad to find that no bones were broken; but a feeling of numbness rendered his limbs almost powerless, so that he was obliged to crawl towards the dead animal.

The young bears growled loudly; but the hunter cared little for these manifestations of anger, and continued his approach. The animals then withdrew to the shelter of the forest, where they gave evidence of their presence by an occasional low moan; probably a call to their mother, whose death they had not yet realized.

On examining the body, which was still quite warm, Pierre perceived that blood trickled from a deep knife-wound behind the shoulder. This was probably the fatal stab which had rescued him from almost certain death.

The moon was now just sinking behind the western forest, and cast her pale light on the stems of the trees at the eastern edges of the opening. Dense shadow veiled all beyond; and against the sombre background the trunks of the birches showed ghostly white, while not a sound broke the intense stillness of the forest. A few stars twinkled here and there among the belts of cloud that stretched across the sky, and looked wan and pale through a thin white mist which overspread the opening.

The night was chill, and Pierre shivered with cold. With some difficulty—for he was still somewhat stiff from the effects of his encounter—he managed to reach the forest, and soon collected a large pile of dry brushwood. This he lighted, having fortunately some matches in his pocket. He then produced his pipe, and, seated on a log near the fire, he mused on the events of the day. He pictured to himself Jake and Gaultier at their camp fire, and their uneasiness at his absence. He thought of Mr. Frazer and his daughter. Would *she* also be uneasy at his disappearance? He tried to answer this question in the affirmative.

Feeling hungry, he helped himself to some slices of the bear, and broiled them over the coals. While thus engaged, his attention was arrested by hearing the rush of some animal behind him; and turning quickly, he beheld in the dim light a noble cariboo buck dashing across the glade, while hard at his heels raced several grayish animals, their mouths lolling open and their teeth gleaming white, as they came within the light of the fire. These Pierre recognized at a glance as the fierce white wolves of the northern forests. Their bushy tails were stretched out straight as they galloped with a speed that seemed unearthly in pursuit of their prey.

Evidently they did not perceive the fire until they were close to it, so engrossed were they in the chase. With a simultaneous rush they swerved aside, but still continued the pursuit. The buck had already disappeared, and Pierre, seizing his rifle, dropped the last wolf by a lucky shot, the animal turning a complete somersault with the impetus of its motion.

The shot, however, was not immediately fatal, and as Pierre approached, the disabled beast bared its gleaming teeth and tried to rush at him. Its back had been broken by the bullet, and finding itself unable to stand, it tried to drag itself into the woods. But Pierre turned it over dead on the spot with a bullet through the brain. He then dragged it to the fire, where he occupied himself after his supper of bearsteaks in removing the handsome skin, which he used for a blanket, having neglected to bring his "five-point mackinaw" from the canoe. Before turning in for the night, the young hunter piled up an immense fire; and then drawing his wolfskin over him, he lay down with his feet towards the glowing coals, and soon fell into a doze.

Although it was now well advanced in the summer, the night was raw and cold; and notwithstanding the great embers, which blazed brightly whenever a breeze waked them up, Pierre shivered in his sleep. A sensation of fear oppressed him; and, full of the consciousness of impending danger, he suddenly awoke with a cry and looked around. The moon had gone down behind the forest, and objects in the open space were scarcely discernible by the feeble light of the stars, which were veiled behind a whitish vapour.

The fire had burned low, and threw a dull glow upon the trunks of the trees in its immediate vicinity, leaving all beyond wrapped in the unfathomable gloom of the woods. An armful of brush soon caused the fire to blaze up brightly; and by its light Pierre saw at a little distance five dusky gray forms which he knew to be wolves—probably those which had passed in pursuit of the cariboo. Failing to overtake their quarry, they had returned to the camp; attracted, most likely, by the body of the bear, as also, perhaps, by that of their companion, both which lay at a short distance from the fire.

At the sight of the freshly-kindled blaze they slunk out of view behind some bushes ere the hunter could seize his rifle. It was probably the consciousness of the presence of these dangerous animals which rendered Pierre's sleep broken, and impressed him with an undefined sense of peril. Strange that our dormant faculties should be influenced by intangible impressions from without, which in our waking moments might fail to secure our attention!

He did not again venture to sleep, but kept up a good fire, at which he sat, having his rifle in readiness, while his eye constantly sought the spot where he had seen the wolves disappear.

Towards morning, fatigued with watching, the hunter took his rifle and left the camp with the intention of reaching the river and rejoining his companions. He walked quietly down the glade, and just as he was entering the woods at the farther end he glanced back, and perceived that the wolves, emboldened by his departure, had emerged from their retreat, and were already loping and snarling round the carcasses.

Not caring to shoot another, he pushed forward as well as the darkness and the difficulties of the path would permit. In an hour he struck the river and followed its course, hoping soon to come within view of the camp-fire of his comrades.

He had not proceeded far when his quick ear detected the approach of a canoe by the dipping of the paddles, while he could also hear the occupants conversing in low tones. Presently the boat shot into view, and he was delighted to find the paddlers were old Jake and Gaultier, who had become uneasy at his prolonged absence, and were now in search of him. Pierre stepped into the canoe, and while Jake and Gaultier paddled back to their camp, he gave them an account of his adventures since he had left them. He was afraid to ask if Miss Frazer and her father were at the camp; but on his arrival there he was much disappointed to find that they had continued their journey to the fort, having been met by a *bateau* manned by French half-breeds, which had been despatched to meet them.

He therefore made no remark; although old Jake, who observed his crest-fallen manner, smiled grimly and said,—

"I guess I feels kinder lonesome now arter the trader and his daurter. I calc'late she thinks hersell some pumpkins, and thinks fellurs like us of no account."

Pierre did not reply, but lay down to snatch some sleep before day, the advent of which was already heralded by the distant howling of the wolves.

CHAPTER IV.

IN a day or two the party approached the junction of the Clearwater with the Athabasca. This spot is called the Forks. Birds of many species peopled the woods along the banks; and the Athabasca itself was thronged with flocks of ducks and swans of several kinds. This river may be considered as forming the head-waters of the Mackenzie, which it joins after leaving the Great Slave Lake, into which it flows, under the name of the Slave River.

Many islands, covered with forest, studded the ample bosom of the stream ; and amidst these the hunters had many opportunities of trying their rifles at the trumpeter swans, which they surprised within range by suddenly rounding the wooded promontories which afforded cover for approach.

Bears, too, were sometimes seen, especially early in the morning, when the party observed them wandering by the edge of the forest, into which they retreated at sight of the boat.

Amongst the wildfowl perhaps the most numerous were the wild geese, of which incredible numbers annually migrate within the Arctic Circle to breed. Of these they noticed several species;—snow-geese, so called from the snowy whiteness of their plumage; brent-geese, the most common kind in Canada; barnacle and laughing-geese were very numerous; and at every meal the hunters feasted on these birds, until they became satiated and anxious for a change of food.

The Indians shoot, snare, and trap immense numbers of ducks, geese, and swans, during the bi-annual migrations. Indeed these people would probably starve at certain periods of the year, if they were deprived by any cause of the means of subsistence afforded by the wildfowl. Deer and other animals are often scarce, and not to be depended on for a livelihood; but twice in the year the ducks, swans, and geese arrive in countless flights, and at these times the natives revel in the midst of plenty. With characteristic thoughtlessness they do not make provision from this bountiful supply for the season of scarcity. Hence, during the intensely severe winters they are frequently in a state of absolute starvation, and are sometimes reduced to the horrible extremity of preying on each other, as we have elsewhere observed.

Among the ducks the youths observed considerable variety of species. Some, and these were the least numerous, were distinguished by red eyes, greenish-black mandibles of a nearly straight form, and a pepper-and-salt coloured plumage. These were the famous canvas-back ducks, the delicacy of whose flavour is supposed to surpass that of all other water-fowl. Others nearly resembling these, differing only in having orange-yellow eyes and concave bluish bills, they recognized as red heads. Besides these there were wood-ducks; king-ducks, so called from their gaudy plumage; harlequin ducks; whistlers, named from the whistling sound made in their rapid flight; shovellers, from the shape of their mandibles; squaw-ducks, or old-wives—a term derived from the almost ceaseless clamour which these birds keep up; and many other kinds.

There are no less than eighteen different species of ducks in the American waters; but it is a question if some of these are not identical with others differently classified, merely varying in some trivial particular which can hardly be held to constitute a difference of species.

The swans were carefully skinned by the hunters at each camp by the way; and such were the numbers in which they met these birds that they soon collected a goodly pile of the handsome "pelts," which they readily disposed of at the fort on the Forks of the Athabasca.

During their descent of the Clearwater, the youths remarked the ragged air which generally characterizes the forest along that river. On the Athabasca, however, the woods presented a marked contrast. Trees of gigantic size were frequent along the banks. There were white spruces, which in this region often reach an altitude of one hundred and fifty feet, and attain a diameter of from three to four feet. The woods were dense and luxuriant, and in many places waved their branches over the waters, affording a grateful shade from the mid-day sun. Our hunters were hospitably entertained at the fort at the junction of the Clearwater with the Athabasca, and here they revelled in unwonted plenty.

For many a day they had not tasted anything more palatable than deer's flesh scorched over the coals, or the monotonous diet of duck, swan, and goose. Here, however, they feasted to their hearts' content on delicious moose venison, the succulent "mouffle" being the most relished part of the animal; on tender steaks from the wood buffalo; and on what they valued even more, delicious vegetables from the garden attached to the fort.

From this land of plenty they were loath to depart; but at length they tore themselves away, and once more floated down the beautiful river.

Long reaches, enclosed between high forest-clad banks, extended before them; the ample bosom of the stream, here some six hundred yards in breadth, being studded with numerous islands, against whose shores the mighty flood breasted with a rushing sound.

Sometimes the high banks gave place to the level plain, and from the soft clay verge came the smell of tar, as if the soil were impregnated with some bituminous substance.

On the fourth day after leaving the fort the hunters determined to camp for a few days by the river. Moose were reported to be tolerably numerous in this quarter, and the woodland cariboo were said to exist in large bands. A hut was speedily constructed of fir boughs, and the baggage safely stowed within. The canoe was placed, bottom up, by the edge of the stream; and the seams, which had begun to leak a little, were well calked with the resin of the *épinette*, or spruce tree.

Early on the following day Jake and Pierre shouldered their rifles and entered the woods, leaving Gaultier in charge of the camp. The two hunters, however, did not mean to hunt in company. By separating they would cover much more ground, and thus have a better chance of meeting with game. Jake took the forest lying down stream from the camp, while Pierre took that above. We will accompany the latter.

For some time the young trapper walked swiftly forward, threading his way among the columnar trunks of white spruce, and creeping through the denser underbrush of young fir woods which had sprung up where the older growth had been cleared out by a forest fire or a hurricane.

At these places the ground was so encumbered by

trees lying at every conceivable angle to each other, and so interlaced with matted twigs and trailing plants, together with the almost impenetrable cover made by the young pines that grew up amidst the tangled mass, that Pierre found it almost impossible to advance. Several times behind the thick cover he heard animals breaking away, alarmed at the noise which he could not avoid making. But he failed to catch even a momentary glimpse of them, so thick was the screen of branches.

At length, hot and breathless, he emerged from these tangled woods, and once more walked with comparative ease amid the open forest. Here and there he noticed tracks of deer, which from their size he knew to be those of moose, but as yet he had not seen any kind of game since leaving the camp.

Light was shining through the trees ahead, and judging that here lay a prairie he advanced cautiously, keeping himself well screened from view. From the verge of the woods he saw a level plateau stretching north and east for a mile or two, backed in the distance by a fringe of trees which extended irregularly along the boundaries of the plain, and were here and there more or less thickly dotted over its surface.

Across this small prairie stretched a line of willows and poplars, with an occasional maple. Behind these Pierre well knew that a stream existed ; and he further guessed that if moose frequented these woods, this was the likeliest place to find them.

The willows grew densely, and offered a secure shelter from which to view the plain beyond, and which effectually concealed the hunter's approach from the gaze of every animal in that direction. Quietly separating the branches, Pierre pushed noiselessly through them, and shortly came upon the banks of a narrow stream whose dark waters flowed sluggishly between high clayey banks. Water-lilies dotted its surface in great profusion; and in several places the hunter noticed that these were much displaced, having been dragged from their hold in the soft bottom and left lying in tangled masses on the surface.

Where the opposite bank dipped down to the stream, affording access to the water, the earth was ploughed by many tracks, some of them so fresh that the water was still actually filling the impressions. Just below this spot the stream made a bend, and on gaining a position from which he could view the lower reach, Pierre was startled to perceive three huge animals immersed in the water, and tossing above its agitated surface their immense antlers as they shook the flies from their heads. Another of the same species browsed off the tender shoots of the willows which projected over the stream from the bank.

In an instant Pierre crouched out of sight, and prepared to approach. Fortunately the wind was in the right direction; and keeping well out of view, the young trapper stealthily reached a spot from which he had made up his mind to fire.

The ground was soft and much encumbered with rotten sticks, the cracking of any one of which beneath the incautious foot would at once startle the wary game. Pierre, however, advanced with the noiseless stealth of an Indian, and in a very few minutes he had the satisfaction of finding himself behind the bush which he had marked as his final cover.

Peering cautiously through the shimmering, waving branches of the willows, he could see the moose still in the same position, with the exception of the one which he had noticed browsing on the bushes along the bank. That animal had vanished. The hunter did not speculate upon this, but singled out the largest head and antlers among the others as his trophy.

The huge beasts had ceased to feed, and stood up to their necks in the cool element, occasionally shaking a head, or twitching an ear, as they were annoyed by the flies which continually torment the Cervidæ. One immense beast towered above his comrades and stood immersed to his throat, facing the hunter at a distance of scarcely fifty yards. This individual Pierre immediately selected as his victim, and he accordingly raised his rifle to fire.

The breeze, which had hitherto befriended his approach, now eddied round suddenly, and bore upon its treacherous wings the taint of the trapper's presence. In an instant the apparently unwieldy beasts plunged towards the bank with mighty splashings and flounderings, throwing showers of mud and water high into the air. The swaying to and fro of the thickly-leaved branches prevented Pierre from getting a sure aim; but just as the monarch of the band reached the farther bank he pressed the trigger.

With a tremendous bound the animal acknowledged the shot, but there the hunter's success seemed to end. A thick fringe of bushes concealed the moose from view, and through this Pierre could hear them crashing as they rushed from the scene of danger.

To cross the deep canal-like brook and follow the game was now the difficulty. After a short search, however, the hunter came to a place where a projection of the bank narrowed the stream considerably. Making a desperate leap from this vantage-ground, Pierre nearly landed on the opposite side. Luckily the water was not here more than three feet in depth, so the hunter escaped with a good splashing.

Climbing up the bank he soon gained the open plain beyond the willows, and at its farther verge he saw two moose making for the woods in a long swinging trot, while the third animal, that at which he had fired, lagged far behind, and sometimes came to a halt altogether.

With a cry of delight the youth ran forward, and soon gained considerably on the moose, who, finding escape hopeless, came to a standstill and faced round suddenly, licking his lips viciously, while his eye seemed to flash with fiery anger. Pierre could now see that his bullet had entered the animal's side too far back to be immediately fatal. From the wound a stream of blood still poured.

Not wishing to come to close quarters with so formidable an antagonist, Pierre halted at some twenty yards from his victim. He raised his rifle in a leisurely way, and took aim. He would have staked his life on the shot, so certain did he feel that the next moment would declare him the victor. He directed his bullet at the junction of the throat with the chest, hoping to pierce the heart or lungs.

As the smoke floated aside he fully expected to see the moose struggling in its death agonies on the ground. But, stung to madness with the pain of its wounds, the huge animal summoned all its remaining strength, and before the hunter could spring aside it had cleared the distance that intervened between them.

Pierre attempted to insert another cartridge, and found to his horror that he had allowed the magazine to become empty. The shot he had just fired was the last in his rifle. Before he could extract a fresh cartridge from his pouch, the moose with frantic energy sprang at him. In vain Pierre attempted to defend himself with his rifle. A toss from the ponderous antlers sent it flying to the distance of several yards; and defenceless and alone the hunter had to face the unequal contest.

Fortunately the crippled condition of the moose prevented it from at once ending the strife by trampling Pierre to death. But such was its activity, despite its

disabled condition, that it was only by the exercise of
the fullest agility that Pierre could save himself from
the infuriated animal, which twisted, turned, and
charged with great rapidity.

At this juncture the hunter glanced hurriedly round
in search of a tree which might afford him some
security. But not one was near enough, with the
exception of a thin, tall poplar. This grew not more
than one hundred yards from the spot. If he could
but reach it! the hunter thought that if once among
its branches he would be safe—for the present, at
all events. This reflection scarcely occupied him an
instant, and he at once prepared to carry it out. The
moose just at this moment stood between Pierre and
the tree, but this was exactly what the young trapper
desired. The beast made a sudden rush forward.
Pierre nimbly stepped aside from the animal's path,
and before it could wheel to renew the attack the
hunter made for the friendly shelter of the tree at his
best pace.

With a snort of rage the awkward, long-legged
animal turned to pursue. Never did Pierre make
such use of his legs. Fortunately for him the race
was short, or he never would have survived the adventure. As a rule, the moose is a wary, timid creature,
flying from danger on the slightest intimation of its
proximity. But when wounded and followed, it will
frequently cast aside all idea of further flight, and then
it fights with the malignant desperation of a demon.

Luckily for our hunter, his last shot was now beginning to tell on his antagonist, so that he was able to reach the tree in time to swing himself upon a branch which grew some ten feet from the ground, just as the moose with a rush passed beneath.

Panting with his exertions, and vexed at the result of his morning's hunt, Pierre climbed higher into the tree, which indeed was so slight as to afford but precarious sanctuary from his powerful foe, should the latter try to overturn it. The branches were weak, and bent beneath his weight as he carefully drew himself upward, while the tree itself inclined slightly to one side.

Apparently the moose perceived this; for instead of plunging round and round below, it now applied its broad forehead to the slender trunk, and pushed heavily against it. A further inclination of the tree was the result of this manœuvre.

Fearful of the consequences, should the infuriated animal succeed in overturning his place of refuge, Pierre descended to the lower branches, and endeavoured to distract the attention of the moose from his task. In his first scuffle with the animal, his revolver and knife which he usually carried about with him had fallen from his belt, and he had not time to pick them up. He was therefore now completely defenceless. The moose, in no way distracted from his efforts to uproot the poplar, horned and pushed so violently that the elastic tree swayed to and fro, and if the hunter had not tightly grasped the branches he would have been quickly shaken from his perch.

Backing from the trunk, the maddened beast suddenly rushed against it with all the force it could command; and with a loud crack several roots burst and shot above the earth. The tree now leaned seriously to one side, and encouraged by this success the moose again charged, tearing off the bark by the force of the concussion. Pierre with terror perceived that the tree was yielding to the pressure, and before he could resolve on what course of action he should next pursue, the remaining roots gave way one by one, and the tree fell to the ground.

With a cry of horror the young hunter gave himself up for lost. The moose sprang forward to the attack; but at that instant the sharp crack of a rifle was heard, and with a mighty bound the huge beast plunged forward to the earth, ploughing up the turf with its ponderous antlers. It was old Jake who had so opportunely come to his comrade's assistance.

Pierre quickly disentangled himself from the branches, and stood over the still quivering carcass of his late antagonist.

"Jehoshaphat!" exclaimed the old trapper, coming forward. "I guess old Plumcentre air yer providence, young fellur. Ef I hadn't put in my say, you'd a gone under—*you* would this hyur day, as sure as beaver medicine."

Pierre expressed his sense of obligation, which the

queer old fellow would not listen to. "Wagh!" cried he, "yer ain't a-talkin' to a tenderfoot from the settlements. In the woods we all helps another, an' no blessed muss about it. Come, old coon," he continued, "I'm a-gwine to raise your nose for breakfast."

So saying, the old trapper unsheathed his shining knife, and separated the "mouffle," or overhanging upper lip of the moose, and placed it in his *possible sack*. Meantime Pierre recovered his arms, and between them the two trappers butchered the carcass and returned to camp, staggering under the weight of as much meat as they could carry. The hide was suspended to a pole cut from the ill-fated poplar; in which position the hunters hoped it would act as a sufficient scare-wolf.

When they arrived at the camp, they found that Gaultier had not been idle. A glittering pile of fish lay upon the bank; and just as they approached the fire, the young hunter drew in a large tittameg, or white-fish, which he threw among the others. That morning the party feasted royally. Old Jake shared his *bonne bouche* with his companions; and being in high good humour, as he ordinarily was when he had done anything unusual, or whenever he was satisfying his appetite on favourite viands, he volunteered to tell the youths his own morning adventures.

"Why," said Pierre, "I thought you had neither seen nor shot anything to-day—except the moose of course."

"Wagh!" exclaimed the trapper, "your tongue wags

faster nor a beaver's tail in flood time! I guess now ef it had been you instead of this child, we'd all on us a heerd tell what ye'd done fast enuff. There's two things," he continued, "a hunter shud never do. One is, to boast o' what he's done; and t'other is, to stir a yard arter firin' without loadin' his rifle. Them two things gets a fellur into wuss musses than a'most anything else—leastways in these hyur diggin's."

Pierre, abashed, said nothing; nor did he remark on the apparent inconsistency of the old hunter's conduct in condemning boasting, when in fact the one thing Jake did best was boasting—if we except shooting, of which he certainly was a master.

While the moose steaks hissed on the embers, and were swiftly vanishing before the lusty appetites of the party, old Jake employed his oracular mouth in the intervals of eating with an account of the following adventure.

CHAPTER V.

"WAL, now, boyees," said the old fellow, "you might make yersells rich bettin' rotten pumpkins agin Spanish mules that I have made a 'raise' this mornin'. I ain't a-gwine to hide my luck. No; thur ain't nothin' mean about old Jake Hawken—that thur ain't. I guess we three fellurs trap on shares, an it'd be raal mean ef I hid my plunder an' kep' it to meself.—Ye rec'lects whur I parted from you?" he continued, turning to Pierre, who nodded in the affirmative. "Wal, I turned down the river a bit, till I kem to the mouth o' a crick which jined the Athabasca from the west'ard. The land about the mouth of this crick wur low, and wur kivered with thunderin' big trees, white spruce at that. I noticed that the banks riz a leetle up the crick, until they got to be like bluffs a'most. Hyur the timmer drew back from the edge, an' the rocks wur bare, 'ceptin' hyur and thur, whur an odd pine or two grew among the donnicks. I wur jest a-thinkin' whether I'd

turn up the crick, or wade it and keep by the main
river, when I noticed in the soft bank the fresh tracks
o' a moccasin. I knowed well enuff 'twur a Redskin
made 'em, an' I skinned my eyes, ye may bet high, to
get a glimp o' the crittur. Now, boyees, don't you
think I hankered arter that Injun's scalp. No! I've
gev up that sort o' bisness sin' last year, when I got to
see how sinful an' wicked it wur to kill our kind.
But this child took a notion that mebbe that thur Redskin wurn't Christianized, an' mout take a fancy to my
old top-knot to fringe his leggin's with. So I jest kep'
my old peepers alive, and follered the trail, which wur
plain to be seed as Chimbly Rock. I warn't long in
kummin to whur the crick cañoned through the rocks,
and hyur I noticed the sign led into the water, which
washed clost up to the face o' the bluffs. The banks
kep' on risin' higher an' higher, an' soon they a'most
closed up a couple o' hundred feet overhead. 'Twur
mighty bad walkin', fellurs, I kin tell yer. The water
wur strong, an' in places wur deep enuff a'most to float
this niggur off his legs. Wal, I wur wonderin' what'n
thunder cud 'a brought that Redskin up sich a horrible
gulch, whur thur warn't light enuff to squint through
hindsights, when, jest as I made a bend in the crick,
what shed I see but that Injun 'ithin a hundred yards
o' me, climbin' up the bluff like a wild-cat torst a hole
I noticed under a rocky ledge sixty feet above the
water.

"I guess I drew back out o' sight, and watched what

wur a-gwine to happen. It wur plaguy hard work, I reck'n, to climb up whur the Injun wur. He tuck a rest every few minutes, and then began agin.

"The cliff wur well-nigh perpendic'lur, an' once or twice I thort he'd lose his balance and fall back into the crick. Jest below him wur a pile o' big stones, agin which the water rushed. Ef he fell on them I guessed he'd be a gone coon in a quarter less'n no time. I wur mighty cur'ous to see what he wur up to, and hardly breathed for fear I'd lose a single bit of it.

"I noticed a line hangin' out o' the cave above, and torst this the Injun dragged hisself. At last he got his claws upon it, and hung upon it, hauling hisself up, hand over hand. I now thort he wur safe; but jest as he brought his head level with the bottom of the cave, the rope broke, and with a mighty screech, which I heerd above the roarin' o' the crick, he fell upon the rocks at the foot o' the bluff!

"Wal, I a'most felt froze to the spot when I saw the poor critter fall; but I made torst him at once and riz him out o' the water when he wur a drowndin'. Blood kem from his ears an' nose an' mouth. He wur jest able to say, 'Wild-cat Paleface's friend. Cache up thur. Paleface can keep all!' His head fell over, limber-like, an' he slipped from my hands as dead as a last year's straddlebug.

"Wal, I wur main sorry for the poor critter. No doubt he had his little store o' plunder cached away up above, an' wur drawing on it to trade some powder

or some sich want at the fort. Wal, thur wur no use
in cryin' over him, an' so I set him up agin the cliff,
and fell to thinkin' how I cud manage to drag my old
carkidge up to the cave.

"I wur determined to take a peep into that Injun's
cache, an' not even what I had jest seen cud change
my mind. Ef I had a rope it 'ud be easy work enuff,
provided I cud hitch it round somethin' up above; but
then I hadn't the rope. While I wur a-spec'latin' on
this differculty, I noticed that the dead Injun had a first-
rate set o' buckskins. I wur tempted to wear 'em
mysell, but my own wur too good to throw off yet a
bit; an' besides, I didn't cotton to the notion o' wearin'
a dead man's plunder.

"I tuck the idee, hows'ever, o' makin' a lasso out
o' the huntin' shirt an' leggin's, an' in the whisk of a
prairie-dog's tail I wur cuttin' them up into strips. I
soon had made the very thing I wanted. But to fix it
wur now the rub. My rope wur nigh forty feet long,
an' would hang low enuff for me to climb up to, ef I
cud only hitch it to the cave somehow.

"Wal, I fixed it at last this-a-way. The cave wur
about twenty feet higher than it wur possible to climb
to; the rock got so smooth, there warn't footin' for a
cat. But in the mouth o' the cave itself a bit o' rock
stuck up like the stump o' a tree. Ef I cud lasso this, I
had nothin' more to do than to haul myself up like a sack
o' flour in a mill. I fixed a good runnin' noose at the end
o' the rope, an' arter a few trials I made it fast at last.

"I wur a bit skeery at fust about swingin' out wi' my whole weight on the rope; but thinkin' didn't make it any easier, an' at last I jest let mysel' go. You bet, boys, my old elbers ached afore I clawed mysel' into that thur hole. Hows'ever, I *did* get in, and looked about me.

"At fust I cudn't 'a seed Pike's Peak ef it had been painted white an' stud afore me. But in a minute or so I got used to the darkness, an' I cud hardly b'lieve my eyes. Thur wur piles an' piles o' the finest furs (and I knows what *they* are, I reckon) that I ever sot my peepers on. The fust lot I got my clutches on wur fifteen o' the grandest black foxes ye ever seed. Boyees, I wur clean 'mazed. Thur wur bear an' beaver in plenty; carcajou an' deer hides, an' all sorts. I guess that Redskin wur an out-an'-out good trapper, an' besides must hev hit a streak o' the tallest sort o' luck. He must have been layin' up them pelts fur years. Thur's no location in all creation where he cud 'a raised all *them* in one season's trappin'. Anyhow, I guess he never thort he wur a-layin' em by fur *me*. No; that he didn't."

Here the old trapper chuckled a little at the idea of falling heir to the Indian's wealth.

"Wal," he continued, "the missioner once said to me, 'Virtue is its own reward;' an' sure enuff, ef I had met that Injun and raised his ha'r as I used to do, we wouldn't now hev a cupple o' hunder pounds' worth o' plunder."

Pierre and Gaultier had listened with breathless interest to the old hunter's story. They now proposed an immediate visit to the cave. To their surprise old Jake seemed embarrassed, and hesitated in a manner very unusual with him. The boys misconstrued the trapper's manner.

"'Tain't no use fightin' agin natur," they heard him muttering; "but yet this coon don't b'lieve in sich things."

"What things, Jake?" asked Gaultier.

"Wagh! young fellur, how d'ye know what I wur a-thinkin' of?" exclaimed the hunter. "Wal, I wur jest a-sayin' to myself that I didn't b'lieve in spooks walkin', an' all sich sort o' rubbish. That's what this nigger wur a-thinking."

"What spooks, Jake?" inquired Pierre.

"Ye see," said Jake, "it's gettin' latish, an' the place is better'n four mile away from hyur; an' agin we got there, what with the nat'ral darkness o' the cave an' the evenin', I guess we mout jest run agin that thur Injun's spook. I've heerd tell they're mighty fond o' hangin' round whur their plunder's cached, or whur they've gone under; an' I guess this location matches both them p'ints."

The boys, who had been better educated than Jake, smiled and interchanged looks, but so covertly that it escaped the notice of the odd old hunter. They said nothing more on the subject; but it was resolved to visit the cave early on the following morning, and to bring away all the treasures it contained.

As the mouth of the creek was down stream, in which direction they were travelling, the hunters broke up camp at an early hour and embarked in the canoe. They were not long in reaching the embouchure of the stream.

Turning up its sombre waters, which flowed sluggishly beneath the heavy shade of overhanging pines, they shortly came to a spot where the shallowness of the stream compelled them to leave the boat and proceed on foot. Alternately wading in the shallows, and creeping round the base of the cliffs to avoid the deep pools which swirled and eddied fiercely round huge boulders fallen from above, they presently arrived at a bend in the course of the creek.

"Look hyur," said old Jake; "hyur's the very spot where I got the fust glimp o' the Injun. Yonder's the cave."

Looking upwards, the youths in truth perceived a dark opening in the face of the cliff, beneath a beetling rock that overhung the entrance. On the summit of the bluffs a few stunted pines were relieved against the sky, stretching their ragged arms over the abyss. Others, having probably been uprooted in a tempest, hung head downwards, or grew at various angles to the cliffs. Both above and below the spot, the waters of the creek rushed over their uneven bed, filling the gloomy passage with the hoarse roar of ceaseless strife against rock and boulder.

It was a wild scene, and was rendered doubly so on

the present occasion by the murky sky which lowered above the cliffs, as well as by the dead Indian, who still retained the upright position against the rocks in which Jake had placed him. His limbs had become rigid, his eyes were open, and he seemed to fix a stony stare upon the party as they approached.

A couple of vultures flapped heavily across the summit of the chasm, their foul instincts having led them to the spot to banquet on the corpse. One of these perched upon a pine which leaned forward from the cliff.

"Wagh!" exclaimed Jake, with strong disgust, "look at that thur stinkin' case. I guess they'd 'a made a meal o' the Redskin ef we hadn't kem too soon.—Hyur's a pill for yer," he continued, raising his rifle.

At the report, which echoed from side to side of the cañon with a thousand reverberations, the ungainly bird dropped from the branch, and whirling down with great rapidity, it fell with a heavy sound upon a pile of boulders which parted the waters of the creek.

The hunters had brought a strong hide lasso with them from the canoe, and old Jake, having attached this firmly to the rope which he had used on the preceding day, and which still depended from the cave, swung himself up with many a kick and scramble. In this position he presented so ludicrous a spectacle that the boys could not restrain their mirth, and burst into shouts of laughter.

"Giggle-goggle, young fellurs, till yer busts. Ye're

welcome to yer fun. See if ye can shin it up more graceful than this coon. I guess ye'll find it pretty considerable o' a climb afore ye stands hyur."

So saying, the old hunter vanished into the cave. He spoke truly when he said that the youths would find the ascent of the rock far from easy. Pierre, who had the advantage of Gaultier in years as well as in muscle, was not long in handing himself upwards, making use of every excrescence or projection to plant his feet upon. But the latter had several times to relinquish the attempt and rest before renewing his exertions.

At length, however, he stood in the entrance of the cave and rejoined his companions. Old Jake's description of the stores which the Indian had accumulated were not much exaggerated. There were many beaver-skins piled neatly one on the other, and all in good condition. Deer-hides and bear-skins had each their respective places, as indeed had all the others, the ill-fated Redskin having evidently been a lover of order in the arrangement of his effects.

In all, the trappers counted one hundred beaver, fifty moose and cariboo hides, twenty-five bear-skins, fifteen black foxes, and twenty various, making a very handsome total. Besides the furs and peltries there was a collection of traps, most of which were in good working order; and on a shelf were a smooth-bore single gun with long barrel, of small gauge, with pouches, some ammunition, and various small articles used by the late proprietor in pursuit of his calling. On the floor of the cavern were the remains of a fire which had evidently been used during the preceding few days.

Clearly the Indian had made his cache his place of residence. Some cooking utensils lay scattered around, and from a peg in a crevice hung the hams of a fine cariboo buck.

As old Jake investigated the condition of each skin separately, and bound them into packs of a convenient size for removal, the examination lasted for many hours. At length all was ready for their departure. Pierre volunteered to make the descent first, and deposit each bundle as it was lowered in a place of safety. With this intention he advanced to the mouth of the cave, when an exclamation from him brought his companions to his side in a moment. While they had been busied in their occupation, the rain had been descending in torrents, and the creek, swollen by the deluge, thundered down the cañon with ever-increasing volume. Small trees and wrack were whirled swiftly by—the former sometimes uprearing themselves in their natural position above the foaming flood, sometimes standing reversed, their roots uppermost, as they were caught in the fierce eddies.

The first thought of the hunters was for their canoe, which contained their stores, and in fact almost the whole of their worldly possessions. It was, without doubt, swept from its fastenings and carried down to the Athabasca, or capsized and sunk among the boulders which everywhere obstructed the channel of the creek.

Peering over the verge of the entrance, the hunters saw that the waters had crept up the bank which just below sloped up from the former level of the creek to the face of the cliff. It was at the highest point of this that Jake had placed the dead Indian, and now the foam-covered stream rose about the body, and gradually reached higher and higher.

"I reckon he'll float out o' this gulch in half a shake more," said Jake; and so, in fact, it happened. The body, disturbed by the lapping of the waves, fell from its position, and being caught by the stream, was quickly whirled along, sometimes disappearing altogether, sometimes visible for a moment as it was borne upon the surging bosom of the torrent. Just at the bend of the creek, where some large rocks broke the water into foam as it bounded over them, the body suddenly rose upright from the surface, with hands outspread, and slowly heeled over, disappearing round the corner.

"Jehoshaphat, fellurs!" cried Jake, "did yer see that? The skunk shook his fist at us, I'm sartin. Ef we're tied up in this hyur trap to-night, as seems most likely, *he'll* walk in among us. That's sure as shootin'."

The youths said nothing; not because they shared the old hunter's superstition, but they were impressed by the solemnity of the scene, and the weird spectacle of the upright corpse, which seemed to toss its arms frantically as it vanished from their eyes.

Abroad, the rain still hissed upon the turbid waters, which had now risen eight or ten feet above their former height, and rendered escape at present impossible. Within, the cave was shrouded in darkness, in which the figure of old Jake was dimly discernible as he groped about among the packs of skins. Suddenly a vivid light flashed through the gloom, startling the party, gleaming on the rifle barrels, and revealing for an instant the most distant corners of the cavern. Almost simultaneously a deafening crash of thunder bellowed through the gorge, completely overpowering the roar of the torrent, and echoing with intensified loudness from cliff to cliff, like the continued discharge of batteries of heavy artillery.

The comparative silence which followed this uproar of nature seemed oppressive by the contrast, although the stream still rushed on with unabated violence at the height of twenty feet above its ordinary level. After a lull of some minutes, a loud roll of thunder again shook the air, immediately succeeded by lightning of intensest brilliancy. Flash followed flash in rapid succession. The rain continued to descend even more heavily than before.—It was now late in the afternoon, and the hunters began to feel hungry. They had brought no food with them ; but, luckily, the cariboo hams were fresh, and each of the party habitually carried about with him the means of making a fire.

Some dry driftwood, collected no doubt by the Indian, furnished fuel, and in a very short time the three trappers were seated round the cheerful blaze, engaged in the pleasant task of appeasing appetites sharpened by long fasting as well as by exertion.

"Wal, I guess this is a snug location now," said Jake, casting an eye round the cavern, which was not so large as to impress its occupants with a sense of discomfort. "Them Injuns ur great at finding out the best places in the woods. I niver seed an Injun camp in an oncomfortable spot; an' the critturs hev an eye for beauty too—they hev so. Ef they kin, they a'most allus pitches thur camp in a nice, cool, green place, with timmer an' water at hand, an' a nice view at that."

"With such taste for the picturesque," said Pierre, "they are certainly less savage than many of the old country settlers who come among us. *They* do not seem to have taste of any kind; and I am sure that with regard to manners, the Indian is infinitely their superior."

"That's true for you," said Jake; "but I reckon, to git a raal Injun, one must leave the frontier behind. Thur's a class o' whites along the border as cud teach the devil himself wickedness he didn't know afore, an' the Injuns are apt to larn all that's bad they sees. Yer raal wild Injun's a gentleman—that is, when he likes to be. On the war-trail, though, I calc'late thur all alike."

"I don't know that we're any better at that time

either," remarked Gaultier; "our rule of action is to take every advantage, and kill all we can. With the Indians, those who make the quarrel go out to fight; while with us they remain safe at home, while thousands of their dupes are being massacred for the sake of an idea. I think our only claim to moral superiority consists in the fact that we do not take scalps—a slender plea to found the claim on."

"I don't hold with yer thur," said Jake; "thur's whites an' whites, an' Injuns an' Injuns. I knows, because I've seed it, that out far in the wilderness the Christianized Redskins are simple, honest, and good; but then thur's more on 'em that's as bad as the worst white a-goin.' An' among the whites thur's some on 'em that's good, an' some on 'em that's bad. I give in, though, that in the States most o' the border whites are main bad."

With conversation such as this they passed the time. Often one of the party approached the entrance of the cave and looked down into the gloomy chasm to note the state of the stream. But night had fallen, and although the moon cast showers of silvery beams which pierced the darkness of the cañon here and there, the bottom was hidden from view. Patches of white foam, dimly visible, floated past with great rapidity; and the noisy turmoil of the water battling its way among rocks and boulders, served to show that as yet descent was impracticable. The hunters therefore made preparation for spending the night in the cave.

There was no scarcity of rugs and wraps, and each having selected the warmest he could find, they laid themselves on the rocky floor with their feet to the fire, and were lullabied to sleep by the drowsy murmur of the torrent.

CHAPTER VI.

IT was late on the following morning when the hunters awoke. The gloom of the cavern no doubt fostered their slumbers, so that it was with a feeling of surprise that Pierre, who was the first to rise, saw from the entrance of the cave that morning was already considerably advanced.

The waters of the creek had now nearly relapsed to their ordinary level; and at this intimation Gaultier and Jake, with many a yawn and stretch, upreared their drowsy forms from the bearskin rugs and set about preparing breakfast.

This was a simple affair. They had neither coffee nor biscuits, and they had to content themselves with dry cariboo venison broiled over their insufficient fire. It may be supposed that they did not linger over their meal, which, in fact, hardly occupied them for five minutes.

They then made preparations to depart. Pierre

cautiously descended to the bottom; and his comrades immediately drew up the rope, and having secured to it a pack of skins, lowered it. In this manner as many of the packs were removed as they could conveniently carry in the canoe, Pierre placing each in a place of safety as it reached him.

Old Jake and Gaultier next descended; and each shouldering a heavy bundle, they commenced to wade down the stream in search of the canoe. In a short time they arrived without mishap at the spot where they had fastened the boat, but not a trace of it was to be seen!

Just here there were shelving banks, which sloped gently upwards from the water, and were covered with low brushwood. The height to which the flood had attained was marked on the branches of these, from which depended wrack of various sorts. After an hour's fruitless search they reached the Athabasca, and here also they could perceive no vestige of the canoe.

"Wagh!" exclaimed Jake, "this tramping has stiffened my old j'ints, an' thur not as limber as they used to be. I reckon we've passed the boat, fellurs," he continued; "an' this coon's gwine to hev a peep behint the brush along the banks o' the crick. It mout be thur."

Depositing their burdens therefore upon a dry spot, they again ascended the creek, keeping this time by the verge of the line of drift rubbish, which plainly indicated the height reached by the flood. Old Jake preceded the others, forcing his way through the tangled branches, and occasionally mumbling his dissatisfaction.

Suddenly he stopped short, with the exclamation, "Snakes alive! look hyur, boys: hyur's that Injun again—we're allus running agin him!"

The lads pushed forward, and were shocked to see the disfigured corpse of the ill-fated Indian wedged between the stems of two small trees. The body had been floating feet foremost, and in passing between these trees the expanded arms had arrested its course. Masses of uprooted sedge, or withered grasses, which had been borne down by the stream, were heaped upon the body, the extremities of which were alone visible.

" I think we ought to bury the poor fellow," said Gaultier, " and not leave him to be the food of vultures."

This suggestion was acted on, and the three hunters, with their knives, soon scooped out a shallow grave in the soft soil, in which the body was deposited. The mould was then replaced and stamped down firmly; a small stick, with a rag fluttering from it, was planted on the grave, to scare away any prowling wolf which might pass by the spot.

"The current seems to have set this way," said Pierre, "since it landed the corpse here; I daresay the canoe will not be far off."

A little further search brought the party to an open

spot, where they perceived the canoe stranded against the verge of the bushes. Strange to say, it had not been capsized nor injured; but the stores, which had been unprotected against the heavy rain, were drenched through, and the boat itself was half-full of water.

Having set matters to right, they lifted the canoe from the ground and carried it down to the creek, which at this place was deep enough to float it. They then returned to the rocks below the cave and loaded themselves with the packs of furs. These they brought to the canoe. After several journeys they removed all the peltries, and embarked.

The passage down to the Athabasca was performed in safety; and having taken on board the furs which they had left here upon the bank, they once more floated quietly down the broad waters of the noble river.

The hunters now held a consultation on their future course. Jake proposed that they should descend the Athabasca to the lake of the same name, and then, entering the Slave River, pass through the Great Slave Lake and the Mackenzie River, and ascend the Liard. This course would, he said, bring them within range of the head-waters of the Youkon River, which would carry them through an almost unexplored country, where game of all kinds abounded.

Pierre, on the other hand, recommended the route of the Peace River, which was long and difficult enough to occupy them during the remainder of the summer.

"We can descend the Fraser afterwards," he said, "and reach New Westminster before winter. If we went north we should have to winter in the mountains, and I do not think that would be prudent in an unknown country, where there may or may not be resources sufficient to support us."

Gaultier did not offer any opinion of his own as to any particular route, but he said that he doubted the wisdom of undertaking such a journey as that which Jake suggested, through regions where probably few white men had ever penetrated, and which must be inhabited by fierce and dangerous tribes.

"Wal, young fellurs," said Jake, "it's all one to this coon whur we goes; though I reckon that ef we want skins we'd better go whur they grows. That's all I hev to say."

"Can we ascend the Peace in our canoe, Jake?" asked Pierre; "I have never been up it further than Fort Vermilion."

"I han't neither," answered the old hunter; "but ef we goes that-a-way I reckon that we'll be able to canoe it for long enuff fust afore we hev to give in."

Finally, then, it was determined to ascend the Peace, and to trust to chance for being able to get through with the canoe.

In the meantime, free from care, the hunters floated down the Athabasca, conversing on the productions of the country, or on their prospects of a successful trip. At times Pierre woke the echoes with a light-hearted carol, in which he was occasionally joined by Gaultier; and as they dipped their paddles they sang in unison an old Canadian boat-song, much to Jake's disgust.

"Wagh!" he exclaimed, after some muttered dissatisfaction, "ye'll scare all the birds off the water with yer squawkin'! I've been a-tryin' to get sight on a swan this half-hour, an' the critters takes to wing jest as I squints at 'em. Ye're enuff to frighten the feathers off a turkey-buzzard!"

Thus admonished, the lads would hold their peace for a time; but under the exhilarating influence of bright skies, and brilliant sunshine lighting up the emerald glades of the forests and sparkling on the waves of the river, they would again incur old Jake's censure by the indulgence of their light-hearted mirth.

Thus they journeyed on. Each succeeding day found them alert at sunrise; and as the fatigue of travelling down stream was inconsiderable, they often prolonged their day's journey until the silver moon sailed above the woods and glanced on the dimpled surface of the water.

One evening as they were landing an unusual circumstance occurred. The place they had selected for their camp was just at the point of a short promontory or bend in the bank which projected into the Athabasca for some twenty or thirty yards. The moon had been clouded for some minutes, but had just emerged from the fleecy vapours which had eclipsed her beams as the party landed on the point. This was but a few yards across; and from an impulse of curiosity Gaultier pushed quietly through the small pines, which thickly clad the shore, and gazed down the farther reach, which stretched away for half a mile, darkened on one bank by the gloomy shade of woods, while the opposite side received the full radiance of the moon.

The distance across was not so great as to prevent the young trapper from observing several animals of immense size standing by the verge of the water. Occasionally one would walk along the beach, and seem to browse; while others advanced towards the river and waded into it until knee-deep, when they bent their heads to drink.

At first Gaultier supposed them to be moose-deer, but he was puzzled by the look of their heads, on which he could discern no such armature of antlers as distinguishes that animal. Quietly retracing his steps, he informed his comrades of what he had seen. From the spot where the canoe had been deposited the strange animals were not visible, and the two hunters therefore followed Gaultier, who led them to the place from which he had observed them. The animals still maintained their position on the beach, but a slight film across the moon rendered them extremely indistinct.

"They are moose," said Pierre; "I can see the horns of that next one—see, the one near that big white pine."

"You must skin yer eyes a deal more to see their horns, I reckon," said Jake; "what you sees is that withered branch hanging down over the critter's head from the tree. I guess I knows now what they ur," he continued: "them's bufflers—wood buffler at that. Hist!" he exclaimed, seizing hold of Gaultier, who was pressing forward from the shade of the trees in order to have a good look; "take kear yer not seen; them bufflers ain't like the plain bufflers—they can see and smell like all creation. I'll tell yer what we'll do: we'll jest slip up the river agin in the canoe, and cross over to t'other side. I guess we'll take the critters in the rear. Anyways, that's our only chance of a shot."

The party silently returned to the canoe, which was placed in the water with the greatest care, so as not to make the least noise. All then embarked, and hugging the shore in order to avail themselves of the sombre shadows of the overhanging trees in case the bison might shift their position and come within view, they reascended the Athabasca for about a quarter of a mile. The canoe was then steered to the opposite bank; and the hunters, taking their rifles, plunged noiselessly amid the dim shades of the forest.

Just here the woods were open, so that they had no difficulty in proceeding quickly and without noise over the mossy ground, which was thickly carpeted with the fallen needles of the pines. Here and there a vista, torn through the trees by some fierce winter tempest, afforded a view of the river, which reflected the mild light of the moon in long streams of silver, edged by the sombre shadows thrown by the opposite forest. A light mist covered the expanse of water, giving a dreamy expression to the scene. The path which the hunters followed gradually neared the river, and rendered caution doubly necessary, as they now approached the spot where the bison were pasturing.

Stealing with the silence of a ghost among the dark tree-trunks, old Jake, who was in advance, suddenly motioned his comrades to stop, and bending his head slightly to one side, he seemed to listen intently.

" Thur hyur yet," he whispered. " Let us creep to the edge of the timber an' gi' 'em goss ! "

Accordingly the two youths stealthily followed the old hunter, each taking up a position at the verge of the cover which commanded a view of the river bank.

As old Jake had guessed, the bison still stood near where they had at first been seen. There were four or five of them, of which number two browsed upon a level sward which intervened between the forest and the water ; the remainder stood at the river's edge, and seemed to have no intention of leaving the spot. Fortunately for the hunters, a cool, fresh breeze blew towards them, thus concealing their proximity from the nostrils of the wary animals.

One of the beasts, which had detached himself from his companions, was gradually feeding towards the forest. Hardly thirty yards separated him from the crouching trappers.

Pierre had marked this beast as his own, and, on the signal to fire being given by Jake, he aimed behind the massive shoulder and pressed the trigger. At the cracks of the rifles the herd of bison turned with extraordinary swiftness and charged towards the forest, leaving but one of their number behind. The animal at which Pierre had fired stumbled heavily forward, recovered himself, and would have followed his companions if the young trapper had not given him another ball at the base of the ear as he rushed past within five yards.

Gaultier and Jake had each disappeared in pursuit of their respective game, and the frequent reports of the rifle of the former proved that he had brought his bison to bay. A loud hurrah from him soon announced his success; and on following up the track, Pierre found him seated, with his sleeves tucked up, plunging his hunting-knife into the throat of the prostrate animal, which still kicked with its hind legs in the throes of death.

Distant yells proclaimed that old Jake was still engaged with his foe; but although the cries continued, the boys remarked that no shots were fired. They therefore followed the sounds, which grew louder and more frequent as they advanced. After a quick walk of about ten minutes among the thick growth of spruces, where the moonlight failed to pierce the heavy foliage, they arrived at the edge of an open space, where the trees had been killed either by fire or by stagnant water—the overflow, probably, of the Athabasca River during unusually high floods. Here the ground was encumbered with trees lying thickly on each other, while several of the largest still stood erect, their storm-bleached branches shining white in the moon-light.

From one of those trees old Jake's cries seemed to proceed, and on looking closely the youths perceived the hunter seated on a large branch, close to the trunk, round which he had thrown an arm to support himself. It was comical to see the old fellow dangling his long legs in air, giving continual vent to prolonged unearthly yells, which echoed far through the surrounding forest.

The lads could not see the foot of the tree which formed the old trapper's perch, owing to the thick entanglement of fallen trees which cumbered the ground in every direction. They guessed, however, that the bison which he had followed had turned to bay, and had forced the hunter to take the first refuge that offered itself. On approaching nearer, the quick snorting and heavy movements of some large animal became audible; they therefore proceeded cautiously, so as to get within shot before the bison could detect their proximity.

Meantime Jake kept the echoes awake calling for assistance. A low whistle from Pierre informed the old hunter of their approach, so he called out,—

" I'm treed by this monstrous beast, and hain't got Plumcentre. Do ee take kear the rotted varmint don't get his peepers on yer, lads, or he'll put ye up a couple o' trees in a brace o' shakes."

This caution was quite unnecessary; but the neighbourhood was so encumbered with fallen trees and brushwood that to advance without noise was almost impossible, and only to be effected by moving with extreme slowness.

Jake was aware of this, and diverted the attention of his jailer by shouting at him, and pelting him with branches, which he broke from the tree. This manœuvre was successful. The bison pawed the ground, and thrashed through the bushes in his eagerness to vent his rage on the body of his taunting enemy.

Under cover of the noise which he thus made, the boys advanced more quickly, and in a few minutes reached a spot from which they could fire at close quarters. Crouching behind a huge log, they waited until the bison turned broadside towards them, and each selecting a spot to aim at, they fired together.

In the damp air and confined space the smoke hung heavy, and prevented them from at once seeing the result of their shots, but a loud hurrah from old Jake, with the exclamation, " 'Thunder! thur's a tumble!'" announced their success.

Jake next descended from his uncomfortable seat among the branches, and unsheathing his long knife he cut the bison's throat and proceeded to extract the tongue.

" I reckon we'll take his skin in the mornin'," he observed; "an' I'll jest rig up a scare-wolf in a minute."

This he effected by taking out the bladder, which he distended by blowing through a straw. He tied this contrivance to a stick stuck into the ground beside the carcass, and having adjusted it to his satisfaction, the old hunter shouldered Plumcentre, having first carefully examined it to satisfy himself that it had escaped all injury. He then left the spot, followed by Pierre and Gaultier.

The tongues of the other two bison were cut out, as well as the choicest parts of the one first killed, which happened to be a fine young cow. A roast was of course the first thing done on arrival at the camp; and during the prodigious meal which followed, each of the hunters fought his battle over again.

In answer to Pierre's inquiry as to how he got treed, Old Jake replied:—

"I guess this nigger hain't often been obleeged to show his tail in that thur ondignified way; but accidents ur sure to happen some time or other to all on us. I've even heerd tell o' a fellur bein' treed by a moose, an' screechin' mighty loud about it, too."

This allusion was taken good-humouredly by Pierre, who laughed.

"Wal, I follered that buffler like a white wolf. I wur determined to hev that buffler, boys, and so I glued myself to his tail, an' tore arter him through the woods. O' coorse, I knowed the varmint wur wounded. I'd let old Plumcentre into him at the fust go-off, an' seed him stumble. But he seemed to get stronger an' stronger the furrer he went, until we kem to that open place whur ye comed up wi' me. All this while I hadn't time to clap the fodder into my rifle; but the

goin' wur so bad for the buffler on the barren that I
slowed a bit, an' loaded up as fast as I cud. While I
wur a-doin' this, the buffler had gained on me, an' wur
ahead somewheres. I cud hear him crackin' through
the trees an' bushes like one o' them railway injins
they hev back in the States, got off the line. I put on
a spurt, and soon agin tackled the critter. I guess he
heerd me a-comin', for before I could cry 'Columbus'
he wur right atop o' me. O' coorse, I pulled on him as
he kem torst me. But 'twur no go. He didn't even
wink, although he got the ball plumb atween the eyes.

" I noticed thur wur somethin' wrong wi' the report,
but hedn't time to calc'late on *that.* No; thur wur
that all-fired beast gruntin' an' roarin' like all creation,
a-pokin' at me wi' his horns as I dodged this-a-way an'
that. I wurn't long in seein' a big tree clost to whur
we wur fightin', an' ye'd better b'leeve I put for it like
a quarter-hoss. I reckin sparks flew from my old heels
as I med that tree, and flew up it like a 'painter' wi' a
pack o' b'ar-dogs at his tail. Plumcentre wur obleeged
to stay below, not bein' able to climb; but ef ye hadn't
come up, I guess I'd made shift to get my claws upon
the old tool somehow, and dropped that rotted bull in
his tracks—I would so!"

CHAPTER VII.

ON the morning following the preceding adventure, the sun had scarcely tipped the tree-tops on the eastern bank of the Athabasca with his rosy beams when the hunters left camp in order to bring in the meat. Old Jake, indeed, found time before starting for a *grillade* of the juicy tongues of the bison; in which succulent repast Gaultier and Pierre were not loath to join. This, however, was only intended as a stay to their appetites, most of these delicious dainties having been consumed at their supper on the previous night.

The amount of food which constant life in the open air renders necessary is prodigious; and, indeed, in the countries of which our narrative treats the chief difficulty consists in supplying the demands of appetite with an adequate quantity of viands. Our hunters therefore had little difficulty in disposing at one meal of the greater part of the three colossal tongues, leaving only the *analecta* of the feast to form a slight refection in the morning.

The air was fresh and balmy as the hunters crossed the broad river, the surface of which was as placid as a mirror, picturing the motionless trees and the dappled sky with exquisite accuracy. On every twig and branch lay a heavy dew, which had been deposited during the night; and the rising sun, glancing through the foliage, glittered on myriads of the diamond drops, which reflected the rays in beautiful prismatic hues.

Old Jake, however, cared little for the picturesque, and anathematized the glittering showers which he brushed from the boughs as he forced his way in the van of the party. The spot where the buffaloes had fallen was soon reached; and here Pierre stayed behind, as he wished to butcher his own game. Gaultier and Jake pushed on, each to find and cut up the animal which was properly his own.

That which had fallen to Gaultier's rifle was first met, and the two hunters were considerably chagrined to find that, despite a scarecrow which had been placed over the carcass, much of the meat had been injured by wild animals during the night.

"The nasty varmints!" said Jake, "hev spiled the best o' the meat. I reckon we were well employed providin' rump steaks fur thur rotted jaws! Ef I cud only introjooce Plumcentre to the skunks, it 'ud take a weight off this nigger's gizzard."

While talking thus, the old hunter was examining

the ground, and presently he lifted from behind some bushes the scare-wolf which had been placed beside the carcass on the previous night.

" I mout 'a guessed that all-fired crittur did the job!" he exclaimed. "Hyur's the thing we rigged up to scare the wolves; an' may Plumcentre turn into a smooth-bore ef he hasn't hidden it behint the bush arter helpin' hisself!"

"What beast do you mean?" asked Gaultier.

"What beast?" replied the old trapper; "I guess thur's only the one hyurabout would play us such a dirty trick. 'Twur a carcajou as did it. I wish thur wur a pound o' pison in his stomach. You bet high he's jest made tracks right away for t'other buffler. I've knowed one o' them horrid brutes to foller up a line o' traps for fifty mile, and dig out the bait, or swaller the beast inside, 'ithout springin' the trigger. When the critter had stuffed hisself an' went off, I guess the wolves fell to an' finished the job. See, they've med raggles o' the hide from the tail to the nose, rot 'em!"

Both hunters now followed their track of the previous night, and after missing the direction once or twice, they came upon the carcass of the third bison. As Jake had apprehended, their cunning enemy the wolverine had found out this also; and, as if in sheer wantonness, he had torn and disfigured the meat as much as possible, and had hidden away the bladder and stick which Jake had planted over the body.

The rage of the old hunter knew no bounds as he surveyed the mischief wrought by the sagacious and sneaking carcajou, and deep were the threats he uttered against the marauding scoundrel.

"Ef I hev to stay hyur till winter," he exclaimed, "I'll trap that varmint. I'll make him smell thunder, or my name's not Jake Hawken. Ye-es! he'll find old Jake's not a snag to run agin' that away. See ef he don't!"

While the incensed trapper gave utterance to these threats, he was busily engaged in cutting out the tongue (the point of which had been bitten off, having protruded beyond the jaws), and sundry other choice bits, which he secured together and slung from his rifle barrel.

Leaving the remainder of the carcass to the wolves, Gaultier and his companion retraced their steps to the canoe. It was Jake's intention to return later in order to rig up a trap near the bison, in which he hoped against hope to catch the wary wolverine.

With this view the old trapper during the afternoon again left camp. At his own request neither of the youths accompanied him, as he feared the cunning carcajou would be likely to take alarm at finding so many tracks in the neighbourhood of the trap. The wolverine has no objection to the trail of a solitary hunter, which, indeed, he actually follows with extraordinary perseverance; tearing open the traps which have been set for the marten or fisher, and either devouring them if

caught, or hiding them away at some distance in the
woods, or even in the top branches of a pine-tree.   He
will thus destroy a whole line of traps ; and this, apparently, from sheer wantonness, as, unless when pressed
by hunger, he contents himself with merely tearing the
captured animal to pieces and hiding it out of sight.
No wonder, then, that the backwoodsmen cherish a
cordial hatred towards the wolverine, and compass its
destruction by every means in their power. So cunning,
however, is this beast, that it is almost impossible to
take it in a trap.   It burrows underneath, and drags
off the bait without springing the trigger ; or if this
should happen, the log-weight falls harmlessly on the
ground.

Sometimes poison has been found effective ; but here,
too, the sagacity of the animal enables him frequently
to detect the danger, and the bait is found by the
trapper untouched, or buried uneaten.   Guns have been
set in vain, the string connected with the trigger having
been first gnawed across and the device rendered useless. The bait has then been safely devoured or carried
off.   Pitfalls have been tried and found wanting.   In
fact the resources of the wolverine are such that he is
fully a match for the most experienced trapper that
ever carried pack or rifle.

To achieve the capture, therefore, of one of those
cunning beasts, is a good test of the hunter's skill and
ingenuity. Consequently the old trapper on the present
occasion felt himself on his mettle, and was determined

to show his younger associates that "not a rotted varmint o' 'em all could fool old Jake Hawken."

On arriving at the spot where the mangled remains
of the bison lay, which indeed consisted of little but
the bones, the trapper first cut down a number of
saplings, which he divided into lengths of about a yard
each. These he planted firmly in the ground in such a
manner as to form a palisade of a semi-oval shape, and
of a length within, about sufficient to admit two-thirds
of the body of a marten, but of insufficient size to
permit the animal to turn round inside. Across the
entrance he placed a small log. His next operation was
to drag up a long branchless pine which lay prostrate
near the spot, and having with much difficulty raised
the heavier end of the stem, he carefully placed it
upon the small log, in such a manner that they were
parallel to each other. A partridge placed as a bait on
the point of a short stick projected into the enclosure ;
the outer end of this stick supporting the butt end of
the heavy tree, and being itself supported by another
short stick standing perpendicularly. Jake next covered
the top of the trap with small branches, pieces of bark,
and leaves, so that no means of access to the interior
presented itself except by the entrance. Having arranged everything to his satisfaction, the old hunter
removed the skeleton of the bison to some distance, and
returned to the camp. As soon as the boys saw him
approaching they came forward to meet him.

"Well, Jake," said Gaultier, "where's the carcajou ?

I thought you went to catch him, and I don't see him."

" Ye'll see the critter soon enuff, young fellur—a considerable sight sooner than ef ee wur to go pokin' round a-lookin' for him yersel'."

" How did you manage, Jake ? " asked Pierre ; " what kind of trap did you make ? You know we are young hands at this kind of work, and expect to learn from your greater experience."

This was a *placebo* to the trapper's *amour propre*, which had been somewhat ruffled by the tone of Gaultier's inquiry. "I reckin," he replied, "that my exper'ence 'ud make a good hunter out o' the greenest tenderfoot iver got loose from his mammy's apronstrings. 'Twould so! But this nigger's not so green as tc expect to take that carcajou the fust go-off. I guess I'll let him nibble at the bait a bit, jest to kinder encourage him. I'll walk over in the mornin' an' hev a squint at what the skunk's been about. I'm a'most sartin he'll chaw up the bait I've sot up—an' I hope he diz! Ef he diz, I reckin this coon'll walk into the varmint pretty slick."

" Why, Jake," said Pierre, " you haven't poisoned the bait, have you ? You know they can smell that dodge."

" I hain't pisoned it," answered the hunter ; " but I guess you'll see soon enuff what I'm up to. Seein's beleevin', they say."

The boys, perceiving that Jake was uncommunicative, allowed the subject to drop; but they were nevertheless very anxious to discover by what method the old trapper intended to capture the wolverine, especially as he had said he did not expect the trap which he had laid to be successful.

Thus speculating, they followed the example of the trapper, and bestowed themselves beneath the shelter of their buffalo robes and blankets, and soon fell asleep.

Pierre and his cousin overslept themselves, so that when they awoke on the next morning they found that Jake had left the camp, and had not yet returned. They got up at once; and when Gaultier went to the river to fill the large kettle, Pierre shouldered the axe, and with vigorous blows soon prostrated a dead pitch-pine, which he proceeded to lop into firewood.

In this task he was joined by his cousin, and the woods around re-echoed the ringing of their axes upon the tough and hard tree. The resinous knots soon kindled a blaze, and the withered branches being placed on this, and the larger portions of the trunk and branches above, a fire was soon made which roared and crackled, sending up forked tongues of flame, which presently reduced the logs to huge glowing embers.

On these the kettle was placed, and slices of the bison were grilled on the coals, or toasted in front of the fire, spitted on pointed sticks. While thus agreeably employed they perceived Jake advancing among the trees.

"He hasn't the wolverine yet, anyhow," said Gaultier. "I wonder how he intends to take him. I don't expect he'll get him, though, for all his 'cuteness."

"You know," said Pierre, "he said last night that he didn't expect to catch him so soon."

Jake now sat by the fire, and Pierre, seeing him in good humour, ventured to ask him for the events of his morning's trip.

"'Twur jest as I calc'lated," he replied. "The reptile bored a hole under the trap from the back, an' took out as fine a marten as I iver sot eyes on, an' I've seed a lot o' the critters. He jest tore him to raggles an' left a piece o' him hyur an' thur round the pen. But he'll try that dodge once too often. He tuck the bait too, but I cudn't see whur he cached that."

While the party continued to eat their meal, a pack of ruffed grouse rose with a whir from some rough grass and sailed away over the trees, but with indications that they did not mean to fly far. Old Jake, uttering an exclamation, seized his rifle, and disappeared in the direction taken by the birds. Before the boys could make any remark on this sudden movement, they heard the crack of the hunter's rifle, and he presently returned in a leisurely manner towards the fire, dangling a grouse by the neck.

"This critter'll make a bait," he observed, as he resumed his meal, which he concluded in silence. The curiosity of the young men was next aroused by seeing the old trapper take from his "possible sack" a piece of stout wire about a foot in length, furnished at one end with a strong hook, such as is used for sea-fishing. After some further rummaging he produced a similar hook, which he proceeded to lash to the other end of the wire with deer sinews. Having accomplished this to his satisfaction, he took up the partridge, and by the aid of a stick he pushed one of the hooks down its throat, leaving the other hook hanging from its beak.

Lest this might excite suspicion, he doubled the wire neatly under the bird's neck, and concealed both hook and wire under the feathers. Having at length adjusted the bait, he again left the camp, and placed the bird in the same position as on the previous occasion.

The trap was re-set, and Jake, not judging it prudent to linger long about the spot, returned to his companions.

Early on the following day he intimated to the youths that they might now accompany him; which they did with eager curiosity to ascertain the result of his ingenuity. As they neared the spot where the trap had been prepared, they perceived an animal something larger than an English fox, stoutly made and with very short legs, hobbling off, but with such difficulty that it sometimes stopped altogether, and sometimes it lay upon the ground and seemed to struggle violently. So engaged was it in its own movements that the approach of the hunters was unperceived.

They dashed forward with a cheer which brought the animal upon its legs in an instant; but before it could attempt escape three bullets passed through its body.

"I guess, wolvy, ye're sorry now ye spiled Jake

Hawken's meat," cried the old fellow, taking up the animal by the tail.—" See, young fellurs," he continued, "this is how I caught the varmint. Ye seed me put them hooks in the partridge?" (The youths nodded assent.) " Wal, then, when this skunk kem along, he jest tried his old game o' makin' raggles o' the bait, an' he got one hook stuck in his mouth, while t'other hung out in front o' his nose. I guess he didn't cotton to that ornament, an' tried to stand upon it to drag it out. That did the bisness, fur he jest hooked his toes to his nose, and couldn't make tracks nohow. I won't say, though, that he wouldn't 'a made away, or leastways cached hisself; but most likely 'twur about daybreak he got caught, and so he hadn't the time. Anyhow he won't run agin this coon for one while. No! that he won't "

Here the old hunter chuckled loud and long at his own superior skill in woodcraft. The wolverine was next divested of his shaggy hide, and bearing this trophy the party returned to the canoe.

It was yet early morning, for the hunters had been early risers. As they had nothing more to detain them at this place, they packed the canoe with all their belongings, and with a certain amount of regret bade adieu to a spot where they had sojourned happily for some days.

But an event soon occurred which banished these feelings and filled them with anxiety. For some days the weather had been intensely hot; the grass and

moss were dried up by a scorching sun, which blazed
with tropic heat in a cloudless sky. The voyageurs
had felt the inconvenience of this, and would have felt
it more but that the nights fortunately were cool, and
enabled them to repose in comfort.

It was the midday halt, and the party, according to
their usual habit, had landed upon a shelving bank,
where the tall grass and foliage seemed to offer a refuge
from the suffocating heat. Just as the camp fire was
kindled, a rushing noise was heard among the trees
behind; and on looking round, the hunters beheld a
cariboo buck bounding along with great speed. Jake
fired, and for an instant the buck faltered in his course;
but recovering almost immediately, he disappeared
among the myriad stems of the forest.

"Kim along, young fellurs!" cried Jake; "he won't
go far with that pill in his innards."

So saying, the old hunter rose, and followed in the
track of the buck with long strides, which the youths
had no little difficulty in keeping pace with.

For some distance the tracks were plainly marked,
as the ground was open and free from brushwood.
Here the hoof-marks were distinctly visible. But
presently the party found themselves descending a
slight incline which sloped towards a thick entangled
swamp, where the trees grew densely and were covered
with *usnea*, which gave a hoary and venerable air to
the woods.

Despite the keenest scrutiny, all traces of the animal

were here lost; and old Jake, grumbling his discontent, surrendered further search, and led the youths back to camp.

As they approached the river they were much alarmed by observing clouds of smoke curling among the trees and inwreathing the forest in their immense folds. Quickening their pace, they soon reached the scene, and fully realized the disaster which had occurred.

We have noticed that the spot selected for the camp was among high grass, which had become bleached by the fervid heat of the sun. While the party were in pursuit of the cariboo buck, the fire had communicated itself to the dry herbage, and in a few moments the flames had spread with lightning-like rapidity in all directions. Already some trees at the verge of the forest were ablaze, and their fierce crackling, in addition to that of the burning grass and weeds, made a noise like the continuous rattle of musketry.

But what concerned the hunters more than aught else was that the canoe, which unluckily had been lifted from the water and placed on the bank to facilitate the inspection of some slight damage occasioned by a graze against a rock, had been wrapped in the flames, and was now completely destroyed.

By great good fortune the stores and furs had been left on the slender strip of shingle which intervened between the water and the camp, and had thus escaped the fate of the canoe. Meantime the flames receded from the spot, and gradually burned themselves out, the inflammable vegetation being confined to the small open space in which the camp had been pitched. Fortunately only some half-dozen trees took fire, and these being detached at a considerable distance from the main forest behind, the conflagration soon died out.

The trappers now found themselves in a very unpleasant predicament. They were many miles from the fort which they had left behind them at the Forks, while at least an hundred miles of wilderness separated them from Fort Chepewyan on Lake Athabasca. Dense forest would have to be threaded, through which it would be almost impossible to force their way if they attempted either to advance or to retreat on foot.

The only alternative was to construct a canoe as best they might, or a raft, on which to continue their journey towards Fort Chepewyan. Once arrived there, they had little doubt that they could procure either another canoe or horses on which they could reach Fort Vermilion on the Peace River.

"Thur's no need o' lookin' so bumfoozled about it eyther," said old Jake, as he remarked the blank expression of his companions' faces. "I reckin we're no greenhorns out for a day's foolin' in the woods. Hyur's trees a plenty, an' we've got our hatchets, I guess. We'll soon trim up a raft that'll carry us down stream like a breeze. Kim, fellurs, git yer axes an' shove."

This appeal roused the youths from their momentary fit of dejection, and under the cheery influence of old Jake's manner they soon recovered their usual good spirits. They accordingly shouldered their axes and followed their veteran comrade, who was already searching for trees suitable to his purpose. In such a place these were not difficult to find. Each selected his tree, and in a short time the ground was covered with logs of dry timber some eighteen or twenty feet in length.

These were trimmed and flattened, and the necessary number being at length prepared, they were conveyed to the water's edge, old Jake supporting the butt end on his shoulder, Gaultier lending his aid in the middle, and Pierre leading. Withes made from the roots of the épinette tree and strips of bison hide lashed the logs together, which finally formed a platform about eighteen feet square.

On this were thrown the tender branchlets of the firs, on which the voyageurs could repose in comfort when not engaged in navigating their raft. Two long slender poles were cut to steer with; and having at length finished their clumsy craft, and taken on board the furs and stores, they shoved off from the bank and floated quietly down stream.

CHAPTER VIII.

FOR some days the hunters descended the placid river,
with no further trouble than was involved in steering
their raft, or occasionally poling where the current,
aided by their own negligence, sent them against the
banks. Reclining comfortably upon the fragrant boughs
of the pines, they dreamily drifted along, basking in the
warm sunlight, and noting with languid interest the
many kinds of birds which peopled the water, and
streamed off its surface in alarm as the raft and its
occupants became visible.

High above, the sun shot fervid rays upon the quiet
bosom of the stream; and whenever a puff of air
blew from the forest, it was laden with the aromatic
fragrance of the pines, which exhaled their perfume
under the influence of his beams.

Pierre, who had often been to the great centres of
civilization, where man strives with man in ceaseless

competition for gain and bread, reflected, amid these scenes of silvan peace, how fortunate was his own lot, which led him from the heartless, artificial atmosphere of civilized regions, to pass his life in the presence of that nature which he loved, and which carried aloft his mind to its great Creator, as often as his eye rested on the myriad works of his hand:—the vast forests which, as seen from some vantage-ground, stretched away into infinite distance; here dense and green, level on top as some richly-hued carpet; there broken into glades where single trees stood forth hoary with the moss of centuries, and whose contorted branches were relieved against the dark background of pines: the splintered peaks, the gray rock-built hills, girdled with forests and capped with changing mists and never-melting snows: the level prairie ocean stretching far and wide, into whose boundless depths the summer sun descends, leaving behind a sky of flame, changing into shades which never have been classified; while upon the far-off verge the tall grass waves against the burnished horizon like the surging of billows on a shoreless sea. These were the scenes which the young trapper yearned for, and it was amid their desert solitudes that his heart could alone find rest.

Gaultier also was influenced by similar feelings. He had been born in the woods of Canada, and from his earliest days had manifested a disgust for civilization, if that can be so designated which consists in outward forms, a modish life, and the substitution of the artificial for the natural. The cousins roamed the woods together, admiring and wondering at the sublime forms in which Nature presented herself—the thundering cascade, the awful precipice, the vast silvan corridors through which the winds moaned, the gloom of night pierced by the lightning of the midnight storm, the pillared vistas of the moonlit forest streaked and flecked by the silver beams which lighted the timid doe or stately buck to pasture.

These scenes had impressed their young imaginations, and filled them with a love of nature which led them from home to undertake long and perilous journeys; in a word, to live as hunters in the western wilderness.

They had the advantage of some education, of which their veteran companion was destitute. But still Jake, in his own rude way, loved nature as truly as did the youths themselves. He was one of a class now nearly extinct—the brave, eccentric Rocky Mountain trapper. A few of these originals still survive the innovations of the times, and year after year retire further before the encroachments of the ever-increasing multitudes who stream westward.

In a few years the romance of the prairies will be a tradition of the past. Nay, the pig has already replaced the buffalo, and the policeman has supplanted the Indian. Already has civilization nearly achieved a conquest over the wilderness; but the world has scarcely become happier. Perhaps Nature will be avenged, and those who rend her will, after having exhausted the physical resources of the country, turn upon and rend each other.

Sunk in their reverie, the hunters allowed themselves to drift with the current; and on rounding an islet in mid stream, they observed, when too late, that they had been perceived by some large animal, of which they had a transient glimpse as it bounded out of sight among the trees on the bank.

"Wagh!" cried Jake; "this comes o' dozin', instead o' keepin' one's eyes skinned. 'Twur mighty like a cariboo buck; an' we'd have got the critter, sartin, if we'd been a leetle on the look-out."

"Well, it's not much matter," said Pierre; "we have plenty of meat for the present, and it would have been a pity to shoot the noble beast merely for its hide."

"I say with you, hoss," replied Jake. "I ain't one o' them fellurs as ur allers lettin' off thur rifles an' killin' off the game. They shud 'a been butchers—that's a fact. Thur not hunters, leastways what this coon means by hunters. I went out in the Rockies a few years agone wi' two Britishers from London, or some sich place. Wal, the way them two got on wur a caution to see. I guess they never before seed game of any kind, to jedge from the way they walked into the bufflers. Ten a-day wouldn't do 'em, nor yet twenty. They left tons an' tons o' prime meat a-rottin' on the prairie, only takin' the tongues. Wagh! it a'most makes me sick to think o' thur doin's!"

"You have no cariboo down in the States," said Gaultier.

"I hain't comed across 'em," replied the trapper; "they are raal handsome beasts."

"Yes," said Pierre; "there are few handsomer animals than the cariboo. You know," he continued, "there are two varieties—the woodland and the Barren Ground cariboo. The former is considerably larger than the latter. Few animals have such an extensive range. It is found in Iceland, and along the northern parts of the continents of Europe, Asia, and America. It is also met with in Newfoundland and in Greenland. In Europe it is known as the reindeer. It has been stated that the cariboo frequenting the sterile regions of the Barren Grounds differs in some respects from the better-known kind, and constitutes a separate variety. Of this, however, no one seems to be absolutely certain. Indeed, I have often observed how little reliance is to be placed on the statements of Indians and hunters on such subjects. These content themselves with killing the game, and unless there is some striking peculiarity observable in the animal, they pay no more attention to the matter."

"Jest so," remarked Jake; "that's dreadful true, I reckin. I wur once engaged as guide an' hunter to one o' them bug-gatherers from the towns as goes about collectin' all kinds o' rubbish, an' fills thur pockets wi' grassjumpers an' straddlebugs. Wal, we wur main hungry one day, hevin' nothin' to chaw 'ceptin' the

parfleche o' our leggins; an' tough chawin' that ur, I
calc'late. We kep' a mighty sharp look-out for game,
you bet high; when on a sudden, jest as we rose the
swell o' the peraira, what shed I see but a small band
o' buffler 'ithin a hunder yards o' us! 'Jehoshaphat!'
I yelled, lettin' loose Plumcentre at 'em, 'thur's buffler
for supper!' 'No, John' (the critter allers called me
John), 'No, John; they are not buffaloes; they are
bison. You should allers call things by their proper
names.' Wal, I a'most fell off my hoss larfin at the
coon—comin' out on the peraira to tell this child what
wur a buffler! It's jest as you say, young fellur," he
continued; "thur's a many as doesn't know half they
purtends."

Pierre and Gaultier laughed loudly at the sample of
ignorance adduced by old Jake; and the former then
resumed his account of the cariboo, to which both of
his companions listened with interest.

"The range of the cariboo," resumed Pierre, "extensive as it is, is of course limited to those regions which
supply it with its favourite food. In Scandinavia it
descends to the high table-lands as low as latitude 60°.
In fact, its range is conterminous with the birch and
willow, and with those lichens and mosses which constitute the chief part of its sustenance. Of these the
Cladonia rangiferina, or reindeer lichen, with one or
two kinds of *cornicularia* and *cetraria*, form the principal."

"Great Columbus!" interjected Jake, "what'n thunder ur them?   I guess the half o' 'em orter choke arey a cariboo as I've seed!"

The young hunters laughed, and without further notice Pierre continued :—

"In Nova Scotia, where the cariboo attains its most southerly limit, it has been seen at Cape Sable, in latitude 43° 30'; but owing to ceaseless persecution it is now becoming scarce in that province, which a few years since was noted for its abundance.   In the neighbouring province of New Brunswick it is still tolerably plentiful; and in the extensive forests of that country I hope it will long survive the continual attacks made upon it, both by Indians, settlers, lumberers, and wandering sportsmen.   The headquarters, however, of this animal lie on the north side of the St. Lawrence, where from the basin of that river, far to the north, stretches a dense forest-covered wilderness of vast extent, which probably for centuries yet will defy the encroachments of man.   To the west of Lake Superior, and following the line of the woods, its range trends towards the Mackenzie Valley, and, crossing the Rocky Mountains, includes the American Territory of Alaska.   That good sportsman and naturalist, Mr. Lord, states that it exists on several ranges of hills in British Columbia. What a vast number of the human race have their wants supplied by this noble deer!   The Lapps use him as a beast of burden; they feed upon his flesh and clothe themselves with his hide.   Their rope and string are manufactured from his sinews; the hind furnishes them with milk and a coarse kind of cheese. In America, the Montaignais and Nasquapee Indians of Labrador, the Milicetes and Micmacs of Nova Scotia and New Brunswick, the Dogribs and the Chipewyans, and various other tribes of the North-West Territory, make it contribute largely to their subsistence. I have observed that the woodland cariboo is much larger than the animal frequenting the Barren Grounds. Of this there can exist no doubt; but upon this difference of size it has been attempted to found the theory of a difference of species. I do not believe that any such difference exists. Want of shelter and consequent exposure to the rigorous winter of those rock-strewn deserts, want of adequate food, and other circumstances, have doubtlessly dwarfed the animal until it might be regarded in the light of a separate variety. The Barren Ground cariboo does not penetrate far into the forest-covered districts contiguous to its natural habitat, preferring clumps of willows or the isolated groups of dwarf pines which derive a scanty subsistence from the sterile soil of those desolate regions. Its range stretches far north, beyond the limits of the forest, embracing the shores of Hudson Bay and the various islands and peninsulas which render the geography of the Arctic coasts of America so confused and uncertain. As described by the traveller Erman, a reindeer closely resembling that of Eastern America is used by the Tunguses of Eastern Asia as a beast of burden. I have made a few notes," continued Pierre, " in this pocket-

THE BARREN GROUND CARIBOO.

book, which I copied from the description of the cariboo by the great American naturalist Audubon. They are as follows :—

" 'Tips of hair light dun gray, whiter on neck than elsewhere ; nose, ears, outer surface of legs and shoulders brownish ; neck and throat dull white ; a faint whitish patch on the side of shoulders ; belly and tail white ; a band of white around all the legs adjoining the hoofs.' "

"That account ain't true all round," observed Jake. "I've often seed a buck, ay, an' throwed him too, wi' his legs an' back as rich a reddish-brown as you'd wish to see, I guess, an' with his rump, tail, an' mane as white as a snow-bank. Them book-makers hain't lived whur the game grows, I reckin, or they'd know more about it."

"You do Audubon injustice there, Jake," replied Pierre, "for he lived the life of a backwoodsman for years. The description I have read for you is merely a general one, and as such you must allow it is singularly correct."

" Wal, I won't say agin it as far as it goes," answered the old hunter ; " but the fellur orter say so, that's all."

" O Jake," said Gaultier, " you ought to write a book. You would have plenty of material in your long life of adventures among the Redskins and wild animals. I am certain it would be a most amusing as well as a most instructive work."

" I wish I cud write," replied Jake, " but this coon's edication wur neglected. When I wur a little chunk o' a lad, a fellur who used to come to my father's house now an' agin offered to teach me how to write an' read ef we'd feed him while tryin'. Wal, the old man thort it 'ud be a fine thing to hev his boy able to read a printed book, an' he agreed straight away. But I guess that fellur gev it up as a bad job. He said the paper looked as if a drunken bat had dipped his claws in ink an' staggered over it. He couldn't make head or tail o' this nigger's fist, you bet, an' so he jest hed to make tracks an' find another log to winter in. Ye-es, that he hed."

Pierre and Gaultier laughed merrily at this termination of their companion's literary career. Presently Pierre continued his account of the cariboo.

"'It is in Lower Canada,'" he said, "'and in the woods of Newfoundland and Nova Scotia, that this deer attains its greatest development. Some have considered that it is an ungainly beast, thick-set and ill-proportioned. But although it certainly loses by comparison with the more graceful species of the Cervidæ, I think these critics are too hard to please. I cannot conceive a finer spectacle for a hunter's eye to rest on than a band of these noble animals bounding swiftly through the woods from the presence of danger. Their fleetness and agility seem incompatible with the idea of clumsiness of form. Probably those who complain of the want of symmetry in the cariboo have never seen the animal in its wild state, trotting springingly with head and tail erect, and apparently braced for any exertion, however arduous, which it may be called on to undergo. It is a singular fact that the horns of the cariboo vary considerably in different specimens. Some are more palmated than others, and are furnished with a greater number and variety of points. There is a similar difference in the size of antlers: those of Newfoundland and Labrador seem to reach a greater size than is observable in the ordinary Canadian variety. But few old bucks retain their antlers during the winter. The does and the young bucks, however, preserve their armature during that season. In spring they fall, when the new antlers grow again in a short time.

"'As I have already mentioned, the food of the cariboo consists in great part of mosses and lichens; and in the winter, when these are covered with snow, the animal uses its hoofs to clear away that impediment, for which purpose they are singularly well adapted.

"'The woodland cariboo has two seasons of migration—in the spring, and again in the autumn. This has been accounted for in different ways. Some have said that the scarcity of food in certain districts necessitates a change of feeding-ground. Others assert that as the migrations uniformly lead to the open plains and sterile hill ranges, the probability is that the animals retreat from the ceaseless torment that they suffer from the flies which abound in the woods. I cannot say which is the true cause; but I have observed, as I doubt not you have also, that even during the winter season the cariboo often leaves a locality quite suddenly.

"'The various bands into which the great herds split up gradually join together, and a district which to-day holds great numbers of these animals may to-morrow be destitute of a single specimen. The cariboo is an extremely shy animal, flying from the neighbourhood of man with instinctive fear. As he needs immense stretches of country for his distant migrations, and as he cannot bear the vicinity of civilization, and requires his communications to be kept open, he will probably soon disappear from those sections where his native forests are becoming circumscribed with a ring of settlements, and retire to the north of the St. Lawrence, where an illimitable wilderness stretches northwards, offering a safe asylum. In fact, he has already disappeared from districts where a few years ago he was abundant.

"'It is a curious circumstance that another animal, also noted for its extreme shyness—the moose—should in these localities take the place vacated by the cariboo, but it is nevertheless true. The moose does not range so much as the former animal, and hence does not require such vast extent of wild country for its support. On the contrary, the moose will increase and multiply in the neighbourhood of roads and settlements, regardless of the distant chopping of the settler's axe, or the roar of the cars along the railway, or the deep bellow of the engine which echoes far through the woods. The slightest scent of approaching man, however, warns the moose to be off; and sharp as is his nose, his ears are scarcely inferior to it in acuteness.

"'The cariboo usually feeds down wind, and as he is furnished with a nose as sharp as that of the moose, nothing can follow on his track without being perceived. To the difficulty of getting within shot is added the difficulty of seeing the cariboo, when skill and patience have at length brought the hunter within range. His colour so assimilates with the hues of the gray lichen-covered rocks or the moss-clad trunks, or, if in winter time, with the alternate flecks of snow and bare brown patches of the tree stems, that the unpractised eye finds it almost as difficult to detect the presence of the game as to stalk it. Yet the very uncertainty of the pursuit invests it with one of its chief charms for the true hunter. For him who looks to certain slaughter as his reward, the shambles, not the forest, is the proper place; the pole-axe and not the rifle should be his weapon.'"

Here ended Pierre's account of the cariboo. His comrades expressed themselves much pleased with the information which he had imparted; and it was resolved that the young hunter naturalist should communicate so much of the history of each animal brought down by their rifles as he himself knew from personal observation, or had learned from others on whose statements he could rely. Pierre modestly disclaimed any intimate acquaintance with the natural history of the animals of America; but Jake insisted that "nary a trapper as he'd ever run agin cud reel off the raal truth about the game like him ; and though he knew a sight himself, he cudn't for the life o' him spit it out like Pierre."

The trapper bashfully agreed to the request, and the subject dropped for the time.

CHAPTER IX.

IT was now evening, and the sun had already sunk beyond the forest on the western bank of the Athabasca. The sky, however, was still aglow with the reflected fires of the sunset, and a holy calm seemed to have descended on the face of nature. Evening breathed a peaceful spirit on the forest and on the river. From the distance came the mournful notes of water-fowl; the cry of the shushuga from the marshes; or from the depths of the forest the fierce yell of the lynx in pursuit of his prey.

These sounds, however, occurring only at intervals, failed to disturb the quiet of the scene. The stately trees on either hand rose, silent and majestic, those on the western bank silhouetted against the heavens, their trunks standing gray and solemn in the gloom thrown by the branches. Before and behind, to distant bends stretched the river, broad and unruffled by rock or shoal; mirroring here the sombre woods, and there gleaming with the reflection of golden cloud or sky.

The hunters lay reclined upon the carpet of fir branchlets, each wrapped in his own thoughts. Pierre gazed abstractedly down the level river which vanished round a pine-clad point: on the left side, deep in mysterious shadows; on the right, giving back the flush of the heavens, which faded slowly to a pale amber.

His thoughts, however, were not fixed upon the scene before him, although they were tinged with the romantic melancholy with which the sight of desert nature inspires those who are most susceptible of such influences.

What could be the subject of the young trapper's reflections? Could it be that he was in love, and that Miss Frazer's was the image which haunted his imagination? That this was the case was rendered probable by the sigh that escaped his lips as he roused himself from his reverie, and suggested to his comrades the propriety of landing for the night.

It was indeed high time, as daylight was fast giving place to the shades of night. The interminable forest shrouded both banks, and it was only after a long search that the hunters found a spot sufficiently open to make a site for their camp.

The raft was tethered to a tree, and the ordinary preparations were made for their evening meal. A huge fire, formed of the whole trunks of several dead trees, the branches and withered sprays being heaped on top, soon roared and flamed, casting a ruddy and hospitable glow far down the dark vista which opened through the forest.

Lairs were made round this at a comfortable distance, and the hunters awaited the boiling of their camp kettle and the grilling of their venison-ribs over the glowing embers.

Pierre, at the request of his companions, occupied supper-time with some remarks on the natural history of the moose, an animal which they had already encountered, and from which the young naturalist himself had had a narrow escape.

"There are probably very few facts in connection with the moose," he began, "which you do not already know. Still it is an interesting subject, and one peculiarly appropriate to our present position.

"While I was at Toronto, after our return from the Saskatchewan last year, I made some notes on this animal, which I will read for you. For some years I have made a habit, as you, Gaultier, are aware, of collecting whatever information I could acquire, either from actual observation or from works on natural history, with regard to the animals which are objects of chase in North America. I have preserved the result in this volume," he continued, producing a manuscript neatly and strongly bound in leather. "I have collected particulars of almost all the principal animals which are usually met in these territories;

and if you can muster patience to listen, I will now give you the result of my researches with regard to the moose. You will observe that I have only noted his more salient features.

"To begin then. The moose belongs to the sub-family of the Alcinæ, or elks, which are characterized by having their horns broad and flat. Of this sub-family the typical representative is the moose. At first sight he seems an ungainly beast, as large as an ordinary horse, and with long disproportioned legs, which give him a shambling and awkward appearance.

"The moose has an extensive range, being found from the northern part of the Scandinavian peninsula to Siberia, and thence passing over Behring Strait into America, it extends to New Brunswick and Nova Scotia. Formerly it was abundant in the State of Maine, and even in the northern portion of the State of New York ; but it has long disappeared thence, and it is now doubtful if it is more than an occasional visitor to the State of Maine.

" Ceaseless persecution, in season and out of season, by settlers and Indians, has thinned the numbers of this noble animal, so that at present few individuals exist in localities noted for their abundance only a few years since. In Scandinavia the limits of the elk (for the European elk and the American moose are identical) have been placed at 58° north latitude. It has also been stated to exist in Finland, Lithuania, and Russia. In Northern Asia it is plentiful in the immense forests which stretch along the banks of the Obi and of the Lena.

"A recent traveller has noted its existence in Amoorland, especially throughout the country bordering the lower portions of the Amoor River.

"In America its range is scarcely less extensive; plentiful along the course of the Mackenzie River, as far north as latitude 69°, it is found in great numbers in the forests of the Peace and neighbouring rivers. It is probable that to-day as many moose are found in the districts watered by the Peace as at any previous period since we have become acquainted with that region. It is a singular circumstance that the moose is not found in Newfoundland, although the cariboo, whose range is more or less conterminous with that of the former animal, is there abundant. This is the more unaccountable, as vast stretches of pine forest, in which the swamp-maple, birch, and willow are plentiful, cover large portions of the country, and seem to offer a home to the moose peculiarly suited to his wants.

"To the north of the St. Lawrence the moose ranges as far to the east as the Saguenay River; although here, as elsewhere, his limits have contracted. Formerly he was found as far as the Godbout River, but he has now deserted that locality.

"In considering the habitat of the moose, whether in Europe, Asia, or America, we find the recurrence of the same features—lonely pine forests intersected by streams and studded with lakes and swamps, which both afford the requisite food and a refuge from the attacks of the insects from which the animal suffers great annoyance. The birch, the willow, the striped maple, as well as the shoots and fronds of several other kinds of trees and shrubs and the succulent leaves and stalks of the pond lily, contribute to the subsistence of the moose.

"In colour, the moose, in common with others of the deer tribe, varies somewhat with the season, and also with the sex. The bull is a tawny brown on the thighs, sides, back, and head; and in some specimens, probably the result of age, this has deepened until it becomes a jet black. Beneath the body the hair is much lighter in colour. The cow is of a light sandy colour above, which fades almost to white underneath.

"The calves of this species are of a sandy hue, and like the young of the ordinary American deer, they are spotted. The spots in the moose, however, are so faintly marked as scarcely to attract attention. As I have observed, the moose is an ungraceful-looking animal. His legs are long, while his neck seems disproportionately short. His ears, which are a marked feature, are broad, and nearly a foot in length. His eyes are small, and are capable of assuming a most malignant expression. The muzzle is square, and is deeply cleft, assuming the appearance of being bifid.

"The upper lip of this animal projects beyond the lower several inches, and is extremely prehensile.

THE MOOSE DEER—MALE AND FEMALE.

Page 150.

With this organ the moose is able to hold on to the boughs and twigs of tall saplings, and convey them within the grasp of his powerful teeth. This lip, or 'mouffle,' as it is technically called, is the *bonne bouche* most highly relished by the moose-hunter. On the throat may be observed an excrescence from which depends a tuft of coarse hair, which is common to adults both male and female. A hogged mane covers the neck and reaches as far as to the withers, or a little farther.

"The horns or antlers of the moose constitute perhaps its most striking feature. They are palmated, and from the outward edge rise the tines or points. From tip to tip these huge horns often measure quite four feet, and a skull with antlers will turn the beam at sixty pounds.

"The female is devoid of antlers. At the age of one year, the young bulls are furnished with two small knobs, scarcely more than an inch in length. At the age of two, these have become elongated to one foot; and in the third year they begin to flatten or palmate. It is not until the bull has attained his seventh year that his head is covered with fully-formed antlers, which then present a truly formidable appearance. From his shortness of neck and his great length of limb, the moose is unable to browse conveniently upon level ground. But from this physical inability he does not suffer much, as grass or lichens form but a small proportion of his food. The shoots

of bushes and trees are his natural fare, and of these
he can partake with ease.

"In April or May the calves are dropped. Sometimes only one is produced, sometimes two, or even
three, make their appearance. The period during
which the young are carried is the same as in the case
of domestic cattle—namely, nine months.

"During the hot season the bull, cow, and calves
remain in each other's company; and again at the
approach of winter several of these families unite and
form bands or small herds. During the heavy snows
of winter these herds occasionally take up their quarters in some particular locality and tread down the
snow over a large space in the forest. These spots are
known as 'moose yards;' and it is in such situations,
when discovered by the Indian or settler, that the
greatest destruction of moose takes place.

"Moose are hunted in various ways. These are
known as, 'still-hunting,' that is, stalking the animal
by means of its tracks through the forest; 'calling,'
which consists in alluring the bull within range, by
imitating the bellow of the cow. This requires the
nicest skill, and no one except an Indian of experience
can hope for success in this branch of the art. The
moose is also overtaken in the snow by the hunter
who is provided with snow-shoes. These preserve
him from sinking, and he can progress with great
swiftness, while the moose flounders heavily along,
plunging up to its thighs at every stride, and soon

becomes exhausted. This occurs all the sooner if the snow be covered with a thin icy crust, which breaks beneath the weight of the animal, and lacerates his legs at every step, staining the snow with his blood. This method is called 'crusting.'

"The moose, when at bay, is no despicable antagonist. With his fore feet he can deal destructive blows, while his ponderous antlers are used for tossing and goring. When the animal, perceiving that further retreat is useless, stops and faces the hunter, licking his lips, and throwing into his little eye a blaze of concentrated malice, it is high time to end the scene by a well-directed bullet.

"Instances have been known in which the hunter has met his death in these encounters—his ribs fractured by the powerful blows administered by the fore feet, and his whole body gashed and torn by the antlers of the infuriated animal. Luckily such instances are not numerous; but the consciousness of their possible occurrence invests the sport with a degree of interest and dignity of which the pursuit of less dangerous game is devoid.

"As might be inferred from the size of the ear in this species, the hearing of the moose is extremely acute, and is only inferior as a detective of danger to the power of scent in the capacious nose. The slightest crackling of a dried stick beneath the hunter's foot, the rustling of the underwood against his person, are conveyed to a great distance in the forest, and apprize

the wary moose of the approach of danger. It is only
during a heavy down-pour of rain that this exquisite
perception of sound seems to become dulled, and at
such times the hunter may hope to approach unheard.
The direction of the wind is, of course, of vital importance in the approach, and this is always ascertained
before commencing operations. The moose, before it
lies down to repose, usually describes a semicircle,
crouching within a few yards of its original tracks,
well concealed by sheltering brushwood.

"Thus the hunter, when pursuing its traces, passes
unconsciously within a few feet of his hidden game,
which escapes while its enemy is puzzling out its trail
round the deflection from its former course.

"The rutting season commences about the beginning
of September, and at this time rival bulls engage in
deadly encounter, for which their huge antlers, now
perfectly formed, are well suited. It is an exciting
moment for the moose-caller on a still autumn night,
when he hears the distant bellow of the bull and the
noise of crashing branches, as the gigantic animal
forces his way through the tangled forest, or smashes
the withered rampikes with his massive horns. The
attendant Indian raises the cone of birch bark to his
lips, and with well-feigned imitation of the call of
the cow, lures the bull within range of the hunter's
rifle.

"In districts where they are not often disturbed,
moose will readily answer the Indian's call; but when

the forests have been much hunted, few animals are so cautious. The slightest variation from the natural sound will cause the wary beast to disappear; and even when he has advanced fearlessly he will suddenly seem to be seized with suspicion, and make a detour to catch the wind of the crouching hunter.

"I have observed that young moose are somewhat later in their season than their elders. Towards the end of October the latter have left the scene, and then the juniors, bulls of two or three seasons, seem to have acquired more caution—perhaps from the reflection that they are left to their own resources. They will readily answer the Indian's lure while they are yet at a distance; but on approaching more nearly they cease their bellowings and sneak cautiously along in the endeavour to catch the wind or get a glimpse of the cow.

"At these times the least sound betrays the hidden hunter, and the game noiselessly retires. The excess of caution which characterizes the moose during the rest of the year seems to desert him in the fall. The hunter at this season will often hear his mutterings and bellowings as he crashes through the forest, often charging brakes of withered trees, whose branches fly with sharp reports before him. He is now in the proper frame of mind to answer the birch-bark call, and recklessly advance to his destruction.

"Sometimes moose, especially if numerous, and in a district not much disturbed, have regular beaten paths leading through the woods towards the bogs and barrens which they frequent, and to which they betake themselves when retreating from danger. These paths are in some places very plainly marked from the passage of the animals; they are also used by bears and other beasts of prey, whose tracks may be observed wherever the ground is soft enough to receive the impression.

"When wandering through the woods, I have on several occasions found the skeletons of two moose, whose antlers had become so firmly interlaced in their encounter, that, unable to extricate them, the animals had perished miserably face to face. I have also found the interlaced horns of the wapiti, which had doubtless met death in the same manner. In the hot season the many species of parasites and insects—such as mosquitoes, ticks, black-flies, and breeze-flies—drive the moose to the lakes and the forest ponds, where they may sometimes be seen standing immersed, with only the head and antlers above the surface of the water. I have even seen a moose in this position frequently submerge his head completely; perhaps partly to rid himself of his tiny persecutors, and also to drag up the tendrils of the yellow pond lily, which I observed he sometimes brought to the surface.

"I have now," concluded Pierre, "read you all the notes which I have made on this most interesting animal."

"Wal, young fellur," said Jake, "that's jest the kind

o' book this nigger 'ud like to be able to read. I'm a'most sorry now I didn't larn while I had the chance. I like to hear about the woods an' the game; I do. I'd never git tired o' listenin' to that sort o' readin'."

Gaultier also expressed himself much pleased, and Pierre's notes were thenceforth regularly read for the amusement of the trappers whenever their situation permitted.

Night had now fallen darkly on the forest. The glow had left the heavens, and in its stead huge clouds swept swiftly across the sky, here and there breaking into rifts through which the stars gleamed wan and faint, to be immediately eclipsed by the drifting vapours. Sudden gusts rushed through the trees and scattered the sparks and smoke of the camp fire, while the wrathful chirrup of the little red squirrel, and the dismal hootings of the owls, seemed to portend a stormy night.

This change was so sudden, so unexpected, that it had taken the hunters quite by surprise. They therefore made what preparations they could for the impending down-pour. After considerable difficulty in the uncertain light of the fire, a hut was constructed of the boughs of the spruce fir, and over this was thrown the skin of the moose, overlapped at the joining by a buffalo robe. Poles were laid against these to secure them from being blown off by the frequent gusts.

The camp fire was next replenished with enormous

logs, which required the combined strength of the
party to lift. Amid the first descending drops of the
storm the hunters retired to their hut; and despite
the howling of the winds and the descent of a pitiless
deluge, they slept soundly until morning.

CHAPTER X.

PIERRE was the first to awake. The clouds of the
preceding night had rolled away, and the sun shone
brightly, although wreaths of mist still hung in the
air above the course of the river. The morning was
chilly, and the young trapper shivered as he raked
together the embers of the camp fire and searched
around for some dry fire-wood to start a blaze. This
was no easy task, as the rain had soaked the dead
trees and converted their "touch-wood" into a dirty
slime. After a little search he was so fortunate as
to find a dead pitch pine which leaned at a considerable angle against a slender spruce. A few blows of
the axe prostrated both, and Pierre soon filled his
game-bag with the resinous knots of the pine, which
are the very best things for kindling a reluctant
fire.

With these he returned to the camp, and with the aid of Jake and Gaultier he soon established a blaze that made the large kettle bubble merrily. Venison was roasted on the coals, and by the time that the sun had fairly climbed the sky and looked down upon the Athabasca, our hunters were engaged in the congenial task of satisfying keen appetites.

After breakfast the party evinced no immediate desire to continue their journey. Jake cut a plug from a large chunk of "James River" tobacco, and having placed it in his mouth, he eyed the scene in a contemplative manner. Gaultier busied himself in arranging some fishing-tackle with which he meditated an attack on the finny denizens of the Athabasca. Pierre reclined upon a bearskin in the doorway of the hut, and gazed vacantly at the river through clouds of tobacco smoke.

Jake was the first to break silence. " I say, fellurs," said he, "we've been lucky lately in gettin' a lot o' furs an' meat. I kinder feels lazy to-day, an' ef ye've no objection, I votes for stayin' hyur an' restin'. We mout hev a squirl-hunt or somethin' o' that sort jest to keep us from mopin'. What d'ye say ? "

It is needless to say that this arrangement chimed in nicely with the feelings of the young men. It was accordingly arranged that a squirrel-hunt should form the chief feature of their day of rest. For this purpose the woods on the opposite side of the river seemed most suitable, as they consisted chiefly of deciduous trees, with many berry-bearing bushes among the underwood.

To this side, then, the raft was directed, and having secured it to the bank they landed, and presently found themselves among the dappled shades of beeches, oaks, and birches. They had not long cast inquiring eyes around the branches when Jake exclaimed,—

"Hyur's for pot-pie!" and suiting the action to the word, the old trapper drew Plumcentre to his shoulder and pulled the trigger. But the nimble little squirrel had been quicker than the hunter had bargained for. Seeing that he was discovered, he laid himself out quite flat along the branch upon which he was perched, and so effectually interposed it between himself and the deadly weapon that the bullet glanced harmlessly from the bough, scattering leaves and bark in the air.

"Do tell!" cried the trapper in amazement; "that ur little chap's the fust varmint that has beat this coon fur long enuff. Do ee try him, lad," he continued, addressing Pierre, "while I slap in the fodder."

The young hunter raised his rifle; but the squirrel, conscious that the least exposure of his body would prove fatal, slipped round the branch, rendering himself quite invisible. So active and alert was he, and so cleverly did he change his position, that it was hard to believe he was really there. Gaultier came to Pierre's assistance, and kept watch on one side, while Pierre moved round to the other.

Round as before came the agile little animal, but to

his dismay he perceived the death-bearing tube levelled at him on this side also. But before Pierre could get a correct aim the squirrel shot down the branch with the rapidity of light, and having gained the trunk, disappeared into a hole which decay had worn in the tree.

"Well, really," said Pierre, "the little brute deserved to escape. But if they are all like that, I fear our pie will not be a large one."

"To think o' the little skunk not comin' down when I pulled upon him," said Jake. 'Tain't a many varmints as kin boast o' that, I kin tell him. May an owl eat him! I've wasted a load upon him, and I can't spare so many o' *them!*"

"Never mind, Jake," said Gaultier; "you can ease your mind on the next squirrel we meet. See! there's one over there, on that oak branch that shows bare over the little birch."

The veteran hunter turned his eyes in this direction, and suddenly stopped.

"Now," said he, "I'll wager this rifle agin a plug o' bacca that I fetches that squirl out o' his boots, an' not touch a ha'r o' the varmint at that."

"I have heard of the shot," replied Pierre, "but I never saw it done."

"I hev, though," answered Jake. "I've seed this nigger do it afore; an' years agone, when I wur a little shirt-tail boy, I've seed it done often by my old man. Hyur goes!"

The young men watched the result of Jake's aim

with interest. His object was to strike the tree against which the squirrel rested, as he sat upon the bough, so close to the animal's head that the concussion would stun him and throw him to the ground. This was a favourite shot with the celebrated Daniel Boone, the pioneer backwoodsman of Kentucky.

After a careful aim, the sharp crack of the old trapper's rifle was heard. The bark flew from the tree at the desired spot, and the squirrel leaped from his perch and fell headlong to the ground, where he was speedily pounced on by the old hunter, who knocked him on the head with the hickory ramrod of his rifle.

" That's what I calls clean shootin'," he remarked as he held up his prize by the tail for the inspection of his companions. "I wouldn't 'a made it, neither, only I didn't like to sit down with the miss I made a while agone."

The youths complimented the hunter, and they advanced again, keeping their eyes well employed in searching the surrounding branches. The next shot fell to Pierre's lot. Pierre tacitly acknowledged a rivalry in the matter of shooting between himself and Jake. He was therefore anxious to cap that worthy's shot by another precisely similar, if possible.

The squirrel which next presented itself was seated upon a small branch high up in an aged oak, and close to the main stem. He thus formed a mark well suited to test the accuracy of the hunter's aim. The distance was fully sixty yards, and, in fact, this was somewhat greater than the range at which Jake had fired.

Pierre slowly raised his rifle, and fixing his eye on the line which seemed to divide the animal's head from the tree trunk, he took a steady aim and fired. A white mark showed out instantly at the exact spot, and the squirrel losing his balance, apparently with the shock, fell from the branch, and from bough to bough, until finally it fell with a dull thud upon the earth. The bullet had not injured the animal, although a small patch of fur had been shot away from the side of its head.

This shot cannot be performed unless the squirrel is actually in contact with the tree. The shock which the tree receives on being struck by the bullet is communicated to the squirrel, which, under favourable circumstances, is stunned and dislodged from its perch.

The hunters continued their sport for some time with varying success. Nearly a dozen squirrels had been consigned to the capacious bag which old Jake carried over his shoulder, when, on halting beneath the branches of a large pine, a rustling among the topmost boughs attracted their attention. It did not seem to be occasioned by a squirrel, as that little creature is so nimble and careful in its movements as scarcely to rustle a twig. By a close scrutiny the hunters distinguished a dark mass at the top of the tree; but so uncertain were its outlines that they could not determine what animal lay hidden there, nor its probable size.

After some hesitation it was resolved that one of the

party should fire at the centre of the opaque body, while the others reserved their shots in case of need. Gaultier claimed the first chance, and accordingly the young hunter threw up his rifle and fired. The branches immediately became much agitated, and presently the dark mass slipped from its position and fell at their feet. It was a Canada porcupine.

"Jehoshaphat!" cried Jake, "hyur's quills a-plenty! 'Tain't waste neither, I guess; he'll make a fustrate stew. Many's the time I've closed my teeth on porcupine, an' thur not sich bad eatin'."

The porcupine was therefore hung up in a tree to await their return, and the hunters, keeping a sharp outlook on all the neighbouring boughs, advanced deeper into the woods. The ground gradually rose, and after some half-hour's walk the party found themselves on the crest of a ridge where the timber grew thinly. On the descending slope a fire had at some former time swept the woods, which had here consisted of pines, the deciduous trees not extending beyond the top of the ascent; and through their bleached and skeleton-like branches the sparkle of water was visible in the valley below. Towards this the hunters directed their course.

Upon reaching the bottom of the hill, they perceived that the waters which had attracted their attention were those of a small lake, fed by a stream that flowed down through the woods at the upper end. A number of mounds, like low, untidy haycocks, protruded above the surface of the lake, and at one extremity the waters fell with pleasant murmur over a dam constructed of the stems and branches of small trees.

It was a beaver settlement, and the lake was the result of the labours of the busy community, which had obstructed the stream and caused it to overflow its banks. None of the animals were visible; but as the hunters pushed their way through the tangled masses of fern which margined the water, several heavy plunges were heard, and the ripples upon the quiet bosom of the lake showed the direction taken by the beavers towards the subaqueous entrances of their dwellings.

This settlement was not a large one, as scarcely a dozen houses were to be seen; but Jake said that during the summer beavers would leave their ordinary place of abode and ramble off to a considerable distance, leading a vagabond existence for some months, when they would again return to head-quarters. He was inclined to think, from the size of the dam, that it must have been constructed by a greater number of animals than one could infer from the number of lodges, and that consequently many members of the community were away on their holiday.

But what could account for the absence of their houses? This difficulty was suggested by Pierre. If the beavers had existed here a short time before, and had left the place temporarily, their houses would remain as evidence of their habitual residence.

"Wal, that's so, sure enuff," replied the trapper; "I can't exactly figure it out yit. We'll take a walk round, an' mebbe we'll find out the reason."

The hunters therefore directed their course towards the upper end of the lake, where the stream issued from the woods, down a glen with smoothly-sloping sides, prettily wooded with pines, interspersed with birches and maples. Along the banks of this stream the tracks of beaver were very numerous.

Continuing to ascend the glen, the party soon came upon another dam, beyond which the glen became considerably wider, the open space being occupied by a lake quite as large as that which they had just left. There were great numbers of beaver lodges, and several of the animals themselves were seen swimming about with all the boldness of conscious security.

This discovery explained the difficulty which had been suggested by Pierre. The colony down stream was an offshoot of this larger community, whose members had doubtless assisted the emigrants in constructing their dam. In fact, they had enabled them to set up in life for themselves.

A question now presented itself to the hunters. They were on their way to the head waters of the Peace River, with the hope of reaching a good game country, where they trusted to collect an ample stock of furs. Here were beavers in plenty, and why continue their journey in search of that which accident had already thrown in their way? The only difficulty was the question of time. To break up the journey, set up camp, and begin trapping in this region, would entail the loss of much time. Besides, it is surprising how easily under such circumstances persons lounge the days away, and finally find the further prosecution of an expedition impossible.

Jake was in favour of staying, and "clearin' out the critters right away;" Gaultier was neutral; while Pierre, perhaps from impatience to arrive as soon as possible at Mr. Frazer's Fort, voted for continuing the journey.

After considerable argument on both sides, Jake finally carried the day. It was therefore determined to camp in the neighbourhood of the Twin Lakes, as Gaultier called them, and to prosecute an attack on their amphibious inhabitants.

Having finally settled this matter, the three hunters left the lakes and proceeded towards the camp, which was several miles away through the woods. So much time had been consumed during the morning hunt, and in the subsequent examination of the lakes and beaver dams, that the declining sun was already beginning to throw long shadows, and shot his beams midway through the foliage. The pools of the stream that connected the two lakes, which at an earlier hour had received a golden tinge from the sunlight, now wheeled in inky eddies round the stones, or flowed gloomily along beneath the pendent branches of the birches. The summits of the trees still confessed the influence of the departing luminary, but in a few minutes the dull gray light which rendered objects indistinct beneath the shade of the forest crept gradually upwards.

The hunters quickened their pace in order to avail themselves of the twilight in their walk towards camp, but darkness enveloped them before they reached it. As they stumbled along over roots and through the tangled brushwood, the various nocturnal noises of the forest added to the wildness of the scene. Owls hooted dismally as they swept the glades on noiseless wing in search of mice or squirrels. The great eagle-owl uttered his maniac screams, while from the distance were heard the sharp bark of the fox, and the wild yell of the lucifee as it bounded in pursuit of its prey.

At length the hunters reached their camp. The fire was out, but a search among the ashes discovered some embers, with the aid of which it was speedily rekindled. Gaultier was cook of the expedition, and to his charge the squirrels were now consigned, Jake and Pierre having first helped to skin them.

Under the clever manipulation of the young cook these succulent little animals soon reappeared in the shape of a savoury pie, which his comrades voted excellent; and in proof of their sincerity they helped themselves to the appetizing mess again and again.

The night was dry and balmy, so that the hunters could repose comfortably in the open air on beds of pine tops; and as they lounged round the cheerful fire, well satisfied with themselves and with all the world,

Pierre was requested to produce his leather-bound volume and to read what information it contained concerning the squirrels of America. This request was readily complied with; and while Gaultier threw more pine logs on the fire, the young naturalist searched out the proper place in his book.

"There are," he began, "not less than twenty different species of true squirrels in North America. If with these we include the 'ground' and the 'flying' squirrels, this number will be considerably increased. The largest, and perhaps the most relished kind, is the 'cat-squirrel.' This, as no doubt you are aware, is the best for the pot of all the tribe, and it consequently fetches several times the price of the common gray squirrel.

"The gray squirrel, however, is the best known representative of the family, as there is scarcely a patch of woodland throughout the country in which it may not be found. Yet, in some localities where this variety was plentiful some years ago, another kind, the 'black squirrel,' is now found instead. It is asserted that the latter drives off the former, as is stated to be the case with rabbits and hares, and the Norway rat and the old brown rat. The 'fox-squirrel' and the 'cat' have often been confounded with each other, whereas they are quite distinct. The 'fox' is larger than the 'cat,' and is also more active, racing to the top of a tall tree with extraordinary swiftness. The latter, on the contrary, exhibits an unusual slowness and caution in its movements among the branches,

FLYING SQUIRRELS.

Page 151.

and rarely ascends a tree to any great height. It is, however, sufficiently agile to slip round a branch or trunk to avoid the hunter's aim. It does not usually take to the first tree at hand if discovered on the ground, but makes for the tree containing its hole, into which it disappears, leaving its pursuer to go in search of a fresh victim.

"The common gray squirrel migrates from one district to another in extraordinary numbers, 'crossing,' says Audubon, 'large rivers by swimming with their tails extended on the water, and traversing immense tracts of country where food is most abundant. During these migrations they are destroyed in vast numbers. Their flesh is very white and delicate, and affords excellent eating when the animal is young.'

"At one time during the last century they were so numerous in a section of New England that a premium of threepence per head was offered for their destruction. In one year this bounty reached the large sum of £8,000 sterling, which shows the number of squirrels destroyed to have amounted to six hundred and forty thousand.

"Perhaps the most interesting species of the *Sciuridæ* are the flying squirrels, so called from a capacity of extending the skin between the fore and hind legs in such a manner as to act as a sort of parachute. They are thus enabled to float, or rather to sail, in a diagonal direction from the top of one tree to the branches of a lower one, often at a considerable distance. Usually this species is gregarious, companies of ten or twelve living together.

"The traveller Catesby, speaking of them, says: 'When first I saw them, I took them for dead leaves blown one way by the wind, but was not long so deceived when I perceived many of them to follow one another in one direction. They will fly fourscore yards, from one tree to another. They cannot rise in their flight, nor keep in a horizontal line, but descend gradually; so that in proportion to the distance the tree they intend to fly to is from them, so much the higher they mount on the tree they intend to fly from, that they may reach some part of the tree, even the lowest part, rather than fall to the ground, which exposes them to peril; but having once recovered the trunk of a tree, no animal seems nimble enough to take them. Their food is that of other squirrels—namely, nuts, acorns, pine seeds, pishimon berries, etc.'

"A kindred variety exists in the Rocky Mountains, which makes very bold flights down the forest-covered slopes, sailing above the summits of the intervening trees until it arrives at the tree which it has proposed to itself as its destination.

"In some sections of America, squirrels, as well as other predatory animals and birds, are a perfect pest from their extraordinary numbers. M. Révoil, in his work on 'Shooting and Fishing in North America,' says: 'Sport is so abundant that the sportsman more frequently finds his ammunition run short than any lack of game. As an example of this, I will quote a passage from a newspaper which I have every reason to believe to be quite authentic. It is an account of a sporting expedition which took place in the county of Shefford (Canada), near a village called Frost. The inhabitants of this place assembled at the Golden Eagle Tavern to consult how best to destroy the vast number of wild creatures which threatened destruction to the harvest of the vicinity; and it was resolved that the marauding birds and quadrupeds should be made the subject of a kind of massacre of St. Bartholomew. Two leaders were appointed to organize the slaughter, and each of these selected seventy-five companions, who for an entire week went shooting under their orders. Messieurs Asa B. Foster and Augustus Wood were the leaders; and on the 19th of April 1856 the game was counted, and the following was the tale :—

	Foster's party.	Wood's party.
Foxes	50	50
Sparrowhawks	50	25
Crows	60	100
Woodpeckers	720	420
Polecats	270	120
Black and gray squirrels	660	673
Red and striped squirrels	41,620	33,150
Weasels	80	20
Jays	2,570	1,860
Owls	160	140
Blackbirds	3	2
Pigeons	—	1
	46,243	36,561
	36,561	

Grand total.................82,804 head.'

"From this table an idea may be formed of the relative number of the different kinds of squirrels mentioned.

" In Europe the common squirrel (*Sciurus Europœus*) is sufficiently abundant in many districts. This graceful little animal measures about eighteen inches in length, including the tail, which probably averages between six and seven inches. The head is capacious, broad above, but at the sides, as well as on top, it is somewhat flattened. The eyes are prominent, are of a dark colour, and are expressive of alertness and intelligence. Standing well up from the head are the ears, which are furnished at the tip with long fine hairs. Generally the fur is of a rich brown-red hue ; this merges into a whitish tint beneath the throat and chest. In the winter, however, the colour of the fur undergoes a change, becoming lighter, assuming a grayish colour.

" The female generally produces four or five young at a birth.

"Ordinarily the food of the squirrel consists of various edible seeds, nuts, and berries, to be found among the woods which they frequent ; but they have been known sometimes to eat birds. In appearance, the squirrel might be selected as the emblem of industry, so alert are his movements, and so keen and intelligent is the expression of his features. His little body is extremely vigorous, and his limbs are elegantly shaped, while his tail, which he jantily holds aloft above his back, is beautifully feathered with long bushy hairs, and adds considerably to the beauty of his appearance.

"He lives among the birds, which share with him their leafy home; and high up on the gnarled branch of some aged oak he may be observed seated upon his haunches, his plumed tail shading his back, holding the mealy acorn or the rough-husked beech mast to his busy jaws with his fore paws.

"It is stated that the squirrel rarely descends to the earth, even to quench his thirst; which it is further alleged that he allays by drinking the dew off the leaves and branches. During the severest winters he lives his usual active existence, leaping from branch to branch in search of seeds or nuts. His nest is an ingenious piece of architecture. It is always dry, even in the wettest weather; and to effect this, the opening, which is placed at the top, is capped by a cone-shaped roof, which effectually excludes the rain from the aperture. This nest is usually composed of small twigs interlaced with moss, the whole being very compact and cleverly put together.

"They also live in holes which age and the corroding influences of the weather may have worn in trees.

"During summer the squirrel hoards up quantities of hazel-nuts, etc., in the hollows or crannies of his tree. This granary he visits in the winter, and draws upon the stores which his forethought has provided. The voice of the squirrel is shrill and inharmonious, and he often utters a kind of grumbling noise through his closed teeth.

"The hardest and smoothest-barked tree offers no impediment to the ascent of the squirrel, which flies up the trunk almost as fast as the eye can follow. At the approach of winter the squirrel sheds his summer coat, and the new hair is of a deeper colour than that which has been got rid of. Taking them altogether, there are few animals which make a more interesting group than the squirrels. They are associated in our minds with the picturesque scenery of our woods, to which they add interest and life; and few among us but can recall many a woodland ramble, enjoyed perhaps when we were young and when life was still a golden dream of the future, when our attention had been arrested by the active movements of the agile little beast as it gleaned its harvest of seeds and nuts, or watched us slyly from behind the shelter of the branches as we paused beneath its tree."

Here Pierre stopped to recover his breath.

"I guess," said Jake, "this coon never thought so much cud be said about sich a little crittur as a squirl. But the longer one lives the more one larns."

"Really, Pierre," said Gaultier, "your natural history is invaluable. How dull we should be without it! I can't imagine, now, how we got on so long without some such aid to pass the time at our camps. But you have not yet told us anything of the porcupines, nor of the beavers, both of which we met to-day."

"I have a few notes here," replied Pierre, "on both; and if you are not tired I will read them for you."

"Fire away—with all my heart," cried Gaultier; "I'm not tired—are you, Jake?"

"No, nor cud a be," replied the old hunter; "I've follered the game these fifty year, an' ain't tired o' the bisness yet, so 'tain't likely I'd be tired o' hearin' about it so soon."

"Very well," said Pierre. "I will go on, then, with my notes."

These, however, we shall reserve for the next chapter.

CHAPTER XI.

"WE will take the porcupines first," resumed Pierre, "as they occur next in my manuscript, although properly they hold an inferior place to the beavers. Both they and the beavers, indeed, belong to the same order as the squirrels, being all classed among the *Rodentia*."

"What d'ye call 'em?" asked Jake. "I hev been, man an' boy, fifty year carryin' a rifle, an' niver heerd tell o' them critters till now. They must be scarce, I reckon, or this child 'ud a run agin some o' them in his time."

Pierre laughed outright. "That is merely a Latin word, Jake," he explained, "to designate a class or order of animals which gnaw their food. You will perceive that the teeth of the squirrel, for instance, are singularly well formed for the purpose of gnawing; so are those of the beavers, and also of the others."

"Wal, go ahead, young fellur," said the trapper;

" I s'pose it's all right what you're sayin', though this child can't figure it out nohow."

"The porcupines, then," continued Pierre, "are a well-defined family, and are designated *Hystricidæ* by the naturalists. They are distinguished by a singular panoply of bristles with which nature has furnished them in lieu of other defensive weapons. These resemble the spines of the ordinary hedgehog of the British Islands.

"There are several different varieties of this interesting group;—such as the African porcupine; the porcupine proper (*Hystrix cristatus*), or the crested porcupine; the tuft-tailed porcupine (*Atherura fasciculata*); and the Canada porcupine, with which we are more immediately concerned. The latter, however, belongs to the sub-family of the *Erethisoninæ*, while the tuft-tail belongs to the *Atherurinæ*. The Canada porcupine is characterized by a flattish skull, a short, close muzzle, a tail of but moderate length, and to some extent prehensile, and with spines of about the same length as the hair. This is the only species inhabiting the Canadian provinces, and it is from this circumstance that it has derived its name. It is a sluggish animal; but as it derives its sustenance principally from the bark of trees, it climbs with great facility.

"From its slowness, as well as from the fact that it does not defend itself, like other animals, with its teeth and claws, one would suppose it must fall an easy prey to the lynx and other predatory beasts; but this is not the case. The eminent naturalist Audubon relates that he found a lynx in a dying condition in the woods, its lips and mouth being filled with the spines which had detached themselves from the porcupine in the encounter, and which had gradually worked their way deep into its assailant's flesh.

"Even the 'painter' has been found in similar plight after a fight with this apparently insignificant creature. The quills have but a slight hold on the skin; and it is possible that, independently of the effect of the encounter, the porcupine is gifted with the faculty of detaching them when they have slightly punctured its assailant.

"These minute spears produce an inflamed wound; and being barbed, they continue to penetrate deeper and deeper into the flesh; which operation is facilitated by the movements of whatever animal has been unlucky enough to receive them.

"The porcupine is very destructive to trees, frequently killing all the trees in a grove, by eating off the bark all round the stem. An individual has been known to remain on one tree for many days, until he had almost completely denuded it of its bark. When the hunter, therefore, passes by one of these animals seated aloft amid the branches, he may leave it unmolested, with the certainty of subsequently finding it still engaged with the same tree.

"The porcupine sometimes gives vent to a peculiar cry, somewhat resembling that of a young child. In districts where the soil is loose and friable, it forms burrows for itself, generally among the roots of some old tree. In these the young are produced, of which the number varies from two to four. In general appearance the porcupine is a liver-brown, the prickles or spines being inclined to white. The quills are used by the squaws as a means of ornamentation; for which purpose they are dyed of glaring colours, and make an effective embroidery for leggings or hunting - shirts. Some of their birch-bark utensils are also embellished with them.

"The crested porcupine (*Hystrix cristatus*) is not found in America, being a native of the southern parts of Europe and of Africa. It has also been observed in many parts of Asia—notably in India, Persia, Nepaul, and round the shores of the Caspian Sea. The spines of this animal are very sharp and strong, and consist of two different kinds. One is long and thin, and forms what may be called the outer layer. The other kind is shorter and stronger, and forms the true defensive armour of the creature. In length these measure from four to ten inches, and are coated with a fine and hard enamel.

"When irritated the porcupine erects his bristly armature, and then—woe betide any animal which has the temerity to attack him! The tail of this species is covered with hollow quills, which make a rattling noise as long as the animal is in motion.

"During the day the porcupine remains in its burrow. But when the shades of evening are beginning to fall, it emerges from its retreat, and goes in search of its food, which consists principally of fruits, roots, or other vegetable matter. During winter, if the weather be severe, it retires to its den, where it remains until the genial warmth of the sun again attracts it forth.

"Some persons have spoken favourably of the flesh of the porcupine as an article of food; but possibly their opinion may have been influenced by previous starvation."

Here Jake interrupted Pierre with the remark,—

"Wal, I hev often closed my teeth on wuss chawin's than porkipines, an' I warn't starved neither. I'd as lief eat it any day as hoss meat, an' I've heern tell that the French eat a sight o' that."

"There is no accounting for taste," said Pierre; "I must confess that I do not relish porcupine much myself, although I have often eaten it when I had nothing else."

"I incline to Jake's opinion," said Gaultier. "I think a stew of the 'fretful' is by no means bad eating, especially if a few pork bones have been thrown in to heighten the flavour."

"I am glad you like it, cousin," answered Pierre, "as you have now an opportunity of indulging your taste. The one you shot seems very fat and heavy."

"Jake and I will lighten him at breakfast, never fear," laughed Gaultier; "but pray go on with your account of the animals."

Pierre therefore continued:—"As in the case of our

own porcupine, the flesh of this species is stated to be well-flavoured, and to resemble veal or pork. The traveller Williamson says of the power of projecting its quills attributed to the crested porcupine: 'With repect to shooting the quills, it is fabulous. Dogs are apt to run upon them; and the quills being sharp, penetrate so deeply and hold so fast as to occasion them to quit their matrices, or insertions in the porcupine's skin. Many horses will not approach porcupines when running, by reason of the peculiar rattling their quills make against each other.'

"The tuft-tailed porcupine is generally characterized by having its body covered with depressed spines, which on the hind part of the back are long, and mingled with the ordinary quills; and by having the tail furnished with spines at its base, covered with scales in the middle, and terminated by a bunch of long, flattish bristles, which the animal possesses the faculty of expanding or contracting at pleasure.

"Little is known of the natural history of this species. A specimen was brought from Fernando Po and presented to the Zoological Society by a Lieutenant Vidal many years since. They are said to be very abundant in the neighbourhood of that place, and to be largely used as an article of diet by the inhabitants.

"I will now read for you," said Pierre, "the few notes I have made on the beaver; and as these animals are so immediately interesting to us, I have no doubt you will patiently hear me to the end.

"In looking at the beaver, two things attract the attention—the broad flat tail, and the webbed hind feet. The former is more than half the length of the body, and coated with scales, which are mixed with short hairs. In the water this animal swims with the greatest facility; in fact it is, if anything, rather more at home in the water than upon land. The teeth of this animal are well formed for the purposes for which they are intended. There are twelve molar teeth, of which the grinding surfaces are flattened; the inside rim or edge of the upper row being marked by one enamelled fold, and the outside edge by three folds. In the lower row this arrangement is reversed.

"The incisor teeth are extraordinarily strong, and are shaped like chisels. With these they are enabled to cut down trees of considerable size, of which they construct dams across streams, with the view of forming lakes, where the depth of the water would otherwise be insufficient to afford security to the animals in their huts. I cannot do better than quote from that excellent and observant traveller Herne a description of the mode of building practised by the beaver:—

"'The situation chosen is various where the beavers are numerous. They tenant lakes, rivers, and creeks, especially the two latter for the sake of the current, of which they avail themselves for the transportation of materials. They also choose such parts as have a depth of water beyond the freezing power to congeal at the bottom. In small rivers or creeks from which the

water is liable to be drained off when the back supplies
are dried up by the frost, they are led by instinct to
make a dam quite across the river at a convenient distance from their houses, thus artificially procuring a
deep body of water in which to build. The dam varies
in shape. Where the current is gentle, it is carried out
straight ; but where rapid, it is bowed, presenting a con-
vexity to the current. The materials used are drift-
wood, green willows, birch, and poplar, if they can be
got, and also mud and stones. These are intermixed
without order, the only aim being to carry out the work
with a regular sweep and to make the whole of equal
strength.

"'Old dams by frequent repairing become a solid
bank, capable of resisting a great force of water and
ice ; and as the willows, poplars, and birches take root
and shoot up, they form by degrees a sort of thick
hedgerow, often of considerable height. Of the same
materials the houses themselves are built, and in sizes
proportioned to the number of their respective inhabitants, which number seldom exceeds four old and six or
eight young ones.

"'The houses are ruder in construction than the dam,
the only aim being to have a dry place to lie upon, and
perhaps to feed in.

"'When the houses are large, it often happens that
they are divided by partitions into two, or three, or
even more apartments, which in general have no com-
munication with each other except by water ; such may

be called double or treble houses rather than houses divided. Each compartment is inhabited by its own possessors, who know their own door, and have no other connection with their neighbours than a friendly intercourse, or mutual assistance in the necessary labour of building.

"'So far are the beavers from driving stakes, as some have said, into the ground when building, that they lay most of the wood crosswise and nearly horizontal, without any order except that of leaving a cavity in the middle; and when any unnecessary branches project, they cut them off with their chisel-like teeth and throw them in among the rest to prevent the mud from falling in. With this are mixed mud and stones, and the whole is then compacted together. The bank affords them the mud, or the bottom of the creek; and they carry it, as well as the stones, under their throats by the aid of their fore paws. They drag along the wood with their teeth. They always work during the night, and have been known to have accumulated during a single night as much mud as would amount to some thousands of their little handfuls.

"'Every fall they cover the outside of their houses with fresh mud, and as late in the autumn as possible, even when the frost sets in, as by this means it soon becomes frozen as hard as a stone, and prevents their most formidable enemy, the wolverine or glutton, from disturbing them during the winter. In laying on this coat of mud, they do not make use of their broad flat tails, as has been asserted: a mistake that has arisen from their giving a flap with the tail when plunging from the outside of the house into the water when they are startled, as well as at other times.

" ' The houses when complete have a dome-like figure, with walls several feet thick, and rising from five to six feet above the water; a projection called " the angle" by the hunters, and beyond the reach of frost; and on this, and also under water, is laid up their winter store, a mass of branches of willows and other trees, on the bark of which they feed. These they stack up, sinking each layer by means of mud and stones, and often accumulating more than a cartload of materials.

" ' Besides these winter houses, in which they are shut up during the severity of the season, they have also a number of holes in the bank, which serve them as places of retreat when any injury is offered to their houses, and in these they are generally taken.

" ' The entrance to these holes is deep below the water, which fills a great part of the vault itself. When the hunter forces the houses of the beaver in winter, the animals swim beneath the ice to these retreats, the entrances to which are discovered by striking the ice along the banks with an iron ice-chisel, the sound indicating to practised ears the exact spot. They cut a hole in the house and surprise their booty. During the summer the beavers roam about at pleasure ; and it is at this season that they fell the wood necessary for repairing their houses and dams, or for building others, commencing the latter about the end of August. Such are the strength and sharpness of their teeth that they will lop off a branch as thick as a walking-stick at a single effort, and as cleanly as if cut with a pruning-knife. Large stems they gnaw all round, taking care that their fall shall be towards or into the water. They rapidly fell a tree the shaft of which is as thick as a man's thigh, or thicker, or from six to ten inches in diameter; and spaces of more than three acres in front of a river have been covered with the timber felled by these animals, though many of the trees were as thick as a man's body.

"'The beaver does not attain its full growth before three years; but it breeds before that time. It produces from four to six young at a birth. The flesh of this animal is esteemed by the Canadian hunters and by the natives as a great delicacy, and its fur is very valuable in commerce. It is from certain glandular tubes that the substance called "castoreum," used in medicine, is obtained, and which (procured from the European variety) was well known to the ancients.

"'In captivity the beaver soon becomes familiar and sociable, and, if permitted, will even in a room exercise itself in attempts to build, using brushes, baskets, boots, sticks, or, in fact, anything it can get hold of for the purpose.'"

"I guess that's so," remarked Jake; "an' I'll jest reel ye off a sarcumstance that happened up to this coon.

'Tis a long time ago now, though. I reckon 'twur the year arter I'd clurred out o' the timber business on the Willamette. I'd med a sort o' shanty fur myself in a crick bottom whur thur wur a sight o' beaver, an' I wurn't long in makin' a purty fair pile o' pelts. The location whur I'd put up my shanty wur a'most level with the crick. I never thort o' thur bein' sich floods in that leetle crick as kem shortly arter; an' so I jest plumped it down beside the water at a place whur it med a deep pool. I used to hev lines into this at night, and in the mornin' I found my breakfast o' raal fine trout cotched ready for haulin' out. Wal, I'd got a young beaver, an' thort I'd make a pet o' the critter, as 'twur right down lonesome in them diggin's, I can tell yer, 'ithout a mortal to open one's meat-trap to from one end o' the month to the other. I slipped a trap-chain round the critter's neck, and tied him up so as he cudn't leave the hut.

" Boyees, 'twur a bad day for this coon that he set eyes on that thur beaver. I reckin ye'll think so too when I've finished. I had a fust-rate axe helved wi' hickory wi' me, an' I jest used to leave it lyin' around any-where till I wanted it. One mornin' I found the handle eat off close up agin the head, an' cut up into small pieces. But that wa'n't all. Great Columbus! how I snorted when I looked over to whur that all-fired crit-tur wur squatted, to see my rifle cut in two behind the trigger-guard, an' packed up wi' my pistols, the axe-handle, four beaver-traps, an' an auger I'd brought wi'

me all the way from Portland, all med into a lodge
which the varmint had been buildin'! I wur jest bilin'
over, you bet; an' I wur a-gwine to fetch that skunk
out o' his boots, when I heerd a rumpus outside that
med me take a squint out o' the door. Jehoshaphat!
that wur a sight met my old peepers then! Thur wur
a tide a-comin' down the bottom, roarin' like all creation, the front wave o' it ten foot high, an' stuck over
wi' chips, sticks, bushes, an' logs, as thick as quills in a
porkerpine. I hed jest one chance. The shanty wur
upon legs; that is, I hed stuck up four posts to make
the four corners, an' hed tree-nailed the planks agin'
'em at a height o' five or six feet above the ground.
I hed did this jest to hev my old carkidge out o' the
damp; an' also, in case o' floodin', to keep myself an' my
possibles dry, as the sile was softish jest about thur. I
wur therefore a reg'lar 'Jake in the box,' as my shanty
wur planked in all round, top an' bottom. I behoped
then that any flood 'ud pass underneath, an' not sweep
the hull consarn along wi' it.

"Wal, I seed at a glimp that I never would hev time
to reach the high ground afore the flood 'ud overtake
me. I hed only jest time to see what wur a-comin',
when the hull thing swep' past, round, over, an' under
me! I reckin I never felt, heerd, saw, or smelt a n'ize
like that! 'Twur like all the fourths of July as ever
kem, put in a box an' busted up together. But the
shanty stood it all elegant. The fust rush wur the
wust, an' arter that the flood settled down a bit,

BEAVERS AT WORK.

Page 168.

though, an' runnin' at that like a mill-race. That hull day it rained bull-dogs, an' I thort torst evenin' that the water wur risin' so high that I'd hev to remove out o' that. Still, as the shanty had stood so well, I didn't like to leave it, specially as all my possibles an' plunder wur lying around.

"I hed so much to do an' to think of that I never thort o' the beaver for a while; an' when I did, you bet I rubbed my eyes! The critter wurn't nowhere to be seed! I guess I soon med out that he'd eat hisself free an' he'd med tracks into the water.

"Hyur I wur, then, 'ithout a sarviceable rifle, alone be m'self fifty mile from anywhur, anchored out in a flood, an' darkness fast comin' on. 'Twur right down ugly to look at, but 'twurn't nothin' at all to what kem arterwards. You'll hardly bleeve me, boyees, when I say that arter takin' a look at how the water wur risin', I stretched m'self on my b'arskins, an' afore long fell fast asleep!

"I don't know how long I wur asleep; but I do know I woke wi' a screech that skeered m'self! I wur all wet, an' I soon med out that the hull shanty wur soakin'. But 'twa'n't that puzzled this coon; 'twur the way the thing wur a-pitchin' an' tossin' an' rollin' from side to side. Jest as I'd steady m'self agin the wall, I'd get a whammel as'd send me kerslap agin the other side; an' then souse I'd go under water, which wur a'most a yard deep over the floor.

"Thur wa'n't a doubt about it: the shanty wur

afloat, an' wur tearin' down the crick to the Dead Hoss Falls, about a couple o' miles below! That wur the sitooation this coon wur hitched to!

"I knew, o' coorse, that ef I got pitched down the falls, the shanty'd be smashed to raggles; an' I guess thur wouldn't be much o' me left arter shootin' down the rocks fur two hunderd feet.

"Thur wa'n't a spark o' light in the sky, an' o' coorse *I*'d nothin' as'd light any more'n a grampus.

"Wal, you'll say, why didn't I make fur the door, an' get straddled on top o' the shanty? That wur the very thing I wished to do, but I cudn't make out the door nohow. The hull box wur pitchin' an thumpin' along, hittin' agin stumps an' rocks in sich a way that I no sooner got on my scrapers than it'd wheel over, an' bang I'd go clur agin the other side! I didn't know, o' coorse, which side wur up an' which side wur down all this time; but arter a spell o' crackin' around in this way, in a suddint thump I got a whammel, an' wur throwed, lucky enuff, slap through the door, which wur now on the under side, like a trap-door in the floor.

"Wal, I thort 'twur all over wi' me. I wur a-goin' down an' down, till I wur a'most stifled. But feelin' I wur free o' the shanty, I struck out an' kem to the surface in time to save m'self from bustin'.

"'Twur as dark as the inside o' a buffler; but I cud jest get a glimp o' the shanty wheelin' around in an eddy. I med torst it, an' soon got straddled on top. I knew by this time that I must be clost to the falls, an'

sure enuff I shortly heerd the roar o' the water tearin'
over them.

"I now thort I mout as well hev been drownded like
a cat in a bag, inside the shanty, as go down the falls.
All at wonst the stream quickened, an' then raced an'
tore down the valley whur the bluffs closed up agin each
other. I thort I noticed a tree now an' agin leanin' out
over the water from the rocks, which wur perpendic'lar,
an' cudn't be climbed nohow. But I knew ef I hitched
my claws to a limb, I'd be able to haul myself up an' git
clur o' the bisness somehow.

"I guess, boyces, that Providence meant me to live
an' be Christianized, an' not to go under while I wur
sich an all-fired pagan. The shanty wur 'ithin twenty
yards o' the brink o' the fall, when it hit agin a rock
that stuck up over water, an' wheeled round torst the
bank, sweepin' me under the branches o' a tree, an'
a'most tearin' me from my hold. You bet, I laid my
hands about me, an' wur soon high an' dry enuff.

"I hed to stay thur till mornin', though, seein' as
thur warn't light to climb the bluffs. Wal, to make a
long story short, I got out o' the fix at last; an' arter
the flood wur gone, I went to the spot whur I'd built
the shanty, hopin' I mout find a leetle o' my plunder
lyin' about.

"When I got thur, you bet, I stared! Thur wur the
legs o' the old shanty standin' four feet out o' ground;
an', boyees, what mazed this coon most of all, each o'
'em had been cut across, jest as neat as ef 'twur done

by machinery! I guess I knew the sign o' beaver's teeth, an' you may stake high I warn't wrong in thinkin' 'twur my pet as hed did it. Ye-es, boyees! I calc'late this coon knows somethin' about beavers— *he* does!"

Here ended Jake's strange narrative.

CHAPTER XII.

EARLY on the ensuing morning, while yet the gray twilight half hid and half revealed the forest paths, the hunters arrived at the scene of their labours.

As beavers always work during the night, it was necessary to begin the work of laying down the traps early, in order that this task might be completed before the shades of evening lured forth the animals to their nocturnal labours.

The party made a cautious circuit of the lake, showing themselves as little as possible; and as they came upon a "run," deposited their traps in it beneath the water and close to the bank. The chain of each trap was secured either to a stout stake driven into the bank, or to a convenient tree-root. A buckskin thong, with a piece of light wood attached, was secured to each trap and formed a float, the object of which was to indicate the position of the beaver, should the latter, as not unfrequently happens, drag away the trap.

By noon the hunters had more than half finished their task, and accordingly they retired a little beneath the forest to rest and refresh themselves with their mid-day meal. From the position they occupied they could command a view of the lake, and while discussing the probable number of beavers they expected to take the next morning, their attention was suddenly arrested by a long, low, and brownish animal, apparently tracking their footsteps by the margin of the water.

" Look yander, boyees," exclaimed Jake ; " jest squint at that varmint. I guess he thinks we've been settin' marten traps."

" A wolverine !" cried Pierre, picking up his rifle.

" Ay," said Jake ; " I guess the skunk'll be welcome to all he'll pick up arter us this mornin'."

They continued to observe the movements of the strange animal, which faithfully followed the route taken by the party in their circuit of the lakes. At each " run " where they had halted to lay down a trap, it stopped for a short time and seemed to search the spot carefully, even looking for some moments into the water. The hunters could see that the stakes to which the various chains were attached did not escape his observation. Several of these he caught between his teeth and shook, as if with the intention of tearing them up. They withstood his efforts, however, and finding this he continued his search.

"He'll come within shot in another minute," exclaimed Gaultier; "let us be ready for him."

But as if aware of the danger to which a further advance would expose him, the wary beast suddenly turned aside from the lake, and disappeared among the trees.

"I reckin now," said Jake, "that the varmint sniffed somehow that we wur hyur. But this coon smells a wuss bother than that, ef we don't throw that all-fired beast in his tracks. I'll bet high he'll watch the beavers, an' make raggles o' all we'll take; an' o' coorse he'll spile the pelts. That's what he's a-gwine ter do."

"We must catch him somehow," said Pierre; "it won't do to throw away all our labour just to keep him in meat."

"Thur's only one way to sarcumvent the skunk," replied Jake. "The hook-an'-line dodge won't answer hyur, I guess. This coon'll jest make a cache in one o' these thick pines, an' watch all night. Ef the varmint is on the prowl at daybreak a-hookin' out any o' the trapped beavers, you bet I'll walk into him purty slick. See ef I don't."

Meditating vengeance against this unwelcome intruder on their preserves, the hunters finished their meal and betook themselves to the lower lake to lay the remainder of their traps. This they accomplished early in the afternoon, and they then returned to the upper lake and helped Jake to make his ambush amid the umbrageous foliage of a large pine which stood a little in advance of its fellows, and in a convenient position for their purpose.

About half-way up the tree a number of branches radiated from the trunk, forming joists on which to lay a flooring of smaller boughs. Upon these were thrown the soft elastic trimmings of the branches they had cut at the back and sides. The thick bushy foliage was bent down, so as to enclose the platform, and effectually to screen off rain and wind.

When finished, the nest presented a most comfortable appearance ; and Gaultier threw himself in an attitude of indolent ease upon the fragrant carpet of spruce branchlets, declaring his intention to share with Jake the pleasure of lying ensconced there during the night. Pierre also signified his desire to remain, rather than return alone to the solitary camp by the Athabasca.

Jake demurred to having so many together, fearing that "the rotted varmint 'ud smell 'em out;" but he offered no strenuous opposition, and it was therefore decided they should all remain.

Their supper was an unusually light one, consisting only of the remnants of their dinner. To this inconvenience they submitted, rather than return to their camp by the river for supplies. Gaultier was much tantalized by observing several fine geese and ducks descend upon the lake, and, unconscious of danger, swim fearlessly within thirty yards of the tree where the party lay concealed. But Jake insisted on their being unmolested, lest the report of the rifle should put the wary wolverine upon his guard, in case he skulked in the neighbourhood. Pierre was even compelled to forego the solace of his fragrant brier-root; and this was the more vexatious as old Jake, who preferred chewing the Nicotian weed to smoking it, chuckled as he made up a plug of "raal James river" and inserted it into his capacious mouth, remarking—

"I guess that pizenous critter'll bust his nose afore he'll sniff this nigger's pipe!"

Evening deepened into twilight, and twilight into gloom. The centre of the lake reflected the diamonds of the sky, while its borders were black with the heavy shadows of the forest. From the darkness below, the hunters could hear the swift footsteps of animals as they came to the water, while the creatures themselves were invisible. Frequent splashes in the lake told of the activity of the beavers; but these also were hidden by the dense shadows.

Presently a pale light streamed high towards the zenith from beyond the eastern trees; and soon from behind the forest rose the full-faced moon, touching with her silver gleam the ripples on the lake, glistening along the western shore, and revealing the gambols of the beavers, which could now be seen in great numbers, —some circling round their lodges, others proceeding towards the shore, while some hopped towards the woods, presumably to cut down timber.

It was a lovely, peaceful scene, that quiet, gleaming lake, set in a circle of dense shadows, hedged in by the virgin woods.   Here and there a hoary tree caught the moonlight on its gray outstretched arms and moss-clad trunk, standing forth like a sentinel, relieved against the sombre background.

The western shore of the lake was visible to the hunters for almost its whole length, fringed by a pebbly beach.   Upon this, and at a considerable distance, some large animals were grouped together near the edge of the forest.   Jake was the first to draw the attention of his companions to them with the exclamation,—

"Gollies! look yonder, fellurs!   Thur's a gang o' moose—five o' them at that.   Ef they'd only kim this-a-way, I guess I'd let that carcajou slide an' go fur one o' them.   Jest to think o' bein' done out o' steak an' mouffle by that rotted critter.   This child ain't a-gwine to stand by an' see it done.   No, he ain't."

The moose, however, did not seem to have any immediate intention of leaving their position, and the hunters continued to regard them with undiminished interest. Gaultier proposed that they should descend, and, availing themselves of the cover afforded by the woods, get within shot of the noble game.   They were just about to discuss this project when their attention was diverted to another channel by a sudden commotion which arose by the verge of the lake just in front of their ambush. The widening circles in the water indicated the exact spot; and looking closely they soon observed a dark object making frantic but vain efforts to leave the lake and climb up the bank, which at this place was somewhat abrupt.

"A beaver!" exclaimed Pierre; "he's caught in a trap."

Gaultier was just about to swing himself down from his perch in order to secure this their first trophy from the lake, when old Jake seized him by the arm and hissed in his ear,—

"What in thunder makes yer want to show yer ugly pictur down thur? Stay hyur, can't yer? an' not start the hull lot o' beaver back to thur lodges."

Somewhat crestfallen at this rebuke, the young hunter again seated himself, and with his companions watched the struggles of the trapped animal. Now and then, at intervals, along the margin of the lake indications were not wanting of the success which attended their first night's trapping.

"That coon's about played out," said Jake, pointing towards the beaver which had first attracted their attention; "I guess he'll go under arter another snort or two. Wagh! he's a'most choked. Did yer hear that ar gulp? I reckin he never was afraid o' water before he ran agin this child."

Presently the efforts of the drowning beast became fainter and fainter, and soon ceased altogether. The water resumed its wonted calm, and nothing remained to indicate that a struggle for existence had taken place in the tranquil and treacherous element.

This scene was being enacted at many portions of

the lake. The traps had been judiciously laid, and the number of beavers which fell victims during the night was very considerable.

Meanwhile the moose had disappeared from the beach, which stretched away in misty indistinctness by the verge of the forest, presenting no object along its expanse to arrest the attention. The night wore gradually away, and sleep overpowered the hunters. Their heads nodded on their bosoms, and one by one they yielded to the drowsy influence.

From this comfortable repose, however, they were rather rudely disturbed by an accident, which might have proved fatal, but which was nevertheless sufficiently ludicrous. A rifle-shot rang out on the still midnight air, and the bough upon which old Jake principally rested, shattered by the bullet, yielded to the weight of the somnolent old hunter, who disappeared from between his companions and fell crashing through the branches.

Fortunately a snag caught the skirt of his buckskin hunting-shirt. Much amazed at his predicament, the veteran hung suspended in mid air, wildly kicking his legs in space, and clutching at whatever seemed to promise a support.

"Git yer shootin'-sticks!" yelled the old fellow; "'twur Injuns, I tell yer. Keep yer eyes skinned, an' make a sieve o' whatever ye kin see. I'm swimmin' down hyur, an' kin find bottom nohow. Great Christopher Columbus! to think o' this old coon goin' under this-a-way. Kim down hyur, one o' yer, an' help me out o' this. I'm dumflummoxed wi' swingin' around."

Much astonished at the sudden commotion, the awakened youths descended to the old hunter's assistance, and after some difficulty contrived to extricate him from his uncomfortable predicament. This was at length satisfactorily accomplished; and on regaining their position the origin of the mishap became evident. Gaultier's rifle was invisible where he had left it; but on searching beneath the tree it was discovered, having evidently been recently discharged.

The incautious youth had dropped it in his sleep, with the result we have already described. We will draw a veil over the scenes which ensued. Old Jake was "over the traces," and many were the hard things said of "tender feet," "greenhorns," and "goneys." In truth, the old hunter was conscious of the ridiculous figure which he had presented, and he felt that his dignity as a veteran mountain-man had suffered some abatement by the incident.

The uproar which attended this adventure having disturbed the neighbourhood, the party decided that to remain longer in their place of concealment would be profitless. They therefore descended, and by the aid of the moon they shortly gathered a mighty pile of withered brushwood, which when lighted threw its ruddy glare far over the waters of the lake, and glowed warmly on the gray and brown tree trunks which stood thickly around.

Jake approached the water and peered keenly into its crystal depths in search of the beaver whose dying struggles they had witnessed from the tree.

"Git me a long saplin', one o' yer," he presently said. "I've spotted the varmint, an' I guess a slice o' his tail will do this coon no harm."

Gaultier ran to do the old hunter's bidding, and between them they soon brought the drowned animal to land, the trap still fast on one of its hind legs.

"Fustrate dog!" said Jake; "pelt's in purty fair order, considering the time o' year. Wough! wough! my beauty," he continued, "I'm a-gwine to go fur yer tail, *I* am;" and having separated that member, he proceeded, much to his own satisfaction, to broil it over the coals.

The odour, which to the old hunter's nostrils was appetizing, soon restored his good humour; and under the benign influence of fat tail he seemed to forget the recent unpleasant episode. Pierre and Gaultier both joined the veteran in his repast, and the rich mess speedily disappeared before their forest appetites.

"Boyees," said Jake, "did I ever tell yer o' my fust tussle wi' a buffler?"

The youths replied in the negative.

"Wal, 'twur more'n forty yeern agone, an' this coon wurn't o' much account then wi' a rifle, I reckin, seein' as I wur so young. 'Twur the fust time I'd ever sot eyes on a buffler, an' so yer may guess I wur green enough fur a jackass to graze on. I think I rec'lects a-tellin' yer about the journey my old man, the old mother, an' all on us med acrost the plains to Oregon. 'Twur that very time the thing happened that I'm a-gwine to tell yer. I wur on the look-out every day for buffler sign o' some sort; an' so, I guess, wur we all, as meat grew scarce in the camp. We'd had an Injun fight—the one in which I wur left 'ithout eyther father or mother, as I bleeve I told yer.

"Wal, the next mornin', arter buryin' the dead car-kidges o' them as had gone under, a big drove o' buffler kem tearin' torst us from the south'ard. Thur wur a swell in the peraira that-a-way that kep' us from seein' the critturs until they wur 'ithin a hundred yards o' the camp.

"Wal, we grabbed our shootin'-sticks purty slick, you bet, an' let the varmints in the front o' the drove hev a taste o' our lead. But 'twur o' no use a-tryin' to turn the critturs. O' coorse, yer knows that a gang o' bufflers goes straight ahead, 'ithout carin' whur they're runnin', when they've got stampeded in airnest. Thur wurn't time to wink when the hull lot wur among the waggons.

"I had got on top o' one o' these, thinkin' 'twur the safest place about; but afore I wur rightly settled the thing wur heeled over an' capsized into the middle o' them. I rec'lects that as plain as if 'twur only yester-day it happened. I felt blamed queery, I kin tell yer, when I wur whammelled over an' fell kerslap into an ocean o' horns an' flamin' eyes an' steamin' noses.

"Ef any one hed been around an' hed seed it, o' coorse he'd a thort 'twur all over with this child. When I kem down, 'twur atop o' a buffler's back I fell; but I reckin I didn't stay thur long. I wur tossed out o' that in the flappin' o' a beaver's tail; an' lucky 'twur fur me, I reckin, that when I slipped off I kem down standin'.

"I tuck an idee at wonst, an' jest laid hold o' a buffler's tail by the root, an' clung on as ef I wur glued to it. The bufflers round on eyther side, I guess, tuck me fur a 'painter' or a b'ar, or some sich varmint, fur they sheered off, an' by-'n-by I wur a-streakin' it acrost the peraira a'most alone wi' my own bull. The crittur hadn't seed me yet. He wur too frightened to wait to see what wur a-clawin' at his tail, an' so he held on, tearin' arter the rest o' the herd, which had wheeled off to one side. I wur safe from bein' tramped to death by the herd, an' I now thort 'twur time to say good-bye to my companion.

"I guess I wudn't 'a taken it onkind o' him ef he'd a let me slip off 'ithout takin' any notice o' me. But that wurn't what he wur a-gwine to do. I wur jest thinkin' o' this, when on a sudden he put down his nose an' gev a hoist to his hind-quarters that lifted me off my legs afore I cud cry Snakes! The tail slipped from my fingers, an' down I kem on the peraira.

"The bull stopped a'most at oncest, looked round, put down his head, shet his eyes, an' kem at me. I hed only jest time to jump on one side when he passed me with a whiz. He wheeled at oncest; an' now, boyees, I gev myself up, fur I seed at that minute another buffler cavortin' torst me, wi' his tail screwed up an' his horns on full cock.

"I wur atween them, an' both on 'em cum a-thunderin' down at me 'ithin ten yards. I cudn't stir no more'n ef I'd froze to the ground. 'Twur jest like that all-fired feel kims over one asleep when a waggon-load o' black cats is drawn up on the bed, an' somethin' awful busts out o' a cloud an' sets a fellur a-hollerin' till he wakes hisself wi' the fright o' it.

"I wur jest in that way, but at the last half-shake I med a mighty jump aside, an', boyees, ye'll never bleeve it, them two bufflers met face to face wi' a crack like an airthquake. Ye shud 'a seen 'em, the way they wur throwed. Both on 'em staggered back an' fell, sittin' on thur hams like dogs; but I guess they didn't stay thur long. They riz at oncest, an' med at each other like game-cocks, snortin' an' plungin' an' pushin' like all creation.

"I wur clean mazed, an' stud a-lookin' on till I tuck a notion that I'd better make tracks fur camp while they'd forgot me. I put out, you bet, like a quarter-hoss, an' never stopped till I got up to the waggons. Hyur I found some o' the mountain-men; an' I cudn't get 'em to swaller my story nohow till I led 'em back to whur I'd left the two bulls fightin'. Sure enuff they wur still at it, an' I crep up wi' one o' the fellurs, an' we each o' us throwed his bull. I wur well out o' the thing, boyees. I guess I chawed that thur buffler's hump that night wi' a hearty appetite. I did so."

Here the old hunter relapsed into silence, occasionally chuckling over the recollection of his early exploits. Pierre and Gaultier confessed that they had never before heard of a hunter being saved from one buffalo by the unintentional intervention of another.

" Ye hain't lived as long in the perairies an' in the woods as this old nigger," replied Jake; " but it seems somehow as if the old days wur better than the new. I hain't," he continued, " had sich close shaves nor been in sich tight places as I used to be, these years an' years. Things are settlin' down and gettin' tamer every day, I think."

" I fancy," said Pierre, " that the game has not now-a-days the boldness it had forty years ago. There has been too much shooting; and no doubt the different animals have learned that discretion is the better part of valour."

" That's so, you bet," replied Jake. " I cud tell yer some queerities that I've come acrost in my time wi' most sort o' critters; but most on 'em happened years agone, an' that jest squares in wi' what yer says."

" What was the tightest place you were ever in, Jake ?" asked Gaultier.

" Wal, young fellur," replied the trapper, " I hain't edzactly figured that out. I've often said to meself that I've had so many near things happened to me that I never cud settle which were the tightest on 'em all. I reckin, though, until I think o' a better'n, that a rumpus I hed wi' the Comanches in the Pan Handle o' Texas will sarve yer turn."

"Wait a bit, Jake," said Pierre; "I'll just throw some more logs on the fire, and we'll have a fresh chaw of beaver while you are telling your story."

The two young men accordingly collected a good supply of fuel, and having put down another broil of beaver, they took their place, turning expectant faces on their veteran companion. The latter seemed lost in rumination while vacantly fumbling with a plug of twist-tobacco, from which he slowly severed a "bite," which he placed in his cheek. At length he broke silence :—

"I guess I hain't never met wi' sich mortal savages as them Comanches; and I've heern Eagle Jack say that he has fout a'most all the tribes in the States, an' gives in that the Comanches beat 'em all fur cruelty. I feels lonesome when I thinks o' poor Jack. He wur an out an' out good fellur, an' many a day he an' this coon spent in company. Ye see we wur reg'lar chums; neyther o' us ever kep' a good thing to hisself, but allers went shares wi' his commerade. We trapped an' hunted, eat and starved together, an' wur a sight fonder o' each other than many brothers. Wal, one day (we wur at Fort Belknap at the time) Jack wur told by a friend that wur dyin' in the fort (hevin' got a ball in his gizzard in a rumpus wi' some o' the boyees) that he knew o' a silver mine in the mountains near the Salado.

"He gev the account o' the place so plain that Jack wur right down sure o' findin' it 'ithout any trouble. O' coorse he tell'd me about it at oncest, and so we jest concluded to slope airly the next morning, afore any o' the boyees 'ud be about an' askin' us awkard questions. We kep' the bank o' the Brazos fur days an' days till we kem to the Saline, which we skirted, an' held on by the Tosohuanuevo, as them ugly Greazers calls it.

"Wal, at the head-waters o' this we wur in a range o' the Guadaloupe mountains; an' a fine location I reckin that wur fur game. One day we kem on a nice valley wi' high grass a'most over the hull o' it, an' a few clumps o' bushes an' trees scattered about every which way through it. In the middle o' this valley we noticed a gang o' buffler, an' o' coorse we pulled up an' agreed to run 'em.

"The wind wur right enuff, an' so, takin' kear to be out o' sight o' the critturs, we dodged torst 'em, an' arter a while, wi' the help o' the timber, we got 'ithin a kupple o' hunder yards o' the drove.

"At a word we clapped in our spurs, an' med at 'em as hard as we cud tear. The beasts didn't smell what wur up till we got 'ithin fifty yards; an' then they wheeled round an' put out in airnest. We laid in our quirts an' spurs, an' you had better bleeve that the way we got over the ground wur a caution. While splittin' along this-a-way, o' coorse we never kep' eye on anything 'cept the bufflers. I reckin 'twud 'a been better fur us ef we had taken a squint around us now

an' agin; but then yer sees we never thort o' thur bein'
anything about 'ceptin the varmint we wur arter.

"Now an' agin I kinder thort I heerd a nize o' some
sort behint us; but 'twur some time afore I tuck a
glisk around to see what it wur. Jehoshaphat! I feels
queery even now when I thinks o' that minute! Arter
us, an' as hard as thur ponies cud go, kem a band o'
Injuns. I gev the wink to Jack, an' he looked back,
an' you bet what he seed didn't please him any more
than it did me.

"Thur wur nothin' to be did 'ceptin to keep on, an'
we gev whip an' spur to our hosses. But I guess the
critturs wur blown already wi' thur quick burst arter
the buffler, an' so we both felt our beasts wur givin'
out fast. The Injuns, when they saw we spotted 'em,
raised all creation wi' thur yells; an' Jack, who understood a leetle o' thur gibberish, med out that they wur
tellin' us we mout as well stop, as anyhow they meant
to hev us and make griskins o' our gizzards.

"By this time we'd left the valley whur we'd fust
seed the buffler, and wur a-streakin' it over a peraira
that stretched torst another range o' hills seven or eight
miles off. We wur well out on this peraira, and wur
hopin' we mout yet reach the other side an' dodge the
varmints among the chapperal we cud see growing on
the hills, or mebbe hide in a cave, when all at once,
'ithout any warnin', we found our hosses stopped short
as ef the critturs wur shot.

"At our feet wur one o' them all-fired gulches (bar-

rancas the Greazers calls 'em), fifty foot deep, an'
stretchin' right an' left as far as we cud see. At the
bottom wur a river, an' we knew from the quiet look
o' the water 'twur deep. I guess the Injuns knew all
about how we wur fixed, fur they yelled an' screeched
wuss than ever, an' kem on like wolves arter a wounded
deer.

"'I guess, old coon,' says Eagle Jack to me, 'I ain't
a-goin' to let meself be tuck by them rotted skunks.
I'm a-goin' to drown, ef 1 must go under.' With that
he riz his rifle an' let drive at the fust up o' the Injuns;
and at the crack, you bet that niggur left his saddle
purty speedy. Wal, I fetched another; an' slingin' our
rifles we jined our hands in front o' our heads, an'
streaked it off the bluff into the water. 'Twur a
fearful leap, I kin tell yer; but thur wur no choice.
Ef we'd gev in, 'twur as likely as not the Injuns 'ud 'a
roasted us alive, as they hed did to some settlers a
short time afore on the Brazos. Arter whizzin' through
the air, hittin' the water at the rate o' a rifle ball, an'
makin' a dive o' twenty or thirty foot deep, 'tain't
likely as eyther o' us felt very clur in the brains.
This old coon wur a'most mazed, an' instead o' makin'
fur the other side, I guess I didn't know whur I wur
a-gwine to, fur I shortly med out I wur a-tryin' to
climb back the very bluff I hed jumped from!

"Eagle Jack got out o' the water and shook hisself
like one o' them Newfoundland dogs, an' seemed no
wuss for his tumble. We squatted clost under the

cliff, hidden by a shelf that cropped out jest over our heads, an' waited. The Injuns o' coorse arruv on the edge of the barranca the minute arter we clurred off it; an' we cud hear the varmints talkin' quite plain, an' wonderin' what'n thunder hed become o' us.

" You may stake high we kep close an' didn't tell 'em ; an' arter a leetle while, as they cudn't see a sign o' us, they toted thurselves right away, an' we seed 'em no more. I reckin they thort we wur killed or drownded with the leap, an' concluded that 'twurn't worth their while to ride round twenty mile, as they'd hev to did, to git down to see what had become o' us."

" What about the silver mine, Jake ? " asked Pierre. " Did you find it ? "

" I guess," replied Jake, " that wur the wust o' the hull business. We cudn't make head or tail o' the country whur we concluded it to be ; an' arter all our trouble an' danger, we jest had to take the back track south, wi' our tails between our legs, as I may say, an' hevin' lost our hosses an' everything we hed, 'cept what we stood up in. 'Twur a nasty job altogether, an' this coon don't overly like to think more about it."

Pierre and Gaultier thanked the old hunter for his exciting narrative ; and as it was now very late, they disposed of themselves for the night as comfortably as their circumstances would permit.

CHAPTER XIII.

THE gray light of morning was contending with the pale moonbeams which still silvered with slanting rays the verge of the forest on the eastern banks of the lake, when old Jake raised his lanky form from the lair in which he had spent the night, and looked around. On the opposite or western shore the prosaic light of day already rendered objects sufficiently distinct to indicate their nature to an observer.

The old trapper had no sooner cast his keen eyes in this direction than he quietly took his rifle, and, with every demonstration of caution, left his still sleeping comrades, and crept stealthily to the cover of the woods. Once within their friendly shelter, he glided noiselessly and swiftly in the direction we have indicated; and having at length reached a spot within rifle-shot of whatever had aroused his attention, he approached the edge of the woods, and looked eagerly along the shore of the lake.

At the distance of some sixty yards, a dark-brown animal was busily engaged in dragging from the water the body of another animal, not much inferior to himself in size. It was the wolverine, busied in his customary practice of counter-working the trapper's ingenuity.

Old Jake slowly brought Plumcentre to his shoulder, and at the crack the nefarious beast sprang from the ground and turned over dead. The report of the rifle awoke both Pierre and Gaultier; and seeing their veteran companion standing on the beach, they soon rejoined him, and congratulated him on his morning's work. After stripping the wolverine of his shaggy hide, the party returned to the camp, and prepared breakfast, during which old Jake recounted the details of his approach upon the carcajou in his own peculiar style.

This was a busy day with the trappers. A visit to their traps entailed the circuit of both lakes, which occupied them until mid-day, by which time they had secured a large number of beavers; and the skinning of these gave them ample occupation until evening.

After setting their traps afresh, they set out on their return to their camp by the Athabasca, intending to revisit the lakes on the following morning. It was late when they left the silvan lake and plunged among the forest shades on their way to the Athabasca.

The prolonged twilight of these northern regions rendered objects sufficiently visible, even at some distance, in the open glades; but within the woods the heavy shadows of the spruces eclipsed whatever remained of day, and in the murky light the eye failed to distinguish anything with accuracy. The dark columns of the trees stretched away into vagueness, while here and there the white trunks of the silver birches seemed to start like ghosts out of the gloom, their shining arms stretched athwart the sable foliage of the firs, and the intricate tracery of their branches outlined against the star-gemmed sky.

From afar down the woods came a sudden cry—a cry so wild and demon-like that the hunters immediately stopped to listen. Again came the hideous wail, resounding sharply through the silent forest.

"A painter!" exclaimed Jake. "I guess the varmint is gettin' peckish, an' he's takin' a poke round fur grub. The very leaves shiver at the skunk's sqwawks, an' nary a beast or bird but does the same when he sings out that a-way."

The animal as yet seemed at a considerable distance, and the party continued their walk, occasionally stopping to listen as the wail of the cougar was borne to their ears. Sometimes the snapping of a twig or the rustling of the branches arrested their attention; and on listening carefully, the nibbling of the Canada porcupine could be heard as he plied his mischievous trade of stripping the bark from the trees.

Frequently small animals skurried past; and on one occasion, apparently on their trail, came the lynx: but although the trappers stepped aside behind the shelter of the nearest tree-trunks, the wary beast seemed to detect the danger, and slunk quietly from the neighbourhood. Hares are numerous in these forests, and furnish the lynx and the foxes with their food. The sharp bark of the latter was heard on every side as they chased the hares through the woods.

On arriving at a small glade, old Jake proposed that the party should halt for a short time, as he believed, from some indications he had noticed during the day, that this neighbourhood was frequented by black foxes. He hoped, when the moon rose, to lure one or two of these very valuable animals within shot.

The open space at the verge of which the trappers stationed themselves measured several hundred yards in length by about eighty yards in breadth. It was covered with greensward, and dotted over with clumps of bushes and some young and luxuriant pines. No resort could be more likely for such small quadrupeds as form the prey of the black fox; and doubtless it was therefore that the old trapper hoped to secure one of those rare and highly-prized animals, whose skins sell for their weight in gold.

Some long grass beneath the spreading branches of a large spruce afforded a convenient shelter. Throwing themselves upon the ground, the party awaited the rising of the moon with as much patience as they could command. The maniac scream of the great horned owl, the yell of the lucifee (*loup-cervier*), and the occasional ghoulish wail of the cougar, accentuated the weird solemnity of the gloomy forest.

Occasionally a deep sighing sound filled the air—the rush of the breeze through the tree-tops, which scarcely swayed to its passing influence. From the glade could be heard at intervals a shrill squeak, which soon caught Gaultier's attention.

"What is it makes that noise, Jake?" he inquired as the sound again reached their ears—this time seeming to come from several directions at once.

"I reckin it's mice," replied the trapper; "an' 'twur them same leetle critters that med me wait hyur a bit. The black fox chaws up them varmints, an' I kinder think we'll see some o' them beauties ef the moon 'ud only show out."

Slowly the time passed to the expectant hunters, until the gradual brightening of the eastern heavens announced the wished-for moonrise. Slowly the pale light stole upward along the sky, and soon the welcome luminary rose from beyond the woods, throwing showers of light upon the sleeping trees, and darting silver spears into their gloomy recesses.

"Now, young fellurs," said Jake, "it's time to skin yer eyes. Jest squint out thur over the grass, an' mebbe ye'll spot a fox on the lope arter them mice."

The young men accordingly cast searching glances down the glade; but in the distance objects were so confused and indistinct that several times mistakes were made, which at length aroused the ire of old Jake.

"Wagh!" he exclaimed, "yer can't see ekal to an owl in daytime. I guess my old peepers kin tell the difference atween a stump an' a fox yit. But," he suddenly cried, "what'n thunder's that lopin' varmint comin' round the brush yonder?"

The young trappers looked eagerly in the direction indicated, and soon observed a large animal stealing forward cautiously from the shelter of some low bushes, and apparently bent on approaching their place of concealment. As far as they could judge in the deceptive light, the new-comer was a long and apparently somewhat clumsily-shaped animal; and from its stealthy, cat-like mode of progression—now creeping rapidly forward, again squatting flat on the ground behind some slight obstruction — it did not require Jake's whispered exclamation, "A painter!" to convince them of its identity.

With breathless interest they watched the motions of the fierce and wary creature. As yet it was evidently unconscious of the proximity of such dangerous foes. Some object in the open glade had fixed its attention; but what this could be, neither Jake nor the two young hunters were able to guess. In its gradual approach it had at length placed itself within easy rifle-shot; but the curiosity of the ambushed party as to its future movements caused them to reserve their fire. They now could observe that the cougar flattened itself out, and almost seemed to sink into the ground; in which position it would have certainly escaped the eye of any one who had not previously watched its motions.

A few yards from the spot where it crouched, there was visible a small projection, which the trappers had regarded as a stump or a tussock of grass. Suddenly the cougar launched itself forward, and, to the astonishment of the hunters, this became all at once animated, and leaped with a feeble scream from its position. Before it had gained half-a-dozen yards, its fierce and active enemy bounded upon it, and in a second the unresisting prey lay still upon the grass. At this moment three sharp reports startled the quiet of the scene, and the cougar, springing to the height of four feet in the air, rolled over on its back.

"Hooraw!" cried Jake; "here's the skunk we heerd a-singin' this blessed evenin'.—Come, my beauty," he continued, as he ran forward, followed by the young men; "let's hev a squint at yer p'ints. I reckin yer didn't know old Jake Hawken wur a-lookin' on at yer —no, *that* yer didn't."

So saying, the old hunter unsheathed his knife, and, with the aid of his companions, in a very few minutes relieved the still quivering carcass of its hide.

"I reckin 'tain't as valeable as black fox," he observed as he folded up the reeking trophy and slung it over his shoulder; "but 'tain't often one runs agin a 'painter,' an' the honour o' the thing must make up for the loss."

The smaller animal next attracted their attention. It was a hare, which the cougar had no doubt tracked from the woods by the scent. This Pierre deposited in his game-bag as a welcome addition to their larder.

The neighbourhood having been much disturbed by this occurrence, the party determined to proceed to the Athabasca without further delay; and after an hour's walking through the sombre shades and moonlit openings of the woods, they at length emerged on the river bank at a spot not one hundred yards from their camp.

This they found exactly as they had left it, no human being, apparently, having passed that way during their absence. A fire was soon crackling and flaming, sending around its cheerful glow; and upon the great embers beaver meat sputtered and the large kettle hissed and bubbled, while the three hunters bustled about the blaze, busily engaged in the pleasant task of preparing supper.

"Who says a hunter's life is not a pleasant one?" said Pierre as he lounged on a pile of soft pine branchlets, within comfortable reach of both the meat and the kettle. "For my part, I feel happy only in the woods."

"Right ye are there," said Jake. "I feels allus as cf a load wur put down on my gizzard when I gets into the settlements. Civilyzation don't pan worth a cent wi' this niggur, you bet. Thur plan o' livin' in houses 'ud kill a hoss; an' as fur thur victuals, I don't know arey a beast a-livin' as cud hold up agin 'em. I wur laid out flat fur a week—an' in a house at that, arter chawin' some fixins I once got at a party. I guess I med tracks out o' them diggins as soon as I cud rise on my scrapers—I did so."

"Life in a crowd is not pleasant," observed Gaultier. "I once had to live in a thickly-settled district for nearly two years, an' I thought the very air would have choked me. Then there were annoyances of different kinds. Money was hard to come by, and meat was scarce. I never lived as well as we do out here, where we have the best of game for the shooting. Pigs and corn and Congress seemed to be the only things anybody cared for; and I was daily disgusted at seeing the few remaining patches of woodland in the neighbourhood hacked down. I was right glad when at last I was able to get back into the wilderness."

"Thur's one class o' people," said Jake, "that orter git clurred out o' the country right straight away, and them's the coons that boss the lumber trade. They won't leave cover for a chitmunk in a few years' time. Why, when I wur a-growin' up younker, I rec'lects rivers, an' big ones at that, whur yer wouldn't see water enuff now to float a chip, an' all o' hevin' the woods cut down. I reckin clurrin off the timber dried the springs. The grand old woods I used to walk in when fust I carried a rifle ur turned into floors an' doors long enuff ago now, I guess. Ef thur's anything this old niggur hates wuss'n civilyzation, it's them lumber thieves that robs the wilderness o' its beauty."

"I heard," said Pierre, "when I was last in Toronto, "that it was intended to bring in a law to check the wanton waste of timber which has laid bare many sections of the country. Inducements have been held out to prairie settlers to plant trees on their farms; but for one tree planted there, a thousand have been cut elsewhere."

"This coon has lived fifty years," said Jake, "an' never did he see a settler plant a tree. I don't b'lieve it's in the critter to do it. No! A settler has but one idee in his brain-box, an' that is that every tree's a rattlesnake standin' on his tail; and the more o' em he chops the more he's pleased."

"I am afraid, Jake," said Pierre, "that you are right. Wholesale waste is their rule. At a meeting in connection with the lumber trade not long ago in Chicago, it was stated that at the present rate of destruction the forests in the United States would be cleared out in about twenty years."

"Wal, I dunno about that," replied Jake. "I knows o' many a mile o' woods whur no lumberman's axe has chopped a tree yit; an' better 'n that, thur ain't a crick 'ud float a grasshopper 'ithin a hunderd miles. Ontil they gits thur all-fired railways into them diggins, thur 'll be elber-room for a hunt. I ain't skeert wi' the thorts that the game an' woods won't last my time; but I guess I kin smell the end o' it for all that—wuss luck!"

"The settlers won't reach where we are now for a good while, anyhow," observed Gaultier; "and I heartily hope they'll never come half-way. What a nice world it'll be when there is not a spot left that doesn't belong to somebody, and not a thing to be seen but bullocks here and pigs there! And that things are coming to this I have no doubt. See the change that has taken place about Winnipeg within the last few years."

"Boyees," said Jake, "yer needn't take on about it. The woods an' plains an' mountains 'll last our time, anyhow; an' let them as kim arter us take kear o' themsells. That's this child's opeenion o' the matter, an' I calc'late it's genuine pheelosophy, as I've hearn some o' them queerities as lives by book-larnin' say."

Having argued the matter to this pithy conclusion, the hunters allowed the subject to drop. The fire was replenished with several giant logs, which soon became a mass of flame, throwing a hot-house atmosphere round the spot.

Fatigued by their day's exertions, as well as overcome by the drowsy influence of the warm camp, the hunters threw themselves upon the lairs which they had constructed, and soon their deep and regular breathing alone disturbed the midnight quiet.

CHAPTER XIV.

OUR trappers remained a week in this neighbourhood, during which time they secured a goodly store of furs. Although it was not, properly speaking, the season for taking the beaver, they nevertheless were unable to resist the opportunity of prosecuting their profession afforded by the well-stocked preserve at the Twin Lakes.

At length the last beaver they intended to take was caught, and the last trap lifted. They collected their various effects, which had been securely stored within the hut built when first they resolved to make a sojourn at this spot. These they placed upon the raft, which had floated by the place, and which they had tethered to a tree; and having taken a last regretful look around the scene of their temporary home, the line was unfastened, and the trappers were once more afloat on the powerful waters of the Athabasca.

After a few days of pleasant travel, they arrived at Fort Pierre, where they were warmly received by Mr. Frazer. Here both the young men found former acquaintances, who welcomed them with acclamation; and many were the stories told of hairbreadth escapes, and adventures by flood and field, that had happened since the friends had met.

At the fort time passed pleasantly. Jake, indeed, who seemed indifferent to all considerations of time or place, provided his wants of meat and tobacco were supplied, resigned himself to the enjoyments of eating and giving or receiving news with great content. As may readily be supposed, Pierre found himself the guest of Miss Frazer's father with a feeling of satisfaction. The fascinating girl whose life he had saved was his hostess, and in her society the days seemed to pass very rapidly.

Each day some new obstacle was discovered to impede his departure; and although some hunting excursions were planned, in which Jake and Gaultier participated, Pierre preferred to act the idler, and spent the time in escorting Miss Frazer to various points of interest in the neighbourhood.

This marked attention on the part of the young trapper did not escape the observation of the residents at the fort. Among these there was one to whom the growing intimacy between Miss Frazer and the trapper was especially distasteful. This was a clerk in the employment of the young lady's father.

As Pierre passed him one morning, the pent-up jealousy which his attentions had excited at length burst forth. The interview took place at a spot on the banks of the Athabasca not four hundred yards from the fort. Pierre having observed that some one was standing motionless by the water, advanced slowly; and when within a short distance recognized his rival, whose name was M'Leod.

Not wishing to appear desirous of avoiding him, the young trapper approached, and courteously bade him good-morning. To his surprise, M'Leod took no notice of his presence, but continued to gaze steadily upon the river.

Suddenly he turned, and in a voice hoarse with passion exclaimed,—

"How dare you speak to me, you sneaking wolf-catcher? With your Frenchified airs and graces you step across an honest man's path, and wriggle yourself into the confidence of people, who, if they knew you as well as I do, would kick you into the Athabasca."

"And if *you* know me so very well," said Pierre quietly, "why don't *you* kick me into the Athabasca?"

"Because I have too much respect for one whose name I will not mention in your presence, to make a brawl with a wandering butcher like you," replied M'Leod.

"You are very careful of your reputation in the interest of others," said Pierre scornfully; "but this shall not serve your purpose. You shall not escape me in this manner."

M'Leod, to the full as hot in temper as Pierre, exclaimed,—

"I do not wish to escape you in any way, or to have you suppose I am afraid of anything you can do. If you think I have said anything which needs satisfaction, I am ready to back with my hand whatever I have said."

"And I am equally ready," cried Pierre. "To-morrow be it, then, at daybreak, in the beaver meadow behind the fort. Our rifles will settle this dispute, and may he who falls find mercy!"

These words Pierre pronounced calmly; and leaving his incensed rival still standing by the river, the hunter returned to the fort. As he left the spot, his quick eye caught sight of a woman's dress among the trees not far from the place where the altercation had occurred; but in the excited frame of mind in which he was, despite his outward calm, he bestowed no attention on the circumstance. How vividly it was afterwards recalled to his mind!

During the remainder of the day Pierre had a difficult part to perform, in the effort to appear gay and unembarrassed in the society of his comrades, while within, the recollection of his quarrel, together with the uncertainty of the result of the impending duel, sufficed to chill his spirits.

He was deprived, too, of whatever of a counteracting influence Miss Frazer's company might have afforded, as that young lady was said to be confined to her room by a bad headache, and even at supper did not appear.

In the twilight Pierre walked along the banks of the Athabasca, which he felt that he at length, perhaps, beheld for the last time. The evening air was calm; the water flowed silently past, reflecting here and there the fading flush of sunset skies; the woods sent forth their resinous fragrance; and across the peaceful bosom of the river the wild-duck led her brood. Nature was at rest; and as the young hunter walked, the holy calm of wood and water seemed to breathe a quiet on his soul, and to still the passions that disturbed it.

Seating himself on a mossy trunk which had fallen forward from the verge of the forest, Pierre cast his eyes into the far-off skies, from which the flaming colours of the sunset were fading into amber and pale gold; and as he gazed he became lost to the present. Visions of the past crowded his mind; and with them, like the scent of distant meadows wafted on the breeze, came the recollections of his childhood and of the teachings of his mother.

Gradually he realized how incompatible with these was his present position; and his moral consciousness being once awakened, the young hunter immediately resolved to be no longer the slave of passion. With this determination he arose, and walked quickly towards the fort. Just as he reached the open space which surrounded the buildings, he saw a figure in the uncertain light moving slowly towards him. It was M'Leod. Full

of his new-born good resolution, Pierre advanced and
held out his hand.

" I have been, perhaps, too hasty, Mr. M'Leod," said
he, "and am sorry if I've given you offence."

" I never thought much of you," was the ungracious
reply; " but I hardly guessed you were so white-livered
as this.   What! you give up your pretensions to Miss
Frazer's hand, and say you are sorry for having entertained them ?"

" You must wilfully misunderstand my meaning,"
replied Pierre, feeling the old leaven of anger rising
within him; " but I cannot even allow you the pretence
of doubt.   I surrender nothing beyond my foolish desire for what is called ' satisfaction,' and which I find
my conscience will not allow me to entertain any
longer."

" Ha, ha!" laughed M'Leod; " that's very good! A
fellow like you pretending to have a conscience! I'll
tell you, my fine fellow, what your conscience consists
of—a very rational love of a whole skin.   That's *your*
conscience.   I shall expect you all the same at the
beaver meadow at daybreak; and," he added in a tone
which left no doubt of his sincerity, "if you are not
there, I will shoot you like a dog wherever I meet
with you.   You shall not stand in my way."

So saying, he turned and walked swiftly towards
the fort, where he was followed, though slowly, by the
young trapper.

It is no disparagement of Pierre's courage to say

that his reflections were not of the most pleasant kind. Conscientiously he disapproved of duelling; yet here he found himself a principal in an affair which, while he heartily condemned it, he could hardly avoid.

He tried to quiet the scruples that assailed him by reflecting that to accept the challenge was the only alternative left to him by the threat which M'Leod had uttered. After much consideration, he finally determined to be present at the place and time assigned; but he was firmly resolved not to wield his weapon in his own defence except in the last extremity. He judged it prudent not to tell either Jake or Gaultier of the unpleasant circumstances in which he was involved, lest their advice and assistance might still further embarrass him; and having left a letter for Gaultier, explaining the unfortunate events which led to his present predicament, Pierre committed himself to sleep with what composure he might.

After a night disturbed with restless dreams, the young hunter awoke. At first he failed to recall his position, or the circumstances in which he was placed. But gradually the unwelcome facts forced themselves upon his recollection; and after the first chilling shock had in some degree subsided, he rose and prepared for the event which was to determine his life or death.

The objections which his conscience had raised on the preceding evening now returned with redoubled force. In vain he opposed to them the specious arguments which at all times have been offered to palliate homicide for a mere punctilio or an idea. These vanished before the criticism of his conscience.

Smothering the suggestions of his better nature, the young hunter left the fort in the gray light of dawn, and directed his steps towards the beaver meadow, which lay embosomed in the woods at the distance of about a mile from the Athabasca. The fog which enwrapped the surrounding scenery was scarcely more chilling to the senses than were the thoughts which occupied our trapper on his way to the rendezvous. The criminality of the act he was engaged in, the uncertain issue of the duel, and the pain it had cost him to keep the matter hidden from his tried and trusted companions, weighed down his spirits and made him completely wretched.

The indulgence of our passions often demands as many sacrifices as the practice of virtue; and yet how many are ready to acquiesce in the one, and how few to follow the other!

Leaden as were the steps which led Pierre towards the place of appointment, he at length emerged from the shades of the forest; and as he did so, his eye fell upon the figure of his antagonist, already upon the ground and leaning on his rifle.

On seeing Pierre approach, M'Leod advanced to meet him, and with an affectation of courtesy touched his hat; which salute was gravely returned by the trapper.

"I am glad," he observed, as he looked insultingly at Pierre, "that you are not such a slink as I took you for. I infer from your keeping your appointment that you still refuse to resign your claim to Miss Frazer?"

"I have already said enough on that point," replied Pierre. "We have come here, I suppose, for another object than mutual recriminations."

"Enough," answered M'Leod. "Your blood be upon your own head. Take your stand by this tree. I will stand beside that pine an hundred yards down the meadow; and at the word 'Three,' we will raise our rifles and fire."

Without a word Pierre placed himself beneath the boughs of a tree which stood by the spot, and watched his relentless adversary as he strode towards a solitary pine, whose scathed and weather-bleached branches stretched like the arms of a skeleton from the lifeless trunk. Upon the topmost twig a vulture perched in an uneasy balance, and with sleepy eye seemed prepared to view the contest, his foul instincts having apparently led him to the spot in anticipation of a meal.

Pierre shuddered as he heard the dismal croak of the ominous bird, which ogled M'Leod without alarm as he approached the withered pine. A thought as swift as light shot through the young trapper's brain—the opportunity suggested it. M'Leod had not quite reached the spot from which he intended to fire; his back was turned, and Pierre stood with rifle cocked and ready. But from whatever source the thought had sprung, the hunter repelled it as unworthy. Another moment and it was too late; M'Leod was at his post; his face was turned towards Pierre, and in a cold, steady voice he called out, " Are you ready ?"

Pierre replied, " Quite ready."

Then came, in the same measured tones, " One—two—three !"

Scarcely had the last word reached the trapper's ears, when a bullet whistled so close past his cheek that he started, and slipping upon a gnarled root, he fell to the earth. At the same instant a piercing shriek rang through the meadow, followed, or rather accompanied, by shouts and oaths uttered in the well-known voice of old Jake. Pierre sprang to his feet and rushed in the direction of these sounds. A horrible foreboding possessed him, which he could not define. He was oppressed by a sense that something terrible had occurred. He scarcely noticed that by his side, running with swift, eager steps, was his deadly enemy, M'Leod.

A few moments sufficed to carry them within the verge of the woods ; and there, stretched lifeless upon the ground, her head supported across the lap of old Jake, lay Miss Frazer, the life-blood streaming fast from a bullet-hole in her breast, and forming a crimson pool among the grass.

With a look of speechless horror M'Leod gazed upon the corpse, fair even in death. A smile seemed to part her lips, and between them her pearly teeth were visible, as when she laughed in life.

"She is dead!" exclaimed M'Leod; "and, gracious Heaven! I am her murderer!"

Here the wretched man threw himself upon the ground, and gave way to the extremity of his grief. He alternately confessed and denied his guilt, and in the inconsistency of his assertions even charged Pierre with being accessory to the dreadful catastrophe. We will draw a veil over the scenes that ensued. Horror-stricken, the three men bore the remains of the young lady to the fort, where the agonies of her distracted father added, if possible, another pang to the sufferings which Pierre endured.

Old Jake showed more feeling on this occasion than either of his comrades had conceived him capable of. He actually shed tears while relating the circumstances which had led him and Miss Frazer to the scene of the duel on this fatal morning.

"The poor young critter," said the old hunter, "kem to me an' telled me that she had seed yer jawin' each other by the bank o' the Athabasca, an' had heerd yer settlin' about meetin' next mornin' to squar' up things in the beaver meadow. 'Wal, Jake,' says she, 'we must stop this. I kin think o' no way o' doin' it, 'ceptin' we goes to the place app'inted an' tells 'em to gev up. I don't think they'll go on with it ef I shows out among 'em, an' begs 'em to be friends for my sake.' Them's the very words o' the dear young critter. O' coorse I wur agreeable, an' as it fell out we wur a trifle too late on the ground. I seed M'Leod throw up his shootin' iron; an' at the crack I heerd the ball take the poor young woman wi' a thud yer cud hear five rods off. 'Twur orful! Boyees, this niggur's seed a many ugly sights in his time, but may I be considerable blamed if any o' 'em kin toe up to the mark wi' these hyur doin's! Wagh! it freezes my old gizzard to think o't!"

The funeral took place at an early hour the next day. Not far from the fort was a small plot of emerald green grass surrounded by trees and traversed by a little brook, on the banks of which, at a spot whence a vista through the trees gave a glimpse of the Athabasca, a grave was dug. A rustic seat stood near, where the ill-fated girl had been accustomed to spend much of her time, occupied with her pencil or with her reading. All the employés of the fort attended; and, rough fellows as these were, the sincerity of their grief was evident.

After the short and simple ceremony, the procession returned to the fort, upon which a deep gloom seemed to have descended. The men stood about in groups, and conversed in low tones; and whenever Mr. Frazer appeared, their sympathy was evidenced by their sudden silence, and the profoundly respectful manner of their bearing as he passed.

This was a day of intensest misery to Pierre. He felt in some sort answerable for the dreadful event, which his conscience told him would not have taken place if he had had the moral courage to obey its dictates. He wandered from place to place, overwhelmed by bitter reflections, and giving way to passionate bursts of anguish.

As the dusk of evening fell upon river and forest, it found the young hunter still listlessly pacing to and fro by the verge of the Athabasca. Here he had, only two days ago, met M'Leod; and here the rash challenge had been given and accepted. His eye involuntarily sought the spot where, as the reader may remember, it had then caught a glimpse of a woman's dress; and as it did so he started. A figure glided through the trees in the direction of the little graveyard, and was lost immediately in the gloom.

Pierre's first reflections were tinged by the superstition so common to most backwoodsmen; but after some consideration he determined to follow the figure. A few minutes placed him by the edge of the miniature glade we have already described. In the failing light he was at first unable to distinguish any object upon its surface; but as he slowly and cautiously approached the spot where the grave had been made, a dark figure was discernible upon the ground. The sounds of heavy sobs fell upon his ear, while the writhings of the prostrate mourner attested the violence of the feelings by which he was agitated. Feeling that he was an intruder on a grief more sacred than his own, Pierre was about to withdraw as quietly as he had come, when suddenly the mourner rose and at once discovered his presence. It was M'Leod. For a moment the two men gazed upon each other across the grave of her whom they both had loved, and to whom their attachment had been so fatal. M'Leod broke the silence.

"Well may you come to grieve by her side," said he, "for you, too, are her murderer. It was my hand did the deed; but you will share my guilt before Heaven. Henceforth we are neither friends nor enemies. As for me, I shall need nothing more."

Appalled by this singular address, Pierre stood without reply. M'Leod seemed by a supreme effort to calm himself, and then, bending forward, he kissed the sod upon the little mound, and walked slowly towards the woods which fringed the Athabasca. Pierre, much moved, retraced his steps to the fort; but M'Leod did not return. From that day forward nothing was heard of him. Whether he committed suicide, or otherwise fell a victim to his grief, was never known.

CHAPTER XV.

AFTER the sad scenes detailed in the last chapter, it is
not surprising that our trappers should find a further
stay at the fort undesirable. They therefore made
every arrangement for their departure on the day following the funeral; and early on the succeeding morning they embarked in a new canoe furnished to them
by Mr. Frazer, and once more floated upon the ample
bosom of the Athabasca. Short as was the time since
they had arrived at Fort Pierre, the sad events that
had occurred during that interval impressed them with
a sense of having passed through an indefinite period
of unhappiness.

During the first days that succeeded their departure,
the hunters—or, more properly, Pierre and Gaultier—
were unusually silent, each reflecting on his share in
the recent tragic episodes. Jake—who, to do him
justice, had evinced an amount of feeling considerable
for one of his class—at length began to get restive

under the gloomy influence of his silent companions.
At first the old hunter had ventured to make an occasional remark, in the hope of starting some conversation. But finding them unresponsive, he broke out
with,—

"This hyur boat ur an undertaker's hearse, it 'pears
to this coon. I'm not agin lookin' sober for a leetle,
now an' agin, when a friend goes under. But the boot's
on the other leg altogether when fellurs makes day an'
night of it, an' puts the sun in their pockets. It ain't
fair, fellurs, I tell yer. Brighten up thur, will yer!
Ef I've got to run this hunt in traces wi' two dummies,
I guess I'm out o' it."

This rough hint had the desired effect, and both the
young men made an effort to shake off the oppression
on their spirits. This became more easy as the distance
between them and the scene of the tragedy increased.
The genial skies, sparkling water, and ever present fragrant forest, helped them to combat their gloomy reflections; and in the course of a week or two they had
in a great degree recovered their equanimity. An
incident or two occurred which broke in upon the
monotonous routine of travel.

It was evening, and the party had landed as usual
about sundown, in order to encamp for the night. As
the sky looked threatening, Jake proposed that they
should construct a good camp to protect them from the
impending storm. To this suggestion both Pierre and
Gaultier assented, and presently the neighbourhood

rang with the merry chink of their axes and the crash of falling pines. A sufficient supply of the umbrageous branches was soon collected, and secured against a framework of poles.

In the art of constructing a rain-proof shanty the hunters were great proficients, so that in a very short time a neat comfortable hut was erected, and a huge fire blazed opposite the door, throwing a ruddy glow upon the river, which was hardly ten yards distant.

Within this snug retreat the baggage was placed; and the trappers were just about to throw themselves upon the carpet of balsam fir-sprays with which they had strewn the floor of the hut, when suddenly an Indian canoe, paddled by a solitary Redskin, rounded the point and made straight for the camp.

In a few moments the new-comer landed and approached the fire. Contrary to the usual Indian custom of waiting for an invitation, the savage seated himself, and after looking furtively at his new associates, said,—

"Hope plenty meat—Injun heap hungry."

"Wal, old coon," replied Jake, "hyur's a griskin o' a deer as wur lopin' airly yesterday mornin'. 'Tain't much, but it's all we've spared. I guess we didn't know yer wur coming', or we mout hev kept a leetle more."

The Redskin did not appear to hear the old hunter's apology, but seized the proffered venison, and devoured it after the fashion of a famished wolf. Before such a vigorous attack the slender supply quickly disappeared; and seeing that no more food was forthcoming, he began to beg for powder.

"Injun got no powder," he said; "deer plenty, but no good for want of powder. Paleface give poor Injun some."

"I don't think we can give you much, Redskin," said Pierre; "we have a very long way yet to go, and will need all we have for ourselves."

"Paleface can get heap more at Fort Vermilion," replied the savage; "he has goods to trade, but Injun poor and has nothing. Trader will not trust him."

"Let us give him a quarter of a pound, Jake," suggested Gaultier; "you have the big horn full, and Pierre and I have plenty of cartridges loaded to last us for a month."

Without replying, the old hunter strode down to the Indian s canoe, and stooping, lifted from under a deerskin a canister of powder, which had evidently not yet been opened. Gaultier, out of curiosity, approached; and while his back was turned, the Indian, believing himself unobserved, seized old Jake's large horn and hid it beneath his blanket. The old hunter, however, had seen this manœuvre, and coming suddenly to the Indian's side, he taxed him with the theft.

"Ye thievin' skunk!" cried the incensed trapper, "d'yer think this old coon's a-gwine to be bumfoozled that a-way? I guess he ain't, by a long chalk. Come! out wi' that horn, or I'll jest put yer an' it together across the fire; an' we'll see how yer likes that per-fumery."

Suiting the action to the word, Jake seized the savage by the arm; when, quick as light, the latter sprang from his sitting posture, flung the large horn into the fire, and rushed towards the canoe, into which he leaped, and with the impetus of his motion sent the light craft skimming out into the stream.

At the same instant a deafening explosion took place, and flaming logs and sparks shot into the air, while clouds of smoke and ashes hung above the spot, con-cealing within their thick wreaths the figures of the trappers, and indeed the whole camp.

From within their dun folds could be heard the wild exclamations of old Jake.

"The all-fired skunk has blown my daylights out clur through my neck. O Plumcentre, my leetle woman, whur ar yer? Ef I'd only my claws on that bit o' iron, I'd make fire streak through that varmint's brain-pan."

As the smoke and ashes subsided, both Pierre and Gaultier were visible rubbing their eyes, and each in his own fashion expressing his feelings.

"It is astonishing," said Pierre, "that we have escaped so well as we have done. There must have been at least a pound of powder in that horn, and I can hardly conceive how we escaped being blown to pieces."

"It had too much room to bust up in," said Jake,

"and that allers takes the bite out o' powder. Ef we'd been in a tight place, you bet we'd hev streaked it among the stars."

"What will you do without your powder, Jake?" asked Gaultier; "you have only the small horn at your belt left now."

"Ef ye'd been in my place," answered the old trapper, "that's all yer 'ud hev; but I guess this child ain't so green as that."

So saying, he held up the Indian's canister, which contained fully as much as the horn that had been destroyed.

The young hunters laughed; and all three set themselves to replace the fire, which had been scattered far and wide by the explosion.

Judging it prudent to leave one of their number to keep the first watch, in case the Indian should return and take them unawares, the others bestowed themselves upon the elastic balsam-sprays, and soon fell asleep.

During the night nothing occurred to disturb the solemn stillness of the woods. The soft plash of the river, the sighing of the wind as it swept over the forest, or the distant bark of the fox, harmonized with the quiet scene, and contributed to its solemnity. Old Jake kept the first watch, and was succeeded by each of his companions in turn. This was their usual arrangement, suggested by Pierre out of deference to the greater age of the trapper, who thus had an undisturbed sleep for the best part of the night.

The cheery voice of the old hunter awoke the young men next morning at an early hour, and announced that as the larder was absolutely empty, the party must hunt for their breakfast. After a refreshing plunge in the deep waters of the Athabasca, the young trappers shouldered their rifles. Leaving Jake to keep camp, they separated, Gaultier following the river in search of water-fowl, while Pierre plunged into the forest in pursuit of deer.

We will accompany Gaultier in his ramble by the river. It was yet gray twilight, but the sky was clear. In its blue depths sparkled stars which were momentarily growing pale. The air was delightfully fresh, and was filled with the fragrance of the pines, which were mirrored faithfully in the river. Soon the sun climbed above the eastern horizon, and shot golden beams into every opening in the woods, glancing with prismatic brilliancy on the dew-drops which studded every branch and spray.

Animated with a happy sympathy with nature, the young trapper cautiously followed the sinuosities of the Athabasca; but the water-fowl seemed unusually shy and scarce. Gaultier was much puzzled by this, as the birds were visible day by day in large flocks; and, in fact, the party had almost got tired of shooting and eating them. Still, in the dearth of other provision, the young hunter was most anxious to fill his bag; and he therefore held on, expecting to come upon a flock of ducks or a swan round each bend in the river.

The mystery, however, was soon unravelled. On running his eye closely down one bank of the river, he suddenly discerned a canoe on the margin of the water, while a thin column of smoke ascended from a fire under the edge of the forest. Two figures sat by the blaze; and although the distance was several hundred yards, Gaultier had no difficulty in perceiving that they were Indians.

Recollecting the unpleasant episode of the preceding evening, the young trapper kept himself carefully concealed, and watched from his ambush the motions of the savages. These presently rose, and having extinguished their fire, they got into their canoe and crossed to his side of the river. Here they disembarked, and lifting the canoe from the water, they carried it into the woods, and placed it behind a bush scarcely fifty yards from the spot where Gaultier lay hidden.

Having accomplished this to their satisfaction, they took their rifles, and with the utmost caution they advanced in the direction of the camp. Gaultier's heart beat quickly as they passed his ambush; but evidently they did not suspect his presence, as they walked along noiselessly and swiftly, keeping under cover of the woods.

From the secret and stealthy mode of their advance so near the camp, Gaultier became convinced of their hostile intentions. He was the more sure of this, as in one of them he recognized their visitor of the previous evening. Filled with fear for the safety of old Jake if these skulking enemies should ambush him at the camp, Gaultier left his place of concealment and followed the footsteps of the savages, taking care to keep out of their sight. This was not difficult, for the Indians only apprehended discovery from the front, to which point, therefore, they directed all their attention. In this manner he dogged them, until, finding themselves approaching the camp, with the position of which they were evidently well acquainted, they skulked with increasing caution from bush to bush and from tree to tree, finally reaching the verge of the open space in which, and close by the river, the camp had been placed.

From the position he occupied, Gaultier could see that old Jake was standing by the verge of the water, and was evidently engaged in fishing, as every now and then he pulled out his line and seemed to be detaching a fish from the hook.

Gaultier was now at a great loss how to act. On the one hand, he had little doubt of the murderous intentions of the Indians; while, on the other hand, he could not bring himself to fire at them until justified by some overt act upon their part; and in the meantime delay might be fatal to old Jake.

While thus uncertain how to act, it occurred to him to put the old hunter on his guard by a signal which they had often used, and with which they were familiar. This was the imitation of the note of the whip-poor-will, or *wawanaissa*, whose plaintive voice had, during the twilight, proceeded from the woods at frequent intervals.

With some misgivings, lest his skill should fail to deceive the quick ears of the savages or to arouse old Jake's vigilance, Gaultier produced the well-known note. At first neither the lurking Indians nor his veteran comrade appeared to notice the sounds; but upon their repetition, Jake glanced quickly to the spot where Gaultier was concealed; and there apparently ended the interest the sounds had excited.

Presently, however, and as if in the prosecution of his sport, the old trapper gradually moved further away, until he reached some stunted bushes which almost dipped their branches in the river. Behind these he seated himself, and from the shelter they afforded he scrutinized closely the verge of the woods where the savages prowled.

From the position which Gaultier occupied he commanded a view of the Indians and also of the bush behind which Jake lay hidden; and as the former had their eyes fixed in the direction of the old hunter, Gaultier was thus enabled to make signals unobserved by them, and which Jake had no difficulty in interpreting. Stooping, to intimate caution, and throwing forward his rifle as if to fire at some object in the open, Gaultier pointed frequently in the direction of the Redskins.

These signs were immediately understood by old Jake, who at once resolved upon his line of action. With his customary caution, he had not separated himself from his rifle: with this in his hand he feared neither beast nor Indian. The old hunter's plan was simply to throw himself at ease upon the river bank, and thus to invite a further advance of his treacherous foes. Thus, when they were once in the open, he could deal with one, while Gaultier attacked the other.

This stratagem had the desired effect. No sooner did the lurking savages see the trapper throw himself upon the ground with his back towards them, than with stealthy steps they crept swiftly towards him, their rifles thrown forward, cocked and ready. Gaultier's excitement was now intense. He could no longer delay his interference without great danger to his comrade. He therefore raised his rifle, and with a steady aim at the foremost Indian, pressed the trigger. At the report, the savage plunged forward on his face, stone-dead; and before his companion could realize what had occurred, old Jake sprang to his feet, and with a well-directed bullet from Plumcentre stretched him lifeless on the ground.

Gaultier ran forward to the spot and joined the old hunter in examining the bodies.

"This is the very coon kem last night an' wasted my powder," said Jake. "I'd swar to his ugly pictur anywheres. I guess he didn't think he wur bringin' this child powder o' purpose to shoot himself. No! *that* he didn't. Only fur yer seein' the skunks, lad," he continued, "they'd 'a throwed me whur I wur fishin'; that's likely enuff, I allow."

"You see, Jake," said Gaultier, "it was Providence that took care of us. We gave the Indian all the meat we had left last night, and that obliged us to go out this morning to hunt for a breakfast. Only for that, we might not have known till too late that these savages were prowling about us."

"Twur queer they didn't notice yer pipin' like the whip-poor-will," replied Jake. "At fust I didn't savy but it wur the bird itself, till I tuck the idee that it didn't pipe so late in the mornin'. 'Twur that as fetched me; an' when I'd got the trail, I seed at a glimp whur it led."

"We had better get rid of the bodies," said Gaultier. "I vote we throw them into the river, and let them float off. It will be easier than burying them."

"I says with you, hoss," answered Jake. "I don't feel cverly inclinated to take much trouble with the skunks; so—hyur goes!"

At the word, the old hunter dragged one of the bodies to the brink of the river, and dropped it into the deep current, where it disappeared with a sullen splash. He then assisted Gaultier to dispose of the remaining savage.

Just as they had accomplished this, they were joined by Pierre, who issued from the forest laden with the choicest portions of a fine buck.

"What was that you were throwing into the river, Jake?" he asked as he approached. "I thought it looked something like a man; but, of course, it cannot have been that."

"'Twur somethin' like that, sure enough," replied Jake, "seein' it wur an Injun—two o' them at that. The varmints thought to make a raise; but I guess they had up-hill customers to run agin. They didn't make much o' the spec'lation. No; that they didn't."

"What does he mean, Gaultier?" exclaimed Pierre; "surely you haven't killed two Indians during my absence?"

Gaultier explained all that had taken place, to Pierre's great astonishment.

"I guess," said Jake, "them varmints 'ud hev whammelled me over ef Gaultier hedn't seed 'em when he did. I'd a-knowed nothin' o' the bisness till thur bullets streaked it through my old brain-box. That's sartain sure."

"Well," said Gaultier, "I think we've waited breakfast long enough, and I vote we just leave these savages where they are, and tackle Pierre's venison ribs."

The hunters accordingly replenished the camp-fire, and in a few minutes the best morsels of the deer were sputtering over the coals, while the large kettle bubbled and hissed, diffusing an aromatic odour of *café noir*, which smelt gratefully in the nostrils of the hungry party.

While engaged with their meal they fought their battle over again for Pierre's benefit, and the latter communicated in return an adventure which befell him in pursuit of the deer whose ribs all three were so keenly enjoying.

CHAPTER XVI.

"WHEN I left the camp," he began, "I struck out straight from the river. You may be sure I kept my bearings well as I proceeded, knowing how dangerous it would be to get lost in these trackless forests. I had some hopes of falling in with a deer before very long, as I noticed that their tracks were plentiful in every soft spot; and, indeed, I once or twice started the animals themselves in the young spruce thickets, but the cover was so dense that I could not see ten yards ahead; and although I heard the creatures bound away, I could not even get a glimpse of them.

"Still, it was encouraging to find that there was no scarcity of game in the neighbourhood. Full of hope, I held on, keeping a sharp look-out down every vista that opened out among the tree trunks. I was not very particular as to what kind of game I brought

back, provided it was sufficiently large to afford us all
a full meal; and I therefore kept an eye out for porcupine sign as well, intending to return straight away if
I knocked over one of these fellows. I hadn't gone
more than a mile when I thought I heard a child cry
a little distance to my right; and you may be sure that
I felt rather startled, well knowing that in all likeli-
hood there was not a child within fifty miles in any
direction.

"Presently the noise was repeated; and, full of curiosity, I immediately proceeded in the direction from
which it seemed to come. I advanced very cautiously,
keeping myself well concealed, and I frequently stopped
to listen for a repetition of the strange cry.

"I soon arrived at the edge of a little glade which
had evidently been cleared in the woods by some terrible storm long ago, as the trees were lying over it,
but so moss-grown and decayed that they crumbled
beneath the foot. Some young pine-trees had grown
up through the entangled trunks, and I soon discovered
that the creature which made the noise I had heard was
concealed behind these.

"I was about to move forward, when I observed that
another animal had appeared upon the scene; and, strange
to say, it seemed to be attracted by the cries which at
intervals proceeded from behind the cover of the pines.
The new-comer was no other than the Canada lynx;
and I guessed by his slouching gait that he was as in-
terested as I was myself in ascertaining what kind of

beast had uttered the cries which had drawn my attention.

" I would have been glad to add the lynx to my bag, but I feared to fire lest the shot should disturb the neighbourhood. I therefore kept myself well hidden from the sharp-eyed beast, and permitted him to get somewhat in advance. This precaution was not thrown away; for in a few moments he had scrambled over the prostrate trees, and I could see him arching himself to spring. In an instant he had disappeared, and I could hear him battling with some animal on the other side of the wind-row. Hastily climbing over the encumbered ground, I soon got a view of the contest.

" The creature whose strange cries had at first attracted me was the Canadian porcupine; and it now occurred to me that here was the opportunity for providing a stew in case nothing better turned up. I was about to sight at the 'fretful' one, when I reflected that I might just as well allow the lynx to deal with him, and reserve my shot for the latter when he had despatched his victim. This was, however, no easy task. The porcupine presented his phalanx of spines to every assault of his adversary, whose jaws soon showed signs of the severity of the encounter. Blood dropped fast from his mouth, while many of the quills had become detached from the porcupine, and penetrating the lynx's flesh, projected like whiskers from round the sides of his mouth.

" For a little while the issue of the contest seemed

uncertain; but the lynx, by a dexterous manœuvre, turned the porcupine over on his back, and in an instant the fierce beast's jaw was buried in the defenceless animal's stomach. The battle was now soon ended; and, seeing this, I drew a steady bead on the lynx, and at the report he rolled over as dead as a door-nail.

"I had hardly observed the result of the shot, when, to my amazement, a fine buck, which had lain hidden near the spot, sprang to his feet and was bounding off, when, by a very lucky chance, I knocked him over. He got on his legs, however, in a moment, and would have made good his escape if I hadn't put another ball into him. I left the lynx and the porcupine where they fell, and butchered the deer, as I knew how hungry you would feel, and made haste back to camp. So there you have my morning's adventures."

"They were more pleasant as well as more profitable than ours," remarked Gaultier. "What do you think, Jake?"

"Wal, I dunno," answered the old hunter. "Once on a time this child wa'n't troubled much wi' shootin' Injuns; but since I got Christianized last year at the mission, I feels as ef I did somethin' that wa'n't edzactly right whenever I throws one o' the critturs. I s'pose it's all squar' this mornin', seein' as we wur actin' in self-defence; but somehow I'd rayther all the same that the thing hadn't took place."

"That is a perfectly natural feeling," said Pierre, "and I feel similarly myself. I am surprised, however," he continued, " that the savages did not notice the whip-poor-will's untimely notes ; the bird is not usually to be heard so late in the morning."

" I guess that dizn't signify much," observed old Jake. " Ef they hed obsarved the crittur's pipe, I reckin Gaultier 'ud hev throwed one o' the varmints, an' I'd hev tackled t'other'n all the same."

" The whip-poor-will," said Gaultier, " is supposed by many to be a bird of ill omen. I know the settlers say that if one of them perches on the wood pile, or anywhere near the house, it portends the death of one of the family very shortly. Those Indians, anyhow," he continued laughing, " might have some reason for regarding the creatures as of evil omen."

" Wagh !" exclaimed Jake, " this coon don't bleeve the leetle crittur purtends to be anything else than what he seems to be. Man an' boy, I've been listenin' to his pipin' these fifty years, an' I never got hurt or harm by it, though I've often enuff seed a hull family o' 'em, as I may say, rollin' 'emselves in the ash-heap 'ithin ten yards o' my old cabin-door. It's jest like them settlers to fix a lie on the leetle varmint. Thur allers tellin' lies, or cuttin' down the trees, or scarin' away the game."

" Pierre, have you any notes in your red book on this interesting bird ?" asked Gaultier.

The young hunter replied in the affirmative; and while Jake prepared himself to enjoy a good " chaw " of " James's River," the book was produced from among

the stores, and Pierre read the following notes for the
gratification of his companions.

"Lawson," Pierre began, "speaking of this bird, says:
'It is so named—whip-poor-will—because it makes
those words exactly. They are the bigness of a thrush,
and call their note under a bush, on the ground, hard
to be seen, though you hear them never so plain.'
Ordinarily, towards the close of April or in the first
week of May, the whip-poor-will arrives in his migration to the middle States. It is remarkable that on
the eastern sea-board this bird seems to fix his northern
limit about latitude 43° or 44°, while in the interior he
pushes his adventurous way many degrees further
north. The well-known writer Nuttall says: 'In all
this vast intermediate space' (between Natchez, on the
Mississippi, and British America) 'they familiarly breed
and take up their residence. About the same time
that the sweetly-echoing voice of the cuckoo is heard
in the north of Europe issuing from the leafy groves,
as the sure harbinger of the flowery month of May,
arrives among us in the shades of night the mysterious
whip-poor-will.'

"I am surprised that the traveller Richardson should
have fixed the limit of northern migration of the whip-
poor-will at the 50th parallel, when, in fact, it is frequently heard at points much farther north. The
truth is that much depends on circumstances—such as
the weather, or the individual propensities of particular
birds. And so we see that multitudes of wild-fowl

breed in the lakes and marshes in all this country, while myriads more continue their flight to the vast wildernesses that lie along the shores of the northern sea.

"It is worthy of notice that the whip-poor-will seems to prefer those woodlands which occupy elevated situations, seldom being heard in low swampy districts. The 'Barrens' of Kentucky are much frequented by this bird, whose somewhat plaintive notes resound from among the pines in every direction. Clayton says: 'Their cry is pretty much like the sound of the pronunciation of the words "whip-poor-will," with a kind of clucking noise between every other, or every two or three cries; and they lay the accent very strong upon the last word, *will*, and least of all upon the middle one.

"'The Indians say these birds were never known till a great massacre was made of their country-folks by the English, and that they are the souls or departed spirits of the massacred Indians. Abundance of people look upon them as birds of ill omen, and are very melancholy if one of them happens to light on their house or near their door, and set up their cry (as they will sometimes do upon the very threshold); for they verily believe one of the family will die very soon after.'

"As you have, of course, over and over again remarked, the whip-poor-will utters his note until midnight, except on bright moonlight nights. He then ceases until again awakened at the approach of twilight. The day is passed in the most secluded parts of the forests. But although thus retiring in its habits, it will emerge from its retreat a little before dusk, and fly about the clearings made by the settlers in the woods, probably in search of the ash-heaps left there from the burning of the logs. In these the whip-poor-will loves to roll, scattering the ashes about and fluttering pretty much as our domestic fowls do under similar circumstances."

Here Pierre concluded his account of the whip-poor-will. Jake remarked that his own experience of the bird confirmed the young naturalist's statements— "though 'tain't allers," he continued, "as them fellurs as writes books agrees with this coon's idees."

"I forgot to tell you," said Pierre, " of a discovery I made just after I shot the deer. I came upon a game-path so well trodden that I determined to follow it for a short distance. As it did not lead towards the river, I felt curious to ascertain what was the attraction which led so many animals in this direction. I therefore followed it up, and shortly saw before me at a little distance a clayey bank which seemed to block up the track completely. This was indeed the case, for here the path terminated. The sides of the bank were well worn, and were pitted with many little cavities, while the ground was trodden almost knee-deep in soft mud, in which small pools of stagnant water had collected. I knew at once what had led the game to the spot. The place was, in fact, a Salt Lick—one of those provisions which Nature has made for the benefit of the animal creation, in localities so far removed from the influence of the ocean that no saline matter can be accumulated in the air."

"I dunno what them things ur," interrupted Jake; "but ef ye hev found a Salt Lick, I reckin we'll walk into the deer fast enuff. They'll come thur in shoals to lick the airth, an' I guess we'll make 'em smell thunder considerable. *That* we will."

"There was one circumstance that struck me very much," continued Pierre. "The animals seem often to die after their indulgence in licking, for there were a great many skeletons lying about the spot."

"Don't ee go to bleeve any sich thing," said Jake. "I hev seed Salt Licks in plenty, an' I niver knew the critturs to die o' lickin' their fill. You bet this coon will figure it out arter hevin' a squint at the location."

"Well," said Gaultier, who had listened with much interest to Pierre's account of his discovery, "as we seem to have eaten enough, I vote we go and have a look at Pierre's Lick. How far is it?"

"Not more than an hour's walk from here," replied Pierre.

The trappers accordingly took their rifles, and under Pierre's guidance set out for the Salt Lick. As they walked along, Jake suddenly asked at what time the moon had risen the previous night. The young men were unable to tell.

"I jest wants to know," said the old hunter; "fur ef it's very latish—an' I kinder think it will—we'll hev to try a dodge I used to practise back in old Massoura. I hain't seed the right thing yet," he continued, casting his eyes keenly round among the trees. "Most o' the timmer hyur is young.—I guess I've jest sighted it, sure enuff," he exclaimed, moving off from the young men, who gazed after him with considerable curiosity.

A huge old tree lay prostrate at some distance, its venerable trunk inwreathed with climbing parasites, which had shared its fall, or had grown up over it and served it as a shroud. Towards this Jake directed his steps. With his hatchet he soon knocked away the luxuriant covering, and with his hands removed some of the decayed wood.

"I reckin," he said to himself, "this'll jest do;" and carrying a handful of the rotten wood, he rejoined his comrades.

"Now, boyees," said he, "ef ye'll take my advice, ye'll give the Salt Lick a wide berth till torst evenin'. The deer'll then be on the move, an' we'll get a grist o' them, I'll allow, by caching near the Lick. 'Tain't o' no use to go thur now."

After a little consideration, both Pierre and Gaultier agreed that their wisest course would be to follow the trapper's advice. They therefore retraced their steps towards the camp, where they arrived, having seen neither bird nor beast by the way.

"What have you got the rotten wood for, Jake?" asked Gaultier.

"I reckin ee'll see by-an'-by," replied the old fellow. "It's a smart enuff trick, an' mebbe ye'll find it useful some other time."

As nothing more could be extracted from him on the subject, the young men whiled away the time as best they could until the lengthening shadows announced the approach of sunset.

"I guess it's about time to make tracks," said Jake. "The night-hawks are skimmin' about, an' thur's leetle more'n an hour till dark arter they kims out."

The young men, on looking upwards, observed several birds, much like the common swift in appearance, but much larger, flying with a winnowing motion round the clearing, uttering at frequent intervals a rapid, abrupt note, resembling the words "*witta-witta-wit.*" These were the *Caprimulgus Americanus* of Wilson and Audubon, a kind of goat-sucker, known variously among the settlers and backwoodsmen as mosquito-hawks and night-hawks. In flying, they may easily be mistaken by a casual observer for the common swallow; but on a close observation a white spot will be remarked on each wing, while their mode of flight differs slightly from the latter, the goat-sucker leaning more to one side, while its tail and wings are much longer than those of the swallow.

While Pierre and Gaultier followed with their eyes the swift movement of the night-hawks, making some such observations as we have given above, old Jake rose from his lair by the fire, and unsheathing his shining bowie-knife, cut a long straight sapling, which he trimmed of its branches, and split at one end lengthwise for some ten or twelve inches. Having effected this to his satisfaction, the old fellow picked up Plumcentre, and slinging that redoubtable weapon to the hunter's "carry," he called to the young men,—

"Drop yer star-gazin' thur, an' step out fur the Lick. I reckin 'twill be as dark as the inside of a tar-tub afore we gits thur."

Seizing their rifles, the lads accompanied the veteran, Pierre leading the way as guide. The sun was swiftly declining towards the horizon, and had already fallen behind the forest, through the myriad vistas of which he shot his beams in sheaves of gold. Here and there a silver birch upon some elevation caught the rays upon its shining stem, and shimmered far through the woods; but more often the topmost boughs of the trees alone were lighted up with the glorious reflection of the west, which gradually deepened till the summit of the forest seemed bathed in carmine. This faded slowly away, and gloom at once seemed to spring forward towards our hunters from among the recesses of the woods. Outside the tree tops a gray twilight gradually prevailed over the lingering daylight, while beneath their tenebrous boughs all was sombre and mysterious.

Pierre and Gaultier, who, as we observed when first

we presented them to the reader,* loved Nature with a deep devotion, drank in the beauties of the scene with ardent pleasure. Jake, however, who seemed case-hardened against such influences, plodded along regardless of aught save keeping his moccasined feet from rough contact with snag or root.

Thus through the darkening forest the three trappers advanced swiftly and silently towards the Salt Lick. As they approached the spot several grayish forms disappeared in the gloom with such swiftness that it seemed doubtful if, in the uncertain light, they were not the creations of fancy. The distant snapping of a twig, however, proclaimed the reality of these fleeting phantoms.

" I guess we've skeered a cupple o' the critturs," said Jake ; " but there's a plenty more o' 'em in the woods."

The hunters now cast an eye round for a suitable ambush from which to fire on the deer, and Gaultier soon discovered a recess in a rocky bank well screened in front by some thick bushes. Jake pronounced this to be exactly what was required. Opposite this spot the sides of the Lick rose perpendicularly to the height of some six or eight feet. Against the face of this bank old Jake planted the sapling to which we have alluded, and taking from his " possible-sack " some shining substance which glimmered with phosphoric light, he placed it in the cleft of the stick at about the height of a deer's shoulder from the ground.

* *Vide* "The Three Trappers." T. Nelson and Sons, Edinburgh.

"Now, young fellurs," said he, "d'yer see that bunch o' rotten wood? I calc'late no deer'll pass atween it an' me 'ithout old Plumcentre hevin' a word to say to him. When the crittur gets atween me an' that shinin' stuff he'll hide it, and at that I pulls the trigger."

The use of this precaution, which elicited the admiration of Pierre and Gaultier, was rendered necessary, as gradually a thick darkness settled down among the tree trunks, and all objects were enveloped in the gloom.

"I don't expect to see more'n a cupple o' deer or so, arter all, until the moon rises," said Jake; "but I reckin' the trouble o' stickin' up that bit o' shinin' stuff ain't much, an' it mout git us a shot or two."

Pierre and Gaultier were of course aware that the moon exerts an influence on the deer, which graze while it shines, and couch when it sets. They kept their eyes and ears on the alert, although the impervious gloom rendered the former of little use. Nestled in their ambush, the hunters waited for a considerable time, with their eyes fixed upon the phosphorescent gleam of the decayed wood, in expectation of game; but in vain. Not a sound disturbed the quiet of the forest save the sigh of the passing breeze. An hour passed, and then another hour, without a sign of life in that vast wilderness. The air was warm and balmy, and the lairs which the hunters had made were soft and comfortable. An irrepressible drowsiness overpowered them, and despite their efforts to resist it, they at length succumbed to its influence, and sank into a profound repose.

ʻThe deep darkness which had enshrouded the woods was at length slowly retreating before the silver arrows of the moon, when the party were suddenly startled from their slumbers by a shriek so dreadful and so near that it seemed as if wrung from some tenant of the infernal world who had visited the upper air. With straining ears the hunters listened for a repetition of the horrid cry. Again it rang through the woods, sending the blood curdling through the veins of the young men, so weirdly wild was the appalling sound. Jake, however, exclaimed,—

"The thing ur a 'painter,' arter all! I guess I thort I wur a-dreamin', an' heerd the war-cry o' the Apachês. I heerd it once on a time, an' I hope I never will agin. Six o' the best mountainy men that ever pulled a trigger went under at that time, an' this coon only saved hisself by hidin' inside o' a buffler carkidge. Ye-es, boyees, the savages cut steaks off that bull, not knowin' who wur inside him. 'Twur lucky for this child that the buffler wur tough chawin', an' that thur wur a sight o' young cow meat around. Only for that, you bet they'd soon hev let daylight in on Jake Hawken."

Pierre and Gaultier listened with amusement to the garrulous old hunter, who never seemed so happy as when recounting his adventures to an attentive audience. The "painter" seemed to have got the wind of the party, for the screams suddenly ceased, and when they were again repeated it was at a considerable distance.

"The only thing that kin hold agin a 'painter' for an ugly screech," said Jake, "is a b'ar at the matin' season. I guess I've heerd some rumpus in my time, but them varmints beat all creation."

"I like to hear the voices of wild nature," said Pierre. "The screams of that cougar now are more to my mind than the squalls of a woman at a piano, with a lot of fellows about her who have no more eye for a rifle or a trail than a turkey buzzard."

"Wal," said Jake, "I don't know much o' peeanies, seein' as thur ain't sich things in the woods or perairas; but I hold wi' yer about the idee o' the thing all the same. This child wur born free as air, he has lived free as air, an' he'll die free as air, whur thur ain't a sight o' men's houses nor laws. I kin hear that back in the States a man can't kill a deer when he likes, nor even yet a peraira chicken. I kin hardly give in to that, though."

"It is quite true, Jake," said Gaultier. "I was once fined myself for shooting a deer 'out of season,' as they call it."

"Well," said Pierre, "where people are numerous, unless some law is made to preserve the game, there wouldn't be a deer or a chick to shoot in a few years."

"I guess," said Jake, "I'd rather pass laws to keep down the number of the settlers. Half-a-dozen o' them varmints is enuff for a county; an' I'd sooner meet a b'ar any day than one o' them. That's a fact."

The moon now ascended above the forest, and threw

a checkered light upon the spot where the hunters expected to see the deer.

"Your fire-stick has not been of any use after all, Jake," whispered Pierre; "and there is light enough now to shoot, if there were anything to fire at."

"It's all-fired queer none o' the varmints hev kem," answered Jake; "but the thing mout ha' been o' use for all that.—What'n thunder's that?" he exclaimed, as a noise like falling shingle reached their ears.

The three hunters listened attentively, and in the deep stillness they distinctly heard a scratching sound, which seemed to proceed from the summit of the bank opposite their place of concealment.

Presently this ceased, and all was as quiet as before.

"I wonder what it can be?" whispered Gaultier. "Can you guess, Jake?"

"I hain't edzactly hit upon it yit," answered the old hunter; "but I hev an idee.—Where around did you see all them bones, Pierre?"

"Just over there," replied Pierre. "Some were on the top of the bank, and the rest were scattered about close by the bottom."

"Then 'tis jest as I thort," said the old trapper. "Boyees, keep yer peepers shinin', an' make raggles o' whatever moves on top o' that bank. It's a car-cajou's cached up there, waitin' for the deer. Kin yer spot the skunk?"

Both Pierre and Gaultier strained their eyes, and keenly scrutinized every uncertain appearance which, under the deceptive influence of light and shadow, assumed a likeness to the body of an animal. But in vain.

"Wal, fellurs," chuckled Jake, "I'd take my eyes to town for repairs, ef I wur ye. This old coon can't see as he used to could, but he sees that rotted carcajou as plain as Chimbly Rock. Look agin."

In obedience to this mandate, the young men again cast their eyes over everything in the neighbourhood— on the ground, on the face of the bluff, on the summit; but no carcajou could they see.

"Wal, yer orter be ashamed o' yerselves to be beat at seein' by one as old as I am. Look at that big limb," he continued, "comin' right out torst us. D'yer see anything roostin' up thur ?"

The young hunters started as they followed their companion's direction, and saw, stretched upon a branch which crossed an open space among the foliage, the sturdy hunched figure of a wolverine plainly relieved against the sky. The distance was about forty yards; and notwithstanding that the wind, such as there was, blew towards them, and that their conversation had been carried on in the lowest whispers, the wary beast seemed to have suspected the presence of danger. They could see him casting his inquisitive glances from side to side; and he occasionally snuffed the breeze with the air of a connoisseur, as if to detect the taint of hidden foes.

Apparently he satisfied himself that his suspicions

were well founded, for he suddenly rose from his couchant position, and commenced to descend the sloping branch.

Before he had gained the tree trunk, three reports startled the echoes; and leaping high from the branch, the wolverine turned a complete somersault, and fell heavily to the earth. The hunters leaped from their ambush, and while the carcass still writhed and twitched convulsively in the throes of death, old Jake unsheathed his hunting-knife and commenced to deprive the carcajou of its shaggy hide.

This operation was soon performed, and bearing the trophy along with them, the three hunters left the Lick and returned to the camp by the river. On the way, while crossing a small glade, several deer were observed flying towards the woods at the farther side. Levelling his rifle at the last, Pierre took a quick aim and pulled the trigger. Before he could see the result through the smoke, old Jake called out,—

"Jehoshaphat! that un's throwed clur. Well done, young fellur! I reckin it's a hunderd an' fifty yards at least. That's the way to make 'em come."

The hunters soon stood over the prostrate animal, which was making frantic but vain efforts to rise. Jake drew his knife across its throat, and wiped the dripping blade with great nonchalance on his buckskin breeches.

"I reckin we'll have a chaw at oncest now," he observed; "but let us hoof it slick away to the camp."

Each shouldered his share of the venison, and staggering along the uncertain paths, the hunters soon traversed the distance which divided them from the Athabasca, whose glittering waters they presently descried through the opening branches ahead. As they approached the camp, two wolves dashed into view from under the shadow of the hut, and disappeared in the forest.

"Wagh," exclaimed Jake, "ef I'd a knowed them varmints wur thur, I'd a let Plumcentre into 'em. That's sartin."

A fire soon blazed in front of the hut, and its ruddy glow diffused a cheerful air around the spot. The moonlight, by contrast, seemed ghastly, wan, and cold; the midnight breeze stirred the surface of the river; the wild howl of wolves resounded through the forest; and that instinctive perception which tells the watcher that midnight has arrived, was felt by our trappers. After supper they replenished the fire, and then lay down in the doorway of the hut, where they soon sank into unconsciousness.

CHAPTER XVII.

WHEN the hunters awoke on the following morning the raft had disappeared! It was Gaultier who made this discovery, and he immediately alarmed his comrades. They had left all their stores, with the exception of a few necessaries, on the raft, as had been their usual practice whenever the night promised to be sufficiently fine to warrant their doing so. Gaultier immediately proceeded to the tree to which the thong that held the raft had been attached. A short examination convinced him that the rope had been severed with a knife.

"It's Injuns, I'm sartin sure, hev done it!" exclaimed old Jake; "an' yer may stake high they've vermoosed with all our plunder. This kems o' not keepin' watch last night. Ef we'd only taken it in turns to keep a look-out, we'd a seed the varmints at their thievin'."

"One thing is quite clear," said Pierre—"they must

have gone down stream with the raft. If we are quick we may yet overtake them."

"Wagh!" exclaimed Jake; "overtake last year's snow! They hain't pulled up yit, you bet, nor ain't a-gwine to, till they puts a hull day's travellin' atween thur kar-kidges an' old Plumcentre hyur. I reckin we're afoot now, an' no mistake, 'ithout eyther furs or food, seein' as them thievin' vagabonds hev toted off all our lead an' powder, 'ceptin' what we hev about us."

Old Jake, having given utterance to these opinions in a melancholy tone, advanced towards the tree to which the raft had been tethered, and from the stem of which still depended a portion of the thong. He examined the latter with eagerness for a few moments, and then rising, he exclaimed,—

"Hurrah, boyees! 'tain't Injuns neyther, arter all. I mout 'a guessed it sooner ef I'd only looked fur meself. See," he continued, as both Pierre and Gaultier rejoined him, "the strip o' hide ur cut clean enuff, I allow; but d'yer see this hyur chawin'?" pointing to that part of the rope which was hanging loose from the tree stem. "I guess 'twur teeth as done it, wolf at that! I calc'late, lads, we've wronged the Redskins this time, an' we'll find our raft somewhere down stream."

This development of the affair was a great relief to the party, and they accordingly lost no time in prosecuting their search for the missing raft. But mile after mile of river-bank was traversed, and still no traces of it presented themselves. The trappers were much puzzled, and even old Jake could not offer a probable explanation of the mystery. The banks on either side of the Athabasca had been keenly scrutinized, but without result; and at length, after many hours of weary walking, the hunters halted, hungry and utterly worn out, without having discovered the least clue to guide their further search.

" Queerest thing this coon seed yet," remarked Jake. " The thing must be over water somewheres, an' it'll be hard lines, but we'll find it."

"Do you think it possible, Jake," asked Gaultier, " that the raft has gone *up* stream ? We have now searched at least fifteen miles from where we camped last night, and it is very unlikely that in such a distance the raft would not have drifted against either bank and been retained somewhere."

" This child wur thinkin' o' that very sarcumstance," answered the old hunter; " but how cud the thing go up agin the river ? That's the diffeeculty, I guess."

" It is quite out of the question," said Pierre, " that the raft could have gone up-stream, barring Indians, and Jake thinks Indians have had nothing to do with its disappearance."

" Wal, I dunno ; it cudn't hev gone up-stream edzactly," answered the trapper, " an' I'll tell yer why. When I fust sot up trappin', I hed as fine a canoe as iver ye sot eyes on ; and one fine mornin' thur wa'n't a sign o' it to be seed, though I searched the hull Willamette valley fur thirty miles below whur I'd been camped. Wal, I tuck an idee that prehaps the boat hed been stolen by some Injuns as lived up-stream some ten mile or thurabouts, an' so I jest streaked it fur thur diggin's. I hedn't med half a mile when what shed I see clost in agin the bank but my canoe, 'ithout a scratch or arey a bit missin' from it! You bet but I wur surprised; an' more'n that, when I found out how the thing hed happened. Ye see I hed left a kupple o' night-lines hangin' overboard, an' a raal sockdollager o' a fish hed put hisself outside o' one o' 'em; an' findin' hisself hitched by the innards, hed mizzled up-stream draggin' the canoe behint him! The boat wur tangled in a lot o' drift-weed an' sich rubbish; an' when I got into it, I felt something a-pullin' an' a-tuggin'. Sure enuff I wa'n't long in findin' out what wur the matter, an' a lump o' lead from my rifle turned up the white o' as big a fish as I've laid eyes on since, though I've seed a-many. Now, young fellurs," concluded Jake, "yer sees a boat, an' mebbe a raft, kin run up-stream now an' agin!"

"We had no night-lines set, anyhow," said Pierre, "and therefore we cannot hope anything from that source."

"No; but thur wur deer-meat aboard," said Jake, "an' thur wur a sight o' ropes, I'll allow. This coon thinks it jest possible that a b'ar has hed somethin' to say to the bisness."

"A bear, Jake!" exclaimed Gaultier; "how could a bear have had anything to do with the disappearance of the raft?"

"I don't say fur sure he has," replied the trapper; "but I won't be surprised ef we finds that a b'ar has sniffed the meat, an' jest walked on board an' got hitched in a noose in comin' ashore. I guess the crittur'd get frightened out o' his senses, an' findin' he cudn't pull the raft ashore, he mout a-swum up-stream a bit."

"I think that is in the last degree unlikely." said Pierre; "and for my part I won't take the trouble of going back to the camp on such a slim chance."

"I agree with you, cousin," said Gaultier; "the thing is hardly possible, and is certainly not worth a walk of fifteen miles."

"I'm a-gwine to walk back though," said Jake; "an' ef ye'll wait hyur, I'll bet a plug o' bacca agin a load o' powder ye'll see this niggur floatin' back to camp afore night." So saying, the old trapper shouldered Plum-centre and disappeared in the direction of the camp of the preceding night.

The young men smiled at the obstinate adherence to his own opinion evinced by their veteran companion, and as it was now waning towards evening, they set about making their customary preparations for encamping. We shall accompany Jake in his search. The first thing done by the old hunter was to scrutinize closely the ground in the immediate vicinity of the tree to which the raft had been moored. The fading light—for it was now some time past sunset—served to show with sufficient distinctness several foot-marks

in the soft soil. Some of these were, of course, those
of himself and of his comrades; but there were others
which were, from the in-toe and the make of the
moccasins, unmistakably those of Indians. The hunter
was much surprised that these had escaped his observation when the disappearance of the raft had at
first attracted attention; but he accounted for this from
the circumstance of the gnawed strip of shanganappi
having suggested the idea of wolves being the perpe-
trators, which diverted his attention from the tracks in
the soil.

"It's Injuns arter all," the old trapper muttered to
himself, as with keen eye he scanned the darkening
bosom of the river and the sombre depths of the woods.

Having satisfied himself that the raft had been
removed by Indian agency, the wary hunter looked to
his rifle and pistols, and loosening his knife in its
sheath, he stole silently among the tree trunks and
directed his course up-stream.

He kept as near the river as he judged prudent, and
as he opened each new reach he searched with careful
eye the banks on both sides for the glare of a fire or
any indication of an encampment.

The twilight, however, soon yielded to the shades of
night; but still the indefatigable old man held on his
way.

He inferred from the foot-marks which he had detected that the Indians were probably few in number,
and that as the raft was heavy, they would be unable to

pole it against the stream for any considerable distance. The further therefore he advanced the more cautious became his movements. Frequently he paused to listen; but nothing broke the silence of the slumbering woods except the rush of the river past the banks, or the occasional sighing of the wind along the tree tops.

For several hours the old trapper continued his search, following the sinuosities of the river, to which he now approached closely, being concealed by the dense shadow of the woods, which rendered him quite invisible at the distance of even a few yards. He had therefore little apprehension of being observed, and walked as quickly forward as the nature of the ground would permit.

The first part of the night had passed, and now the pale light of the moon stole from between the rifted clouds, and gleamed on gray tree trunk and shimmering river with ghostly whiteness, necessitating greater care on the part of the trapper in concealing himself from the observation of any prowler in advance.

At the place where the hunter now found himself, the trees receded somewhat from the water, and between them and the stream lay a level space, encumbered here and there with piles of drift-timber or flood-wrack left by the subsidence of the river.

While Jake debated whether to venture across this or to skirt it within the shelter of the timber, an Indian suddenly appeared from behind a heap of drift-wood and advanced towards the river. Presently two others followed, and joined him at the water's edge.

At this instant the moon, which had been wading through fleecy vapours, shone out clearly, and enabled the hunter to observe that a raft lay moored by the bank. The distance which separated the trapper from the party was scarcely one hundred yards, and in the brilliant moonlight he had no difficulty in recognizing the raft, and even the piles of freight with which it was loaded.

Jake's first impulse was to attack the savages; but upon second thoughts he decided to postpone hostilities for the present. While uncertain how to act, the Indians, who had been conversing in low tones, stepped upon the raft, and picking up the sweeps, they pushed out into the stream and commenced poling upwards.

Crouching carefully out of view, the hunter left the beach, and having gained the woods, he kept pace with the raft, which the savages impelled slowly and with difficulty against the current.

Suddenly Jake found his further advance intercepted by the waters of a small stream or creek which joined the Athabasca. The banks were high and clayey; and the water, which flowed sluggishly, seemed deep and impassable.

Much chagrined by this unexpected obstacle, the hunter was about to make a detour in search of a fordable spot, when glancing towards the raft he was surprised to observe that the Indians had pushed it towards him, and evidently meditated poling it into the mouth of the creek.

Bending out of sight behind a clump of brushwood, Jake could presently hear the grating of the sweeps against the raft, and the rustling of the branches which it forced aside in its passage.

In a few moments the savages were abreast of him and immediately below him. With bated breath he listened as the party passed, and cautiously rising he could perceive the raft slowly driven up the narrow creek by the three Indians, who each applied his strength to a long pole or oar which he plunged against the bottom. The trees which grew on either bank closed their branches overhead, and completely over-arched the stream, which here and there glittered as a moonbeam fell through a chink in the foliage, and elsewhere was black as ebony.

For a little time the trapper watched the retreating raft; and as it passed beneath the chinks in the foliage through which fell the silvery light of the moon, he noted that the various articles of the freight, the bundles of furs and their other effects, were still intact, and piled together in the centre.

Jake was now somewhat puzzled as to what course to pursue. In his old scalping days no difficulty would have presented itself. The circumstances would have afforded a perfect justification, in his eyes, for the immediate despatch of the Indians. But since he had become a convert to Christianity he had developed a conscience, and he now felt the embarrassment consequent upon this novel acquisition. He was therefore at a loss how to act. He reflected that to expose his presence to the Indians would be dangerous in the highest degree, and could lead to no good result, while, on the other hand, he did not as yet feel justified in solving the difficulty with his rifle.

While the old hunter speculated thus, the raft had rounded a sinuosity of the stream, and vanished from his eyes.

Cautiously advancing, Jake presently arrived at the spot where a few moments previously he had beheld the raft disappear. To his astonishment no trace either of it or of the Indians was visible.

The old man cast a keen glance down the stream, which at intervals was illumined by the moon, but in vain. He listened intently for several minutes; but in the breathing stillness not a sound save the drowsy rush of water at a great distance could be detected by his straining ear.

For a moment the hunter was oppressed by a superstitious awe. He had heard of the apparitions of Indian spirits which haunted the scenes of their earthly deeds. Those phantom figures that had passed his ambush, and had thus unaccountably disappeared, perhaps they were the unquiet spirits of braves who had long since gone to their account. But these were passing apprehensions.

" Wagh ! " exclaimed Jake to himself, " this coon don't

give in to sich things. I reckon them three wur the
very skunks as lifted our plunder, an' ef thur above
ground thur bound to show."

With a determination to prosecute his search, old
Jake advanced stealthily, keeping as near the creek as
the nature of the ground would allow, and the while
glancing sharply to right and left, expecting each
instant to detect the savages lurking beneath the
shadow of the banks.

At the bend in the stream, where its farther course
became visible, the hunter paused a moment in surprise. He could see down the creek for a considerable
distance; but, as we have seen, the raft and its occupants were nowhere visible.

While carefully separating the branches as he
passed through them, a twig snapped sharply, echoing
in the death-like silence from bank to bank of the
stream.

The hunter suddenly ceased to move, and listened
intently. A distant rustle caught his ear, and then all
was still. He was about to move forward again, when
a flash shot out of the thick brushwood which lined the
brink of the creek, some hundred yards away, and at
the same instant a bullet hissed so close past his head
as actually to carry away a lock of hair from under the
verge of his coonskin cap!

Jake was too experienced in the arts of Indian war-
fare not to know what course to take. The moment
the report of the rifle reached him he sank out of sight

behind the brushwood, and moved neither hand nor foot, lest the slightest motion of his enemies might escape him.

For an hour the trapper lay perfectly still. During that period nothing disturbed the quiet of the woods. The alarm which had been occasioned by the report of the rifle seemed to have subsided, and again the ordinary noises of the forest were audible—the bark of the fox, the call of the loon on the neighbouring Athabasca, the scream of the heron, or the plaintive cries of the water-fowl. Jake, however, was not to be betrayed into a fancied sense of security. He lay still in his ambush waiting with the patience of the cat for the appearance of his foes. At length the bushes on the opposite bank of the creek at a spot about one hundred yards distant rustled violently, and immediately the trapper beheld the raft impelled from their shelter into the stream. The three savages were upon it, and in a moment they had pushed across the creek, where they plunged amid the trees, and were lost in the dim shades.

No noise betrayed their whereabouts; but Jake well knew that to discover him, alive or dead, was their object. The moment, therefore, that he beheld the Indians disappear deeper into the woods, as if to take his position in the rear, Jake left his ambush, and descending the steep bank of the creek, he dropped into the water.

This was deep; but the old hunter was a good swimmer, and cared little for his immersion, although it occasioned him some trouble to hold his ammunition and rifle out of the water with one hand while he swam with the other.

To gain the raft was the trapper's object, and towards this, therefore, he directed himself. Fortunately the distance was trifling, so that within the space of a few minutes from the time he left his ambush he found himself once more in possession of the raft, and surrounded by the valuable stock of furs which constituted the freight.

Jake was well aware that time pressed. At that very moment the savages were crouching stealthily towards the spot he had lately occupied, and discovery would certainly follow if he remained longer in the neighbourhood. He therefore seized one of the long poles with which the Indians had navigated the raft, and with one vigorous push he shot the unwieldy vessel across the creek to the point at which he had seen it emerge a few minutes previously. Here, to his great surprise, he discovered a hidden channel, completely overarched by the underwood and smaller trees which grew thickly among the taller growth. Into this with considerable difficulty he pushed the raft, and once more breathed freely.

" The varmints thort to sarcumvent old Jake Hawken!" he chuckled; "but they'll find him a rayther uphill customer, I reckon! He, he! they ain't a-gwine to make much out o' this speculation, I guess!"

At this moment the murmur of voices fell upon his ear, and presently from his ambush the hunter could see his enemies gesticulating excitedly, as they held a council by the verge of the creek. One of the number pointed backwards through the trees, as if to emphasize a statement that the trapper had escaped in that direction, while the others from their manner appeared to imagine that he had gone down the creek towards the Athabasca.

They now approached the spot where they had left the raft.

"Thur'll be lightnin' around loose now," thought Jake, "when the critters find the raft gone."

A sudden halt, and an ejaculation of surprise and disappointment from each simultaneously announced the discovery. Then like hounds on a lost scent they divided. Two ran down the creek towards the Athabasca, while the third searched the upward course of the stream.

"I guess I sweeps stakes this time," exclaimed Jake, raising his rifle. The third savage was now plainly visible as he stood close by the verge of the water and gazed earnestly down the stream.

A sharp report, a frantic cry, and a heavy splash startled the echoes. The Indian fell forward into the creek, the waves made by his fall gradually subsided, and again the moonbeams rested peacefully on the quiet surface of the water.

"The niggur brought it on hisself," muttered Jake

sternly as he pressed home the well-leathered bullet
into his rifle.

Scarcely had the trapper completed the loading of
his rifle when the two Indians who had gone down
towards the Athabasca returned, attracted by the shot.
From his place of concealment Jake could see them as
they cautiously pushed their way through the under-
growth, the moon occasionally gleaming on the barrels
of their rifles, which they held ready to be discharged
at a moment's notice. Exactly opposite the mouth of
the hidden cove a shelving bank gave access to the
water, and here the two Redskins halted. Jake could
hear their expressions of surprise at the disappearance
of their companion (to whose rifle, apparently, they
ascribed the shot which they had heard) as they keenly
scanned the moonlit reaches of the creek. They stood
side by side at the water's edge, fronting the lurking
trapper at the distance of hardly fifteen yards. Jake
was aware that it now had become necessary to shoot
both the savages; but as his rifle was a single barrel
he could not hope to dispose of both at one shot until
they were one behind the other. He therefore reserved
his fire and waited his opportunity.

Little did the savages suspect the imminent danger
of their position as they stood full in view, just where
a sheaf of moonbeams fell through the overhanging
branches.

Presently, having satisfied themselves that their
comrade was not in the immediate vicinity, they turned

to ascend the bank. This was the moment for which
old Jake had waited. As the Indians climbed the
slight declivity they fell into line, and at that instant
the hunter pulled the trigger. The hindmost savage
sprang from the ground, and rolling down the bank lay
motionless with outstretched arms by the verge of the
creek. The other dropped his rifle, and after falling
once or twice, reached the bushes on the summit of
the slope, where he finally fell, incapable of further
effort.

Concealment was, of course, no longer necessary.
Jake therefore took a pole, and forced the raft out into
the stream. As he left the friendly shelter of the cove
he observed an Indian lodge on a little open spot
adjoining the water. This clearly was the hut of the
three ill-fated savages. Jake leaned a moment on his
oar debating whether to visit the hut and appropriate
to his own use the effects of its late owners; but being
anxious to rejoin his friends, he decided to postpone
this proceeding for the present. He therefore used his
pole vigorously, and soon entered the broad stream of
the Athabasca. Here his labours were confined to
keeping the raft to the centre of the river, whose
powerful current bore him rapidly downwards. In
about three hours he had the gratification of seeing the
glare of a camp fire reflected upon the river, and with
an exultant shout the old trapper directed his raft
towards the bank, where he was immediately met by
Pierre and Gaultier, who pressed him with eager in-

quiries as to his adventures.　We need not recapitulate
these; but we may observe that they lost nothing of
excitement when detailed by the garrulous old fellow,
who relished nothing so much as "reelin' off his doin's"
to an attentive audience, while satisfying an appetite
which seemed well-nigh insatiable.

CHAPTER XVIII.

THE party did not continue their journey on the
following morning. The excitement and labours of
the preceding night had disposed old Jake to take a
little more rest than was his wont, and the forenoon
was therefore well advanced when that individual set
about preparing his breakfast. Both Pierre and Gaultier had risen long before, and were gone, by Jake's
direction, to the Indians' hut, as they considered it very
probable that these savages had lived an isolated life,
and had neither squaws nor relatives who might fall
heirs to their possessions. The young men consequently considered these as their legitimate spoils.
They were likewise anxious to ascertain what had
become of the third savage whom Jake had seen fall
desperately wounded in the bushes. On arriving at
the scene of the encounter, which they had no difficulty in discovering, they found the bodies where they

had fallen. That of the third Indian was leaning against a tree, to which the ill-starred wretch had dragged himself in his last moments. He presented a hideous spectacle. Blood had welled in torrents from a bullet-wound in his back, and had stained the grass and weeds all round, as well as all his person. His eyes were open, and seemed fixed with a malignant scowl upon the hunters as they came towards him. The lower jaw hung open, and they could perceive that his mouth was filled with clotted blood, which had dropped in copious gouts upon his chest and thighs. The features were convulsed, and assumed in their contortion a demon-like expression.

Shocked at so dreadful a spectacle, the young men turned to examine the other savage. He seemed to have died peacefully. Indeed, his death was instantaneous, as we have seen. Pierre and Gaultier appropriated the arms of the dead, and leaving the bodies as they lay, they directed their attention to crossing the creek, which, although not more than fifteen yards in breadth, was too deep to be crossed on foot.

This difficulty, however, they soon surmounted. On the top of the bank, and close to the brink, stood a pine which rose probably to the height of seventy or eighty feet. With their keen axes they soon felled this across the creek, in this way making an effective bridge by which they gained access to the farther side.

They immediately proceeded to examine the hut,

which had apparently been unvisited since the death of its owners. The interior resembled that of an ordinary Indian lodge. In one corner they found a goodly collection of skins, among which were several of the highly-prized silver fox. Some of the peltries were almost valueless. These they rejected, and finding no other objects worth removal, they shouldered the packs into which they had bound the hides, and again crossing the creek upon their impromptu bridge, they wended their way towards the camp. It was late in the afternoon when they arrived at a spot about a mile distant from the encampment. Here, feeling fatigued with their walk, as well as by the weight of their burdens, they disembarrassed themselves of their loads, and flung themselves upon a grassy bank which commanded a good view of the river both up down its course. Pierre produced his pipe, and having filled it from his otter-skin pouch, he surrendered himself to its quiet enjoyment. At this spot the river was several hundred yards across, the farther bank being covered with trees almost to the edge of the water. While vacantly gazing through the wreaths of smoke, Pierre's eye was suddenly arrested by an object which moved behind some bushes near the verge of the opposite bank. For some moments it remained stationary; but presently it advanced from its shelter, and both the hunters immediately observed it to be a bear. The animal apparently had not perceived them, as it came boldly forward to the water.

" I declare," exclaimed Gaultier, " he's coming across! Let us hide."

Both the young men accordingly crawled behind a bush and watched with interest the progress of the animal, which had plunged into the river and was now swimming with powerful strokes towards them.

" He'll land within ten yards of us," whispered Pierre; " don't fire till he comes ashore, and then blaze at him."

Gaultier nodded assent. In a few moments the bear raised his dripping form from the water, and stood directly before the hunters. At this instant both fired together; and as the smoke cleared away, the bear was observed lying lifeless by the edge of the water. Pierre's bullet had pierced its skull, while Gaultier's had penetrated the neck, severing the spine in its passage.

" It is lucky," said Gaultier, " that we encountered this fellow so near camp. I would not have liked to have had his hide to carry much further, as our other loads are quite enough."

The two hunters set about skinning the bear, which operation they performed in a very few minutes. They then shouldered their loads and set out for camp, which they reached without any further adventure.

Jake had been expecting their return, and had the forethought to prepare a good broil of venison ribs; to which the hungry trappers did ample justice.

When they had satisfied their appetites and reclined on the grass near the fire, Gaultier proposed that Pierre should read his notes on the bears of America; which proposition was seconded by Jake. The young hunter made no objection. and opening his manuscript he began :—

" I will take the common black bear first, as he is more widely distributed and is therefore more generally known than either of the other species. In colour, as his designation implies, he is ordinarily a deep black ; but is furnished with a yellowish-red patch upon the muzzle, upon which also the hair is smooth and short. This patch, however, is not invariably present, as instances are not wanting in which it has been absent. The colour, too, sometimes varies, approaching more nearly to brown in some specimens than in others. Occasionally animals of this species have been seen with dashes of white, but these are very uncommon ; others have been observed of a cinnamon colour. Upon these differences of hue in the pelage some have founded the theory of a difference of species. But such persons cannot have had much practical acquaintance with the subject. I have myself seen a bear as black as jet followed by cubs of a different colour—"

" I reckon that's so," interjected Jake ; " an' this niggur has seed a brown b'ar wi' cubs as black as the pelt ye fetched in a while agone. It's all a chance what colour the young uns takes to, though, o' coorse, black's the most nat'ral."

Pierre continued—" The black bear devours roots of

various kinds, which he skilfully grubs up; nuts and fruits, as well as fish and flesh. He is, in fact, omnivorous. He has also been known to eat heartily of carrion; but, as a rule, he prefers a vegetable diet. Some individuals, however, have developed a partiality for a meat diet, and will brave every risk to satisfy the craving. These will boldly invade the settler's sheep or hog pen and seize a victim, which they will convey to the nearest cover, and there greedily devour it alive; for the bear, unlike other carnivorous animals, does not kill his prey outright, but rends and devours it while still screaming and struggling for its existence."

" I need not remind you," said Pierre glancing from his book, " that the black bear is fond of honey. To discover a bee-tree, indeed, is one of the chief aims of his life. As he is a very expert climber, thanks to the strength of hug with which Nature has supplied him, he can ascend the tallest and smoothest trees with ease. He thus has no difficulty in prosecuting his never-ending search for the hives of the wild bees, which are usually the holes worn in some patriarch of the forest by the corroding effect of the weather or by internal decay. If the entrance to these stores is too small to admit his head, he soon enlarges it with his powerful claws. His thick fur is a perfect defence against the attacks of the enraged insects, whose buzzing legions the robber regards with the profoundest indifference. But should a sting be inserted in a tender part, such as the eye or lip, the bear immediately retreats to some neighbouring

A BEAR IN THE HOG PEN.

Page 274.

branch for a short space until the irritation subsides, when he again advances to the attack.

"The habitat of the black bear is very extensive. As he affects the woods both for the shelter they supply as well as for the fruits, larvæ, nuts, etc., there to be found, he is seldom met with at a distance from timber. In all the large forest-covered districts, therefore, of North America, from the Atlantic to the Pacific, both in the United States and in Canada, the black bear is more or less plentiful.

"The open prairies, the arid deserts which stretch along the Rocky Mountains, as well as the gloomy passes and timbered valleys among these hills, are the home of the fierce grizzly bear. In Canada another bear, considered by some to be identical with the *Ursus arctos*, or brown bear of Northern Europe, is found ranging over the sterile regions known as the 'Barren Grounds.'

"In these desolate regions, too, is found the Polar bear, whose geographical distribution has, it is supposed, no limit in a northern direction.

"The advance of civilization has, of course, thinned the numbers as well as restricted the range of the black bear. Two centuries ago the vast region between the Atlantic and the western limits of the forests beyond the Mississippi formed a habitat peculiarly well suited to the requirements of this animal. But it has disappeared from many districts before the encroachments of the settlers upon its woodland haunts, although there are still but few states which do not possess some tract of wild country which affords shelter in forest or mountain fastness to animals of this species. In some states it is probably as plentiful as ever. The cane-brakes and forests of Louisiana, Texas, Florida, Mississippi, and Alabama are well stocked with bears, which afford exciting sport all the year round to the hunters of those regions.

" In the cold climate of the north the black bear retires to the shelter of a hollow tree or log, or if this be not conveniently met with, to a cave, where it lies torpid during the winter months. Sometimes its retreat is of a very primitive character—merely the shelter obtained by squeezing its body under the lee of some fallen tree. The snow speedily covers it up, and the bear will thus repose in somnolent inaction until the returning warmth thaws its covering, when it emerges from its retreat. At this time it is in a state of great emaciation. The Indians say that a bear which retires to its den at the beginning of winter in a poor condition will not survive until spring. They further assert that the immense mass of fat which surrounds the body of the bear at the time of its retirement, after having revelled among fruits, nuts, roots, etc., during the summer and autumn, forms its means of subsistence during its torpidity by becoming absorbed into the animal's system. Both these statements seem probable enough.

" The pursuit of the black bear is a very favourite

amusement with the settlers in the backwoods. The animal is chased by dogs, which soon cause it either to 'tree' or to come to bay in some spot where it can defend itself with advantage. The hunter then steals up, while the bear's attention is drawn off by the dogs, and delivers the fatal bullet from a distance of a few yards. Should the incensed animal, however, get the hunter within his clutches, he will make him pay dearly for his temerity in venturing to such close quarters.

"When the bear takes refuge from his pursuers in a cave or in a hollow tree, he is forced from its shelter by smoke. Sometimes he is taken in pens, or is caught beneath a ponderous log, so arranged as to fall on the springing of a trigger to which the bait is attached. But it must be confessed that these methods of capture do not recommend themselves to the true hunter, who trusts chiefly to his rifle to win a victory over the denizens of the wilderness.

"I have observed that at the approach of cold weather the bear sometimes retires to a cave in which to hibernate. Should the hunter discover this retreat, and be sufficiently courageous, he will enter, and by the light of a torch attack the bear in his den. Sometimes the passage is so low and narrow that the hunter has to crawl forward, pushing his light along in front of him. To do this the more easily, the torch—usually a rough candle made of wild bees' wax, tempered with bear's grease or some similar substance—is fixed in a block of wood, to serve as a rude candlestick. When at length the lair is reached at the farthest recess of the cave, the bear may be observed cuddled up comfortably with his snout buried between his fore paws. The hunter now selects the spot at which to aim ; and if, from the position of the beast, this be not sufficiently exposed, he will not hesitate to whistle in order to wake the bear. The latter startled from its profound repose, its eyes dulled by sleep, and its faculties inert from imprisonment, sits blinking at the unwonted apparition, and probably shuffles forward to sniff at the candle. This is the hunter's opportunity. Lying (as I have supposed) on his face in the narrow passage, incapable of an expeditious retreat, his life may truly be said to depend upon the success of his shot. Should he fail to bring down the bear at the first fire, the beast, maddened by the sudden wound, springs upon his victim, who literally lies at his mercy. Risky as this mode of attack may appear, but few accidents have occurred to those whose nerves have been sufficiently firm to allow of their undertaking it. But the hunters of the West are not men to be easily unnerved, under any circumstances.

" When the bear, therefore, advances to the light, the hunter raises his rifle steadily, and draws a bead upon the small pig-like eye. A stunning crash follows, the pent-up echoes reverberating like a thunder-clap through the ramifications of the cavern, and the bear falls forward with his skull shattered to atoms by the unerring bullet. The candle is extinguished; but the hunter possesses the means of relighting it, and having done this, he proceeds to drag the carcass from the cave. If this be impossible, either from the narrowness and inequalities of the aperture, or from the weight of the bear, he flays the carcass where it lies, and effects his retreat, dragging with him the hide and grease and such other portions as he fancies. In several journeys the whole is removed. Probably no method of bear-hunting affords such thrilling anecdotes of peril as this."

"Ye may take yer davy o' that fur sure," exclaimed Jake. "This coon 'a many times follered up a b'ar, an' each time he declared it'd be the last. 'Twur once or twice near bein' the last, sure enuff; but a fellur forgets them things when he's on hot b'ar sign an' 'ithin reach o' pelt an' karkidge."

"I'm sure, Jake," said Gaultier in a coaxing tone, "you have had many tussles with bears under ground as well as over, and Pierre and I would like to hear an account of one."

"Wal, young fellur," answered the hunter, "as we're talkin' o' the varmints, I don't care ef I diz tell yer o' what happened to me the very last time as ever was, I follered a b'ar into his cave. 'Twur ockard, ye'll allow, an' no two sayin's about it, I guess. I wur out west in the Medicine Bow Range, an' hed fixed a pretty tall heap o' b'ars durin' the fall. Wal, one day arter snow time, I wur trackin' up a wapiti bull as hed carried away a pill from Plumcentre in his innards, an' wur failin' fast on the trail, when what shed I come upon but a b'ar's snore-hole; that is, o' coorse, the leetle hole the varmint's hot breath melts up through snow over whur he's cached below. Arter finishin' wi' the bull, I kem back an' tuck a view o' the sitooation. I clurred off the snow from whur I expected the mouth o' the cave to be, when what wur my surprise to find thur wa'n't no cave to be seed! Thur wur a small hole about the scantlin' o' a mouse-hole down through the ground, an' twur up this the varmint's breath hed come.

"'Jehoshaphat!' cries I, 'this niggur's not as hefty as he used to was; but his carkidge'd never get down thur!' So I sets to work, an', sure enuff, I med out the mouth o' the cave in the face o' a leetle bank clost by. At fust I thort o' lightin' up stink-plants an' stinkin' the b'ar out; but on second thorts I concluded I'd take a look in on the crittur, as the cave seemed purty roomby. Wal, I poked in, an' lit a bit o' candle I luckily hed in my possible sack.

" I soon found that the cave narrered, and got so low at that, that I hed to go it on all fours. The travellin' wur main bad, fellurs, I kin tell yer; fur, yer sees, the water hed kept droppin' through above, an' med pools hyur an' thur along the floor through which I hed to drag my old carkidge, till I wur as wet as a gudgeon. I didn't mind that so much though as keepin' my candle lightin' an' old Plumcentre dry. So I crawled along, an' arter a leetle time I kem to whur the road split, one passage goin' straight on an' t'other'n goin' off to one side.

" 'Twur hard to tell which way to take; but arter a leetle speculation I concluded to foller right ahead—an' right that wur, I reckon! In two minutes more, in scroogin' round a corner, I kem bang upon an all-fired big b'ar 'ithin three feet o' Plumcentre's muzzle! Boyees, I seed at half a glimp that b'ar wur a grizzly!

" At fust the varmint wur dozin' sound enuff; but he wur rolled up in sich a tangle that 'twur hard to say which wur head an' which wur tail. Anyways, afore I hed much time to find out, the b'ar he riz up his head, an' you'd better bleeve the start he gev wur a caution.

" His leetle peepers wur blinded wi' the light, an' he kep' blinkin' an' starin' while I sot down the candle an' got Plumcentre ready.

" 'Twa'n't a long shot, you bet! But when I pulled the trigger I thort all creation busted up all round! The n'ize wur dreadful in sich a confined place; but it 'twa'n't that skeert this coon. I hed hardly heerd the report when the b'ar wi' a roar med at me. The candle wur out, an' the varmint tore over me, a'most squeezin' my innards out, as thur wa'n't room fur two in the passage. Wal, fellurs, I felt as ef every bone in my body wur broke; an' as fur my old phisog, I thort it wur clean ground off me agin the bottom o' the cave. The b'ar wur somewhur behint me, as I cud hear him snortin' like all creation; but I wur fortunate, I guess, that the lump o' lead hed done his business. Ef it hedn't, you'd 'a never knowed Jake Hawken. I cudn't turn round to see the b'ar, the cave wur so narrer; so I jest crep' forward a bit till I got into the b'ar's lair, which wur a bit wider. I then turned round an' lit my candle agin, which I wur lucky to lay my claws upon as I groped along on all fours.

" I soon med out that the b'ar wur dead; but the critter hed dropped in the narrowest part o' the hull cave an' plugged it up as tight as a ball in my old rifle barrel!

" Thur wa'n't no gettin' past him, you bet, so I hed to set to work wi' my bowie; an', fellurs—will yer bleeve it ?—I wur four mortal hours hackin' an' hewin' at that thur carkidge, an' carryin' pieces o' it back out o' the way, afore I cud squeeze meself past it! The hide, o' coorse, wur cut to raggles, an' o' no account at all; an' so I hed nothin' to show fur all my trouble an' danger, 'cepting what blood an' grease wur plastered over my old duds. I kem out o' that cave, boyees, as dirty a case as ever ye sot eyes on! I didn't care fur that though, seein' I wur so well out o' the bisness; fur ef I'd knowed 'twur a grizzly as wur inside I'd never have ventur'd in; that's a fact." Here ended Jake's account of his adventure.

The remainder of the day was spent in making pre- parations for departure; and when these were completed the hunters retired early to rest, as they anticipated a fatiguing day's journey on the morrow.

CHAPTER XIX.

THE day broke gray and chill. Heavy clouds obscured
the sky towards the north-west, and from their gloomy
fields irregular masses became detached, and were
hurried across the sky by a fierce wind. Sudden
squalls tore through the woods as if in search of the
weak and decrepit members of the forest, which parted
with their branches or fell entire before the vengeful
spirit of the storm. The embers of the camp fire were
seized by the gusts and whirled into the faces and
against the persons of the hunters, who with difficulty
achieved the cooking of their simple meal.

They soon left the camp, and committed themselves
to their raft, which tossed unpleasantly upon the
agitated surface of the water whenever the fierce
hurricane howled along the course of the river.

All day they drifted with the current, and towards
evening landed near the debouchure of the Athabasca

in the lake of that name. The night was spent as usual, and in the morning the journey was continued. But the storm still raged, although the direction of the wind had changed, and rendered the task of crossing the lake both difficult and dangerous.

Jake, however, anticipated a quick run across to Fort Chepewyan on the farther shore, where he looked forward to a fresh supply of tobacco and other necessaries, which had become exhausted on their somewhat protracted journey.

While the raft was under the lee of the forest, the full force of the wind was not experienced; but once beyond its shelter, the party began to regret the indiscretion of having ventured upon so large a lake when lashed into fury by a storm. The seas were short and choppy, and whenever the wind attained its utmost force, the water broke in a deluge over the raft, sweeping away some articles which had been carelessly secured.

Towards the east and north-east, as far as the eye could reach, extended a waste of green foam-crested billows, rising in angry undulations against the leaden horizon, while behind the distant forest receded rapidly, and soon a surging world of hungry waters surrounded them on every side. Both Pierre and Gaultier shivered as the tempest tore the spray from the crests of the waves and hurled it over them in sheets, drenching them to the skin. The raft laboured heavily, hardly rising over the billows, which indeed had full play over its surface; so that it was with genuine satisfaction that they beheld the opposite shores of the lake gradually becoming more and more distinct, and soon they could distinguish the more prominent features of the coast.

In little more than five hours from leaving the mouth of the Athabasca they landed on the northern shore of that lake; but at what precise spot they could not determine.

Their proper course would have been north-westerly to reach Fort Chepewyan; but they had been driven much to the eastward by the tempest, which had veered from north-west to west during the previous night.

"'Taint o' much account whur we ur edzactly," said Jake. "I reckon we kin make tracks out one location as well as out o' another."

"At any rate," said Pierre, "we must remain here until the storm abates. To-morrow we must search the shores to the west, as I am certain the fort lies in that direction."

"This coon don't know what ye're a-gwine to do," observed Jake; "but he's a-gwine to see arter hevin' somethin' to chaw. That ar lake wur a caution! an' now we're safe o' it, I feels kinder peckish!"

The provisions were soon produced, and notwithstanding that their exposure to the waves had somewhat damaged them, the three hunters made a hearty meal.

Wood was next cut, and a huge fire made in a

sheltered nook. Round this the party stood drying their clothing, which was thoroughly saturated with the spray.

During the night the storm moderated, and at daybreak perfect quiet prevailed. The lake, however, was still much agitated, and they judged it prudent to remain in camp until the waters had relapsed into their normal quiescence.

Shortly after breakfast Gaultier drew the attention of his comrades to a huge bull moose which, unsuspicious of danger, had emerged from the cover of the scattered clumps of pines and willows on the lake shore, and now stood about three hundred yards away, close to the edge of the water. Pierre took his Winchester, and resting one elbow on his left knee as he sat, took a steady shot at the animal's shoulder.

"Great Christopher Columbus!" cried Jake, "that thur lump o' lead has did the bisness!" and in fact the party observed the moose to give a tremendous bound and then to fall, its head and shoulders in the lake, while its hind quarters lay upon the pebbly beach.

They immediately set out for the spot, and soon were busied in flaying and cutting up the gigantic carcass.

The district round Lake Athabasca is a favourite haunt of the moose, which is also plentiful along the courses of the Peace and Mackenzie rivers.

The Fur Company's posts in these regions are chiefly rationed with his flesh, for which nearly five hundred moose are annually required by those stations which lic along the Peace River. Athabasca exports on an average the skins of some two thousand moose yearly.

The extraordinary powers of hearing possessed by this animal have been already alluded to. It is on those days when the elements are in a state of disturbance that there is the best chance of approaching unperceived. When the rain has rendered the fallen *débris* of twigs, the dried leaves and herbage, soft and pliant, and when the wind howls through the forest, swaying the branches against each other, and filling the air with their rustling, the moose-hunter leaves his camp with the assurance of being enabled by the uproar to steal unobserved and unheard on the gigantic game. Notwithstanding the great numbers of moose annually destroyed, they still exist in great plenty throughout the vast regions of the North-West.

Another animal formerly numerous has, however, much declined in numbers of late years. This is the wood-buffalo. One of the original explorers of these countries found their droves darkening the meadows of the Peace district; but now few survive. Unusual severity of the weather is alleged as the cause of their disappearance. In 1793 they ranged in large herds along the shores of the Peace River; in 1826 Sir George Simpson ascended this stream, and found that the buffaloes had almost become extinct.

At the present time they exist in scattered bands on the banks of the Liard River in the sixty-first degree of north latitude. Preferring the dense entangled forest to the open prairie; larger, darker, and more ferocious than the buffalo of the plains; keener of eye and of scent, it is asserted by the Indians of these solitudes that, although differing as we have noted, the two varieties are but the descendants of a common stock.

Towards noon the waves upon the lake had subsided sufficiently to induce the hunters to continue their journey. The sail which old Jake's ingenuity had improvised from a moose skin was spread before a favouring breeze, and under its influence the raft glided along the picturesque shores at the rate of some five miles an hour. During their sail the party had an opportunity of observing the great numbers of waterfowl which frequented the shallow water near the shore. Swans of different varieties, geese, and ducks croaked, flapped, and flew on all sides; and in a few shots sufficient were secured to last them for some days. Several bears were also seen; but these, unfortunately, had observed the uncommon apparition of the raft and its occupants, and had discreetly retired behind the shelter of the woods, where the trappers did not feel disposed to follow them. The remainder of the day was passed in this manner, and at sundown, as was their habit, the hunters landed and made their camp for the night. Just at this spot a stream of some width joined the lake, and at a little distance up its course they observed several of the dome-shaped lodges of the beaver. The animals themselves were invisible; but the widening circles in the water betrayed the fact that they had betaken themselves in sudden fright to the shelter of their houses at the approach of the trappers. Throughout all this region beavers are numerous. Along the shores of the Peace River (which flows into Lake Athabasca by way of the Slave River at its western extremity) nearly thirty thousand of these animals annually fall victims to the wiles of the Indian hunters. Still their numbers do not seem sensibly diminished, and during the open season on the river their splashing and gambolling may be heard during the night, if the traveller lies awake in his camp.

The black, the brown, and the grizzly bears here also roam in great numbers, making it one of the most attractive fields for the adventurous sportsman to be found now-a-days on the American continent. In autumn these bears are extremely fat, owing to the abundance of fruit which grows all over the country. The saskootum berry grows in vast profusion over the hill slopes, and on these luscious dainties the bears revel day by day until they become absolutely unwieldy through excessive obesity.

At the camp the trappers had an opportunity of remarking the mingled ferocity and curiosity evinced by a huge grizzly. The animal emerged from a gully of some considerable depth, which at this season was dry, but which no doubt in spring at the melting of the snows poured a rushing flood into the waters of the lake. Some hundred yards separated the animal from the camp, the fire of which he almost immediately observed, for he turned and regarded it steadily for fully a minute. Neither of the hunters stirred. The bear evidently had had but a very limited acquaintance with the human species, as he did not appear to realize the risk he ran in exposing himself so freely.

The fire and the motionless figures seated round it seemed to rouse his curiosity, and after taking a good survey of the strange objects, he threw himself from his erect position upon all fours, and advanced towards the camp, now and then giving vent to a growl of dissatisfaction.

When within fifty yards matters began to look serious. Clearly the grizzly meant action, for his growls became more frequent and savage, and a row of shining teeth displayed themselves which suggested to the trappers the advisability of taking measures for their safety.

"Don't 'ee go fur to fire!" exclaimed Jake in an excited tone to Gaultier, who was poising his rifle for a shot. "Remember the blessed muss yer made at the Buttes on the Saskatchewan last year wi' bringin' a grizzly tearin' down on us. No, sir! I guess we'd better get aboard o' the raft, an' then we'll walk into the coon all together."

This advice was acted on. Hardly had the hunters pushed off from the beach when the bear charged the camp, and began to satisfy his curiosity by pulling about the different articles which had been left lying round the fire. The large kettle especially seemed to interest him; and much to the amusement of the party he inserted his nose into this, which happened to be filled with hot water. A loud snarl, accompanied by an ungainly start, testified to the animal's surprise. He immediately seized the kettle as if it were a sensient enemy, and in an instant capsized the contents over himself! A loud shout of laughter from the trappers drew the attention of the enraged animal towards them, when he ran to the water's edge, and without hesitation plunged in, evidently with the intention of attacking the raft. But alas for poor Ephraim! Three rifles which seldom varied from their mark were directed upon the massive forehead, which, elevated above the waves, presented a perfect target. The three reports seemed as one, and when the smoke cleared, the feeble splashing of the bear as he endeavoured to keep afloat served to show that he no longer meditated fight. The raft was immediately poled towards him, and Jake had just time to fling a noose over the grizzly's head as the carcass began to sink.

The hunters again landed, and with considerable difficulty they contrived to drag the dead bear upon the beach, where they busied themselves in removing the hide.

The grizzly bear has an extensive range. It is found throughout the solitudes of the Rocky Mountains (with an occasional hiatus) from the great bend of the Rio Grande in the south to at least the sixty-second degree of north latitude. It is also common in the plains eastward of the mountains. It is singular that these animals have been observed in the sterile deserts of interior Labrador, on the east of Hudson Bay, while in the vast intermediate space none are found until within some three or four hundred miles of the Rocky Mountains.

Mr. John Maclean, author of "Twenty-five Years in the Hudson Bay Company's Service," states that he undoubtedly received the hides of grizzly bears from the Indian hunters of Labrador, and notes the fact as a curious one.

The grizzly is a gigantic animal, and attains his fullest size towards the southern limits of his range. In general, however, he may be stated to weigh some eight hundred pounds, and in length he attains from eight and a half to ten feet. His massive fore arms are furnished with terrible claws, six inches long, which cut like chisels when the monster makes a blow with them. The strength of this bear is tremendous. With a stroke of his ponderous paw he will disable a buffalo bull, and then drag away the carcass with almost as much ease as a cat can carry a rat. A noted hunter named Dougharty once shot a huge bison, and having left the carcass in search of aid to cut it up, on his return was astonished to find that it had been removed during his absence! He had some difficulty in following the trail; but at length he discovered the body of the bison in a deep grave, excavated by a grizzly which had abstracted the carcass. Unlike the black bear, the grizzly does not hug his victims to death. A blow or two from his formidable paw usually is sufficient to kill or cripple his antagonist. His first instinct, as we have seen, on perceiving a strange or unusual object is to uprear himself on his hams and take a steady stare. He then seems to make up his mind for an attack, and rushes straight on, regardless of every consideration save that of gratifying his ferocious propensities.

It seems the grizzly possesses a mobility of claw denied to the other varieties of his tribe. He can move each of his claws independently, so that when searching for larvæ in the decayed fragments of a dead tree he can crumble the wood to atoms by moving his claws in succession.

"Old Ephraim," as he is familiarly styled by the hunters of the West, impresses a profound respect for himself upon the inferior denizens of the wild. Wolves will not venture to touch a carcass which has been left by him, although every other carrion which falls in their way is greedily devoured.

Another peculiarity of the grizzly has often been noted—namely, that of burying either the bodies of his victims or of those which he casually comes across. This has often been taken advantage of by hunters whose every other resource had been exhausted in a contest with this animal. Feigning death, the bear ceases hostilities and drags away the body of the hunter, which he buries in some convenient spot. Several adventures of this kind had befallen old Jake, which he recounted for the amusement of his companions. One of these we reproduce here :—

"'Twur jest three yearn ago," began the trapper, "that I wur out in the Wind River mountains prospectin' partly fur gold an' partly fur pelts. Thur wur a sight o' elk that winter in the valleys, as the snow wur deep above, an' druv down the game, which kem in also in troops from the plains eastwards. Wal, I hed poked out as sweet a location as ever ye seed—a leetle valley hedged in by thunderin' big hills on all sides, 'ceptin' torst the south, an' wi' timber scattered over it jest like it'd be planted o' purpose fur shelter. Thur wa'n't much snow on the ground hyur, an' when the sun shone bright, ye'd a'most think 'twur summer instead o' its bein' winter. Wal, I guess 'twur the warmth o' the sun as fetched out old Eph from his cave or whursomever he'd toted his old carkidge to. I wur lookin' arter my pelts, an', o' coorse, never thort o' a grizzly standin' on his hind legs 'ithin ten yards o' my back till I heerd a sniff an' looked round. Boyees! a fellur sometimes feels blarmed queer out in these diggin's; but I wish I may never feel agin what I felt when I squinted around an' seed that b'ar—a raal buster— squatted on his hams, an' wuss'n all, wi' my rifle on the ground clost to him! Hyur wur a blessed go. Ef I'd had that leetle gun in my hand I'd a felt a weight off my gizzard ; but thur wa'n't no help fur it. I hed no tree to run to, nor hed I eyther knife or pistol. I'd left

the hull kit o' 'em at the shanty, which wur about a
quarter o' a mile or so away, as I expected to be back
in five minutes, not meanin' to go far. I guess the b'ar
seed how I wur sarcumstanced, fur he kem at me as
hard as he cud go. I hed heerd o' hunters foolin' b'ars
into a notion they wur dead, an' seein' as I wur jest as
good as dead m'self, I thort I'd try the trick. 'Twur as
good to be chawed lyin' down as standin' up, an' so I
fell stiff, 'ithout a kick or a stir, afore that b'ar's nose.
I expected to feel his claws or teeth tearin' me open
every second; but, fellurs, he didn't touch me hardly.
He sniffed round me; an' through my eyelids, which I
had a'most closed, I cud see him a-sittin' up an' goin'
on so clumsy an' funny wi' his fore legs, that only it
wa'n't a larfin' matter I'd a larfed outright. Arter a
leetle bit o' dum play the varmint let hisself down on
his legs agin, an' caught a holt o' me by the shoulder,
carryin' me as easy as a feather. I wur took in this
way about a hundred yards, when the b'ar let me go,
an' scraped sand an' dirt over me till I wur covered a
foot deep. I thort I'd never be able to hold in fur
coughin' an' wheezin' when the crittur wur heapin' the
rubbish atop o' me. But I guess a fellur never knows
what he kin do till a grizzly's got a holt o' him. I lay
dead thur fur a full hour 'ithout darin' to stir hand or
foot. O' coorse I cudn't see a bit, bein' covered up wi'
airth an' sand; but at last I began to get tired o' the
bisness, an' took a heave, throwin' off the stuff. Thur
wa'n't a sight o' the b'ar to be seed! I didn't stay thur

longer, you bet, an' shortly hed my claws on Plumcentre agin.

"I follered the b'ar's track, which wur as plain as Pike's Peak, an' overtook the varmint at the bottom o' a deep gulch. He hedn't seed me as yit, so I clomb the bluff to a ledge thirty foot over the bottom, an' took a rest off a rock at Ephraim's brain-box. I reckon that b'ar gev a jump. He wa'n't throwed though. He spotted me at once, an' kem torst the bluff, but cudn't climb nohow. I slapped in the fodder as fast as I cud, an' next time med a good shot. The b'ar wur stretched out as·stiff as an ice-chisel, so I kem down an' riz his ha'r. Ye-es, I guess b'ars hed better leave Jake Hawken alone—that they hed!"

This opinion was shared by both Pierre and Gaultier.

CHAPTER XX.

THE next day the hunters arrived at Fort Chepewyan.
They did not meditate a long stay; indeed, their chief
reason for stopping was to replenish their stores, which
had become alarmingly low.

They also "traded" their stock of furs, for which
they received a very considerable sum. Some days
were passed pleasantly among the employés at the fort,
hearing news, and giving in exchange their many
adventures by the way. They were hospitably entertained by the gentleman in charge of the post, who
seemed to think that he could never do enough to
render their stay agreeable. It was therefore with
regret that they tore themselves away from a real roof
and real beds, to which they had been so long unaccus-
tomed, but which on that account were all the more
valued. Before again venturing on Lake Athabasca

they provided themselves with an excellent canoe, and having stored it with a full supply of provisions, they set out for Fort Vermilion on the Peace River.

They steered a westerly course, favoured by a good breeze, until they struck the debouchure of the Slave River, up which they turned. Late that evening they reached the mouth of the Peace, which does not debouch (as many suppose) into Lake Athabasca, with which it communicates only by way of the Slave River, and, in high water, by the channel of the Quatre Fourche.

The Peace flows through the Rocky Mountains for some three hundred miles, receiving on its way the waters of innumerable smaller streams. It is doubtful if such stupendous cliffs as frown down upon the last hundred miles of this river exist elsewhere upon the American continent. This awful chasm is six thousand feet deep, and at the bottom the water flows along as black as ink in the gloomy shadow of these inaccessible cliffs. After leaving the mountains, the Peace winds for five hundred miles through a deep narrow valley, sunk nearly eight hundred feet below the level of the surrounding plateaux. It next descends to a lower level, and, enclosed by banks of no great height, it traverses a fine alluvial valley densely wooded. Here its waters, once rapid and turbulent, become calm and slow, and wind their way along until, at the end of a course of eleven hundred miles, they discharge themselves through a delta into the Slave River.

In a course of nine hundred miles, but two obstructions to navigation occur. One owes its origin, at two hundred and fifty miles from the mouth of the river, to a ridge of limestone rock, which occasions a short rapid and a fall of about eight feet. The second obstruction is met with at the entrance to the vast cañon at the mountains, where a portage of ten or twelve miles becomes necessary. Through the mountains it flows deep and silent, creeping along by the bases of the immense cliffs, and affording a good waterway to the canoes of the hardy employés of the Fur Company.

The shade of approaching night was already descending on the landscape when the hunters directed their canoe to the bank. They felt in unusually good spirits, and the young men awoke the echoes with their shouts and boat-songs. The easy motion of the canoe, the facility with which it could be steered and navigated, offered a grateful contrast with the lumbering raft to which they had been condemned for so long. Pierre's pipe, too, for some time empty, was now in full blow, while old Jake's jaws wagged (as he said) as fast as a beaver's tail in flood-time. Tea, that cherished beverage in the Western wilderness, sugar, salt, some preserved vegetables, and biscuits, had been added to their stores, and it therefore was little wonder that the party felt elated.

Those of my readers who have actually experienced what it is to run short of these supplies on a journey through the wild West will sympathize with the

trappers in their joy at having their exhausted stock
renewed. To celebrate the occasion in a fitting manner,
it was decided to have a great feast. Fish had been
procured by a Buell's spoon-bait, which Gaultier had
paid out astern as they descended the Slave River;
Pierre's rifle had laid the feathered tribe under contri-
bution; while just as they landed on the banks of the
Peace, a huge moose, which swam across the broad
stream in front of the canoe, succumbed to a well-
aimed bullet from Plumcentre. Jake was in high glee,
and presented a gory spectacle as he butchered the
immense carcass.

A prodigious fire soon cast abroad a ruddy glare over
the surface of the river, and striding round the blaze
the hunters toiled in cooking fish in a large kettle,
grilling goose and duck, mouffle and steak, which hissed
and sputtered on the embers.

A kettleful of tea washed down these dainties, and
when finally the shanks of the moose were grilled on
the embers, and yielded up their rich store of marrow,
the hunters, one and all, lay back on the loppings of
white spruce, incapable of further effort.

" I guess I feels kinder comfortable now," said Jake;
" thur's few things to ekal moose meat, I reckon."

" I think mountain mutton is better," observed
Pierre; " I once lived on it for three months and didn't
get tired of it."

" Did yer ever eat musk-ox ?" asked Jake. " Thur's
not a many critturs on this great continent that I

heven't chawed, an' one o' 'em is musk-ox. I'm cur'ous about it."

" I have tried it," answered Pierre; " but I did not like it. It tastes too musky; the young does, however, are the best. They are very curious creatures, and seem like relics of the antediluvian world rather than animals to be met with in our humdrum days."

" What sort ur they ?" asked Jake; " I hain't never seed the varmints."

" In appearance," answered the young trapper, opening his manuscript book, " they bear a general resemblance to a large sheep. In fact, their scientific designation (*Ovibos moschatus*) recognizes their relationship or at least similarity to both the ox and the sheep. They are furnished with hair, however, instead of wool; and this grows to a great length, almost touching the ground as the animal stands. In looking at the horns, we are reminded of the Cape buffalo, as these formidable-looking weapons are in both similarly joined together at their bases, and effectually protect, by a mass of bony substance, the foreheads of the animals from any ordinary injury. As is the case with other species, the horns of the female are somewhat smaller than those of the male, nor do they meet so perfectly over the forehead. In both sexes the latter is much arched; and as a defence against the rigorous weather of its habitat, the face is thickly covered with hair to the end of the muzzle. The tail is very short, and exhales a very disagreeable smell of musk, with which the flesh of the animal is also impregnated.

"This quaint-looking animal is only to be met with in the high northern latitudes of America. Some have asserted that it is also to be found in Arctic Siberia; but it seems probable that this is erroneous. The mistake is most likely attributable to the fact that several skeletons of the animal have been carried by icebergs which have drifted westward from our own northern coasts, and have been deposited on the shores of Siberia.

"The musk-ox is an active animal. Its legs are short; but, notwithstanding this, it can run with great swiftness, and can clamber among rocks and hills with ease. Sir John Richardson, describing it, says:—

"'One pursued on the Coppermine River scaled a lofty sand-cliff, having so great a declivity that we were obliged to crawl on hands and knees to follow it. These oxen assemble in herds of from twenty to thirty about the end of August or beginning of September. The females bring forth a single calf about the end of May or beginning of June. Herne, from the circumstance of few bulls being seen, supposes that they kill each other for the cows. If the hunters keep themselves concealed when they fire upon a herd of musk-oxen, the poor animals mistake the noise for thunder, and crowd nearer and nearer to each other as their companions fall around them; but should they discover their enemies by sight, or by their sense of

THE MUSK OX.

Page 301.

smell, which is very acute, the whole herd seek for safety by instant flight. The bulls, however, are very irascible, and, particularly when wounded, will often attack the hunter and endanger his life, unless he possesses both activity and presence of mind. The Eskimos, who are well accustomed to the pursuit of this animal, sometimes turn its irritable disposition to good account; for an expert hunter having provoked a bull to attack him, wheels round more quickly than it can turn, and by repeated stabs in the belly puts an end to its life.' "

"Had you ever an encounter with one, Pierre?" asked Gaultier.

"I have had a good many," answered the latter smiling; "and I will tell you of an adventure which befell me some years since when pursuing a band of these animals. At that time I was stationed at Fort Reliance, which is to the east of Eastern Slave Lake.

"A party of us went out for the purpose of procuring a supply of fresh meat, as the stock at the fort was becoming exhausted. Musk-oxen had been seen a few days before, and we took the direction in which they were supposed to have gone. After a very fatiguing march through rugged valleys, and over stony, sterile plateaux, where the vegetation consisted chiefly of the *tripe de roche* and a few stunted willows in the bottoms, we suddenly came upon the musk-sheep in a little sheltered valley where some dwarf willows surrounded a large pool.

" Unfortunately, just as we rose over the crest of the hill the band saw us, and immediately took to flight, racing up the steep sides of the valley with extraordinary swiftness. One of the herd, a large 'bull,' for a moment was brought to a stand by an almost perpendicular rock, from which he slipped back on attempting to scale its slippery sides. The distance which divided us was about two hundred and fifty yards. I therefore raised my rifle, and at the report the animal seemed to stagger, but recovered himself immediately, and disappeared behind some projecting rocks. My companions were meanwhile engaged with other members of the herd, as I could hear distant shots. I lost no time in gaining the place at which I had seen the musk-ox disappear, and to my surprise I discovered a passage leading through the rocks, and issuing at the other end in another small valley similar to that I had left. I looked eagerly round in quest of my game, and presently espied him making the best of his way among some boulders towards the top of the ridge which hemmed in the valley. I immediately gave chase, as I perceived that the animal was evidently wounded, and here and there on the stones I observed that the trail was marked with blood. I therefore held on, and I soon found that I was overhauling the beast, which now walked more slowly and occasionally stopped altogether. When I got within about three hundred yards, he seemed to be aware, for the first time, that I was following him. He attempted to go on more quickly; but probably finding this inconvenient, he turned aside among some immense rocks, which seemed to have rolled down from the surrounding heights, and was lost to view. Thinking that I now was certain of him, I ran forward with increased eagerness and soon reached the rocks. Just as I was about to turn the corner of a huge boulder, the musk-ox, which must have been lying in wait for me, suddenly charged with such ferocity that before I could raise my rifle it was dashed from my hands, and I was myself knocked backwards with great violence among the rocks. The infuriated beast butted at me with his huge horns as I lay on the ground, and several times pounded me beneath his hoofs. Two or three times I attempted to rise, but was as often knocked down again.

"I almost gave myself up for lost, when, looking round for some place of refuge, I suddenly noticed a recess close to me into which I might squeeze myself. Taking advantage of a stumble made by my adversary, I sprang into the friendly nook; and as I did so I heard, just behind, the hollow crash of the musk-ox's horns as he came in violent collision with the rocks. I was now safe for the present at any rate. My savage jailer glowered at me from under the penthouse of his shaggy brows, enraged at being cheated of his victim. The recess in which I had taken refuge was a cleft in an immense rock, and looking upward I could see the sky. I now thought that I might scramble to the top by working with my arms and legs against the sides of the cleft, just as a sweep ascends a chimney; but I was so much shaken and bruised from the pommelling I had received that I was hardly equal to the task. At length, however, I stood upon the summit, which was fully twenty feet above the ground below. I was now much amused to observe the rage into which my escape had thrown the musk-ox. He plunged round below, making frantic efforts to spring up the rock; and finding this impossible, he seemed to challenge me to descend, by making threatening motions with his head and feet and then glaring savagely at me. I soon began to wish the affair ended. I had no weapon, except my rifle, and that lay among the stones at the foot of the boulder, and directly in front of my enemy. To regain it before being again assailed would be impossible.

"On crawling to the very verge of the rock, I saw the rifle underneath. Fortunately, it seemed to have met with no injury, and was favourably placed for recovery, if I had anything long enough to reach it. On searching my pockets I found some deer-hide thongs; but on attaching them together I found they would only reach half-way. I therefore sacrificed a moccasin, and with the strips of hide thus obtained I fashioned a kind of lasso, furnished at one end with a running noose.

"After several fruitless attempts, which were regarded by my friend below as a covert attack on himself, I had the satisfaction of seeing the noose settle round the barrel of the rifle, and on carefully tightening the string I hauled up the gun.

"When the musk-ox saw this manœuvre he charged the rifle as it swung clear of the ground, and might have seriously damaged it had I not quickly pulled it out of his reach. He hit the rock with great force, and staggered back from the effects of the concussion. I was now, of course, extricated from my predicament. The ox looked up at me, as much as to say, 'You had better come down,' when he was met with a ball between the eyes, which turned him upside down on the spot. I then clambered down from my perch and butchered the brute. As I said, I don't care much for musk-ox in general, but I did eat that fellow with a kind of relish."

"That wur likely, you bet!" exclaimed Jake. "This niggur hev chawed varmints wi' double the pleasure arter bein' nigh done fur by 'em."

"Come, Gaultier," said Pierre, "tell us about your first fire-hunt. I don't think you ever told Jake about it."

Gaultier laughed and complied readily.

"It is only fair," he said, "that I should contribute my share to the general amusement, although my adventure was not so thrilling as those with which Jake regales us; nor even as yours with the musk-ox, Pierre.

"I was staying with a friend some years since," he

continued, "near the Upper Ottawa, which was then a first-rate place for deer. We decided one night that we would have a fire-hunt, as a relative of my friend's was coming from Ottawa on a visit, and my host was anxious to have a fine fat buck to help the entertainment.

" The night was very favourable—that is, it was as dark as a wolf's mouth—and after supper we left the house, and having provided ourselves with a bag of pitch-pine knots and an old frying-pan, we got into a canoe and dropped quietly down the river. There were few settlers in those days round my friend's neighbourhood; but among the few who had found their way up there, was an old gentleman who had formerly been an officer in the French army. I had often heard of him, and from all accounts he was a queer old fellow. His house stood very near the river, but divided from it by some brushwood, through which grew a few tall trees. All these particulars I learned afterwards. Well, we put up our birch-bark screen so as to intervene between us and the light of the blazing fire-pan, and, crouching behind its shadow, we keenly scrutinized the bank of the river, expecting each moment to catch the gleam of an eye peering at us from among the foliage.

" We had not proceeded far when my friend drew my attention to a bright, glistening object, apparently at the verge of the water. ' It's a deer,' he whispered; ' take a good aim, and be sure you drop him.' Following the direction of his finger, I observed the glittering orb, and I immediately drew a bead upon it with my rifle. At the report the eye disappeared. On landing we discovered the animal, which was a fine buck, lying dead on the ground, shot through the brain. We threw him into the boat and continued our voyage. The next shot fell to my companion's lot, and as he was an old hand at this game he brought down a large doe; but we regretted this circumstance, as we found she was accompanied by her fawns. However, there was no help for it, so we placed her in the boat and again dropped down the river. You may ask why it was that we did not return now that we had got two deer. But I believe hunters are never satisfied; and, besides, there was something so fascinating in this sport that I said nothing, and was ready to assist my friend in any amount of slaughter.

" I was eagerly on the outlook for the reflection from another eye, and scanned the shore closely. Several times I was about to fire, but was prevented from wasting my shot by my more experienced companion. At length an unmistakable eye presented itself; the colour was the same, and the same steady stare too. I raised my rifle, and as I did so I thought I heard my friend say something; but I did not wait to hear what. I pulled the trigger, and along with the report I thought I heard an unusual noise—something very like the crashing of glass. My friend was in fits of inextinguishable laughter. 'What have you done?' he cried; 'you've smashed old ——'s' (naming his neighbour) 'parlour window, as I'm a sinner!' At this moment a tall figure in white appeared in front of the house, which I could now dimly discern through the bushes, and came running towards us.

"'Here he is himself! pull for your life!' exclaimed my comrade; and instantly he capsized the pan of blazing knots into the water and seized his paddle. A few strokes placed us under the shadow of the opposite bank, from which we could hear the old Frenchman venting his rage in all manner of strange words, and threatening vengeance against us. An unlucky laugh on the part of my friend revealed our whereabouts, when instantly the irascible old colonel discharged his smooth-bore at us, the charge rattling about our ears, but fortunately without doing us any injury. As we gave no sign, he soon took himself off to bed, from which he had evidently sprung on hearing the shot followed by the smashing of his glass.

" We were glad to be out of the scrape so easily, and we paddled homewards the moment we heard him bang his door behind him."

The party now began to yawn and stretch—evidences of fatigue. They therefore heaped the fire with fresh fagots, and bestowed themselves in the most comfortable postures which their ingenuity could suggest. Shortly, sounds indicative of profound repose alone disturbed the silence, if we except the deep murmur of the river or the wail of the wind through the tree-tops.

Although our hunters could sleep soundly they possessed the faculty of waking at pleasure, and were habitually early risers. The sun, therefore, had not yet thrown his beams up the broad bosom of the Peace when they were astir and preparing for their departure. A canopy of fleecy vapour hung above the course of the river, and from behind its opaque wreaths could be heard the quavering cry of the loon, the quacking of ducks, and the gabble of geese. A breeze soon sprang up and cleared away the fog, revealing the flocks of waterfowl, as well as the heads of several beavers that were swimming at a little distance. At the appearance of the hunters the beavers dived, and the geese and ducks, with harsh cries, rose into the air and disappeared beyond the trees.

The distance still to be traversed before reaching Fort Vermilion was nearly two hundred miles; but the river was slow and deep, and the labour of paddling the canoe was trivial. The party therefore addressed themselves to their work with light hearts, and the graceful little boat flew up-stream, impelled by the sinewy strokes of their practised arms.

For some days they paddled onward, halting only for their meals and for the night. Game was plentiful along the banks of the river; they frequently saw moose dash away into the woods, and on every hill-side bears of several kinds seemed busily engaged in grubbing for roots. Wildfowl, in countless numbers, streamed off the water at the approach of the canoe, and filed away to other haunts to seek refuge from man's intrusion.

On the north-west and south-west shores of Lake Athabasca the wood buffalo and the moose are still tolerably numerous, and furnish the staple of subsistence to the employés at the Fur Company's forts, as well as to the natives of these districts. To the north of the Peace is the true home of the reindeer. Some twenty or thirty miles north of Fort Vermilion lies the range of the Reindeer Hills; and from their summits, some fifty miles to the south, beyond the Peace River, stretching from east to west, may be seen the Buffalo Mountains. These two chains may almost be said to form the geographical limits of the animals whose names they bear. Of the reindeer and the buffalo Colonel Butler says :—

" It is singular how closely the habits of those two widely differing animals approximate to each other. Each have their treeless prairie, but seek the woods in winter ; each have their woodland species ; each separate when the time comes to bring forth their young ; each mass together in their annual migrations. Upon both the wild man preys in unending hostility. When the long days of the Arctic summer begin to shine over the wild region of the Barren Grounds, the reindeer set forth for the low shores of the Northern Ocean ; in the lonely wilds, whose shores look out upon the archipelago where once the ships of England's explorers struggled midst floe and pack and hopeless iceberg, the herds spend the summer season subsisting on the short grass which in a few weeks changes these cold gray shores to softer green.

" With the approach of autumn the bands turn south again, and, uniting upon the borders of the Barren Grounds, spend the winter in the forests which fringe the shores of the Bear, Great Slave, and Athabasca Lakes. Thousands are killed by the Indians on this homeward journey ; waylaid in the passes which they usually follow, they fall easy prey to Dog-rib, and Yellow-knife, and Chepewyan hunter ; and in years of plenty the forts of the extreme north count by thousands the fat sides of cariboo piled high in their provision stores."

It will therefore be evident how important a place these two animals hold in the domestic economy of the inhabitants of these untilled solitudes. White man and Redskin alike depend upon them for their daily food ; and in seasons when from any cause the buffalo is too far south on the plains, or the reindeer does not appear at the usual season, famine stares each one in the face, unless goose and duck, whitefish and salmon, have been secured in extraordinary numbers to meet the deficiency.

CHAPTER XXI.

ONE evening our hunters landed as usual to camp for
the night. The spot which they had chosen was at
the foot of a slight eminence which sloped back from
the river, and was covered with dwarf cedars. Plenty
of dry drift timber lay piled along the banks, and
afforded an unlimited supply of fuel. This circumstance formed their chief reason for selecting this particular spot.

Jake left his young friends busied at the fire, and
shouldering Plumcentre directed his steps towards the
crest of the rising ground, saying that he "mout hev
a chance o' throwin' a lump o' lead into some varmint."

He had not been absent for more than a few minutes
when the report of his rifle was heard; and almost immediately afterwards the old hunter appeared on the

top of the slope running towards the camp as fast as his long lean legs could carry him.

As he came he shouted, "A b'ar! a b'ar! Git yer shootin'-sticks; he's arter me!" And in truth the young men at that moment observed a bear of the brown variety appear in hot pursuit, lumbering after the trapper at a kind of cow gallop. Jake no sooner reached the camp than he placed himself in rear of his comrades, when he used the utmost despatch in the loading of his rifle.

Meanwhile the bear, on seeing three enemies where he had only looked for one, came to a halt, and seemed to be considering the situation. His uncertainty, however, was soon dispelled, for he came forward uttering savage growls, but again halted when only some thirty yards distant. At this instant Pierre and Gaultier levelled their rifles and fired. Before they could see the effects of the shots the bear was in their midst, and with a loud snarling roar seized Gaultier in his deadly embrace!

The young trapper's rifle was dashed from his hands, and he himself thrown to the ground, while the infuriated beast attempted to seize his face in his mouth! Throwing down his rifle, which he was afraid to use, so confused were the motions of the bear and its struggling victim, old Jake drew his shining bowie, and leaping forward got astride of the bear, and fastening one hand in its shaggy hair, drove his sharp knife home repeatedly with the other. The maddened animal turned on its new aggressor; but old Jake kept his seat despite its utmost efforts to dislodge him. Blood poured in streams from the wounds inflicted by the hunter's blade, and dyed the ground at the scene of the struggle.

While the bear's attention was centred in old Jake, Gaultier scrambled from underneath the animal's legs; but overcome by a sudden faintness he reeled forward, and would have fallen had not Pierre caught him in his arms.

Finding that he was getting the worst of the encounter, the bear now made an effort to escape; but Jake stuck to his seat manfully, and fairly rode the terrified animal off the ground, stabbing him as he went. For fully fifty yards did the wretched beast survive to carry his fatal rider. At length the trapper's knife, directed with more judgment, found a vital spot, and the bear fell dead.

Jake immediately returned to the spot where Pierre sat supporting Gaultier. He procured some water from the river, and bathed the face and temples of the young hunter, who soon regained his consciousness. An examination showed that he had suffered no injury of a serious nature. As soon as his comrades were relieved of any anxiety on this score, they proceeded to examine the dead animal. The carcass was covered with blood, which still trickled from not less than fifty wounds, inflicted by the old trapper's knife. The hide was valueless; but old Jake observed, "The varmint's hams ur worth takin';" and he accordingly proceeded to secure them. Having accomplished this task, they returned to the fire, and eagerly discussed the adventure.

"Jest as I topped the rise," said Jake, "I seed the varmint down below at the other side. Thur wur plenty o' cover, an' so I slouched along, keepin' well out o' view till I jedged I'd got far enuff. I put up Plumcentre, an' let drive at the b'ar's skull so as the ball'd range across fur the off eye. But jest as I pulled the trigger the b'ar moved his head, an' I med a bad shot. I hedn't time to wink when he swung round an' kem at me, an' as I knew I'd reach camp afore he cud come to grips, I thort I'd git ye to help me. That's how I brought the varmint arter me."

This incident afforded Pierre an opportunity of giving a short account of the brown bear (*Ursus arctos*), whose habits are substantially the same as those of others of the tribe. We will therefore only remark that this animal flies contact with man (except when attacked and wounded), and frequents the wildest and most inaccessible regions. It dwells in caverns, clefts in the rocks, or in such hollow logs as it finds scattered through the virgin forest. It sometimes even excavates a hole for itself in which to pass the winter. During this season, in common with its kindred, it passes a considerable time in a state of torpidity. In proportion to its size the eyes are small; but whatever disadvantage might arise from this circumstance is counterbalanced by the acuteness of its nose and of its ears. The hide is tough, and is of considerable thickness, and is covered with a dense coat of hair. From a study of the teeth it might be supposed that the diet of the brown bear, as indeed of the other varieties also, consists chiefly of vegetable substances. But the fact is that they are indifferently either carnivorous or frugivorous. When attacked, these animals defend themselves in an upright position, giving terrible blows with their powerful fore arms. When the bear emerges from his winter quarters he is at first in capital condition ; but a few days' exposure to the air reduces him to the merest skeleton.

It has been observed that if the bear removes the litter which he had provided during the previous winter, he intends to re-occupy the same quarters; on the other hand, if he allows it to remain, it is an indication of his intention not to return.

While Pierre was making these remarks, both Jake and Gaultier were busying themselves in getting supper ready—a task which had been so unceremoniously interrupted. Night soon descended on the scene, and under its shadow the wolves, whose distant howls had been heard for a little time, approached, and fought over the carcass of the bear. In the dim light their fleeting forms were faintly discernible, and the hunters took advantage of their boldness to approach a little nearer. A united volley stretched three of their number dead upon the ground, much to old Jake's delight, as he nourished a grudge against the whole tribe which seemed incapable of being satiated.

He begged to be allowed to skin the wolves which had fallen to the rifles of his comrades.

"It does this niggur good," he said, "to rise the pelts off the varmints—thur sich sneakin' thieves, an' hev played me a purty trick afore now. I reckin though they hain't made much out o' rubbin' up this child's fur the wrong way."

"What did they do to you, Jake?" asked Gaultier.

"What did they do!" cried the old trapper as he forced the skin from the back of one of the wolves, the beast's body lying across his legs, which were stained with its blood. "This is what the skunks did, an' I guess 'twur enough to make me hate 'em as long as I live."

Here Jake paused, and after mumbling and muttering a little, proceeded :—

"I wur camped upon a peraira near Clerk's Fork o' the Yallerstone," he began, "an' hed good times, I reckin. Thur wur a sight o' game ; an' this niggur, you bet, wur thick fat wi' dint o' the best eatin' in the mountains. I hed to keep my eyes skinned though, fur Injun sign wur plenty, an' from the heights I one day seed three smokes, o' coorse risin' from as many Injun fires. They wur a long way off though, I reckin ; but still I knew the skunks 'd not be long in huntin' me out ef once they got my trail. I wa'n't a-gwine to clur out o' sich diggin's anyway, ef I knew it ; an' so I took chance, an' stayed. Wal, as it turned out, 'twurn't the Redskins, arter all, as kem near sendin' this coon under—'twur wolves as did that. I hed been out arter sheep in the mountains, an' hed got one thunderin' fine ram. I cut up the critter, an' threw him on my old mustang's back, an' sot out fur camp.

" 'Twur jest about nightfall when I clomb up to my saddle, an' as the way wur longish I let the old mar' know as 'twur best to be steppin' out. I hed tied up the mutton wi' strips o' hide, an' somehow one o' the pieces hed got loose, an', unknownst to me, wur draggin' arter the hoss along the ground. That wur the sarcum-stance as fetched the wolves.

" Wal, from time to time I thort I heerd a whimperin' an' a yowltin' behint; but 'twurn't much, an' o' coorse I'd heerd the same every night, as the wolves chased the deer or the rabbits, an' so I never minded it. By'n-by, however, I guess I minded it. 'Twurn't long until the n'ize got louder, an' kem nearer, an' all o' a suddint thur wur a yowl out o' a hunderd throats close behint, an' at that the old mar' put out like all creation. Boyees, I guess this coon has knowed what goin' means now an' agin, but it wa'n't nothin' to this.

" Rocks an' trees passed like a whiz, an' the very stars 'peared stretched out like ropes o' light along the sky as I ripped along under 'em. 'Twur main bad ridin' too, I kin tell yer. Thur wur steep places whur the old critter hed to jump down five or six feet at a time ; an' at that the lumps o' mutton 'd whammel agin this child's back, an' once I wur struck on the head, an' as near as cud 'a be pitched out o' the saddle. I

held on though, you bet.   All this time the wolves wur
hard behint us.   I cud hear the fierce whimperin' o' the
critters ; but I guess the speed wur too great fur 'em to
waste thur breath in reg'lar cry like hounds.   'Twur a
silent, detarmined race fur life or death, an' the varmints
did all they knew to overtake us.   I soon found out
that wi' the weight o' the mutton an' o' m'self the mar'
cudn't hold out much longer.   I cud hear the poor
thing breathin' thicker an' thicker ; an' as often as the
wolves 'd give a yelp I'd feel her shake like a leaf, an'
then she'd put on a trifle more speed ; but 'd lose it agin
in a minute.   The wolves knew this as well as I did,
fur they began agin to yowl ; an' I now seed two o' 'em,
one on each side, lopin' along wi' thur tongues out, an'
the hot steam risin' like a fog out o' thur mouths.   I
began to give in 'twur time fur this child to go under.
But one clings to life all the same, an' so I laid my
quirt into the mar', an' even pricked her on wi' the
p'int o' my knife.   The poor critter wur near played
out, an' already the wolves wur crowded around, when
all at once what shud I see right under the hoss's nose
but the edge o' a bluff wi' a river five hundred foot
below !   Thur wur a few pines hangin' everywhich way
over the edge ; but I hedn't time to wink when the
mar' arruv on the brink, an' went over !   I've felt some
considerable in my time, but never anything ekal to
that.   As the mar' went over, fur she cudn't stop herself in time, she gev an unairthly screech—sich a
screech as I hope I'll never hear agin.   It rang in my

ears fur many a day, an' the sound o' it hain't left 'em yit !

"Jest as she wur gwine over I threw myself off, an' fell so clost to the edge o' the bluff that my legs hung over as I turned a somersault upon the ground wi' the toss I got. I hedn't time to cry mercy when I wur surrounded wi' wolves, thur teeth gleamin' an' eyes shinin' like coals o' fire in thur heads. I med through 'em wi' my bowie, an' lucky it wur, I reckin, fur this coon that thur wur a few o' them piñons growin' on the bluff, or *he'd* never 'a knowed what to-morrow wur like. I clawed up into a pine, an' ef thur hedn't been a wolf nearer'n Jerusalem that climb 'ud 'a been danger-some enuff. The tree wa'n't a big un, an' it leant out over the barranca, so that when I got squatted at last, my legs wur swingin' above the river five hunderd foot below !

"O' coorse I'd lost my rifle—that hed bust off my back when I fell, an' wur lyin' somewheres along the top o' the bluff; but I hed my pistols, an' I kep' loadin' an' firin' wi' them till I'd throwed a good wheen o' the wolves. Torst morning, seein' as they wurn't likely to make a 'raise' by the spec'lation, the band took thur-selves off, arter chawin' up every one o' the lot I'd killed.

"That's thur style, I reckin. Anyhow I got clur m'self; but fur the fright an' the loss o' my mar' I hev med the varmints pay dear since. Nary a wolf comes 'ithin reach o' Plumcentre 'ithout gettin' a lump o' lead ;

an' I bleeve that leetle gun remembers that night as well as I do, an' ud go herself at the skunks even ef thur wa'n't no old Jake Hawken behint her to pull the trigger."

Here the hunter ended his narrative.

The remainder of the night was devoted to repose, and it was well on towards noon the next day when the hunters left the camp and continued their journey.

We do not propose to chronicle all the adventures which befell our travellers on their way to Fort Vermilion. They had several exciting encounters with bears, which, however, uniformly ended in a victory for the trappers; and once or twice they narrowly escaped having their canoe dashed to pieces against floating logs, borne downwards by the current. These were the ordinary incidents of travel, and as they resembled in all respects similar occurrences already described, there is little use in detailing them for the reader.

The success which had attended their hunt even thus early, and the unlooked-for good fortune which made them heirs to the valuable stock of furs secreted in the cave by the Indian whose tragic end old Jake had witnessed, rendered our trappers careless of prosecuting their journey for the present beyond Fort Vermilion.

That post was now but one hundred miles distant, and each day the hunters felt that their protracted journey came nearer and nearer to its termination.

They were therefore in high spirits, and looked forward to a rest from the tedium of their journey, or rather to a change of their somewhat monotonous routine.

One evening, while seated by the camp fire, the hunters observed a small animal stealing along by the edge of some brushwood not far from the river bank. At first, owing to the grass being somewhat high, they were unable to recognize the creature; but presently it came directly into view, and they at once perceived it to be an ermine weasel.

It was evidently in pursuit of some small quadruped or bird, as it ran the scent with eagerness, sometimes stopping for a moment as if uncertain, and again running forward with swift, stealthy steps. The trappers had hardly made these observations when it suddenly sprang forward, and at the same instant several grouse rose with a whirring noise and disappeared behind the woods, leaving one of their number struggling and fluttering in the clutches of the ermine. The fierce little animal soon ended the contest by crunching the bird's head between his sharp teeth; and he was just about to drag the body into the bushes, when Jake ran up and secured the bird as a titbit for his supper. The weasel looked as if half inclined to fight; but on second thoughts he took to his heels, and vanished in some long grass.

"I think," said Gaultier, "that those little fellows change their coats in winter. What does your red book say about them, Pierre?"

The latter produced his volume and read the few notes he had made.

"The ermine (*Mustela erminea*)," said he, "closely resembles the common weasel, and is, in fact, related to it. It attains the length of about nine inches; but this measurement does not include the tail. As you can now see (from the specimen you have before you), its colour at this time of the year is a beautiful brown on the upper parts, and below is a yellowish white, the tail being terminated by a black tuft.

"While thus coloured it is called a roselet. At the approach of winter this coat gives place to another of pure white; but the black tip of the tail remains unaltered. It is a common animal in the northern districts of both Europe and America, and is of course very destructive to small quadrupeds as well as to most birds. Were its coat to retain its summer hue during the winter, the ermine would certainly starve to death, as its colour would be too noticeable to allow it to surprise its prey on the spotless white of the snow. In addition to this, it has been remarked that its white fur enables it to maintain a more equable temperature during the severe cold of the Arctic winter than if it were furnished with a darker covering.

"The ermines are also allied to another animal, which indeed forms a member of the same group. This is the pine marten (*Martes abietum*); so called from being supposed to eat the seeds of the pine cones. Its diet, however, is not so innocuous, as it devours squirrels, birds, rats, mice, and also eggs whenever it can find them. In size it is much larger than the last-mentioned animal, and its general colour is yellowish, dashed or blended here and there with a blackish tint; the tail is long, well feathered, and pointed. It is by no means unusual to find some individuals whose fur varies somewhat from the general rule both in colour and fineness.

"As the animals and birds which furnish the pine marten with its food frequent thick woods, it is consequently in these that it is most commonly found. It robs the nests of the wild bees as dexterously as the black bear himself, and will devour fish, insects, and even reptiles readily. Squirrels often fall a prey to this predatory beast, and their nests are frequently appropriated by it.

"The pine marten, according to Audubon, produces from four to seven young at a birth, and generally in a hollow log, a hole under a rock, or in a burrow.

"The fur is of some value, but is inferior to that of the sable marten. Sir John Richardson says: 'A partridge's head with the feathers is the best bait for the log traps in which this animal is taken. It does not reject carrion, and often destroys the hoards of meat and fish laid up by the natives, when they have accidentally left a crevice by which it can enter.'

"When hard pressed, the marten can show fight much after the fashion of a cat when attacked by a dog; that is, it shows its teeth, erects its fur, arches its back, and emits a hissing sound. When attacked by a dog it will seize the animal by the nose, and hold on with such tenacity as frequently to drive the assailant from the field. In some instances the marten has been domesticated; but it rarely or never becomes docile.

"I think now," said Pierre, "that is all of importance which there is to tell concerning this animal."

While Pierre had been communicating these particulars, his comrades had been busy with frying-pan and kettle, and had prepared the evening meal.

They were about to partake of this when they observed a canoe approaching them paddled by two men, whom they soon recognized as belonging to Fort Pierre.

They soon brought the canoe to the bank, and joined the trappers at their supper. They brought the sad intelligence of Mr. Frazer's death. He had been utterly cast down by the terrible event which deprived him of his daughter, and had been wasting away day by day, until he finally died two days before these voyageurs had left the fort.

On the following morning the hunters and their new allies left camp together and set out for Fort Vermilion. The miles flew swiftly by, and just as evening descended on the river the canoes rounded a bend, and the stockades of the fort became visible at a little distance. In a few minutes their long and toilsome journey was over, and surrounded by a crowd of voyageurs and half-breeds they vanished through the gateway of the fort.

They remained at this post until the shortening days warned them to continue their journey before the ice stopped the navigation of the Peace. They pushed forward with the utmost despatch, and reached Dunvegan the very night a fierce cold sealed the river with a three-inch crust of ice. Here they wintered, occupying themselves in trapping the beaver, the sable, and the other valuable fur-bearing animals of the country.

At Dunvegan we take leave of our trappers with feelings of regret that we shall no more share their perils by flood and field, no more listen to the tale of hairbreadth escape or wild adventure round the camp fire.

If the young reader has had a love awakened or a taste fostered for the beauties of God's creation by the perusal of these pages, the object which the writer proposed to himself has been attained.

THE END.

www.ingramcontent.com/pod-product-compliance
Lightning Source LLC
Chambersburg PA
CBHW031143120726
47905CB00006B/1801